THE APPRENTICE JOURNALS

BY

J. MICHAEL SHELL

T0314904

Published by
Dog Horn Publishing
45 Monk Ings, Birstall, Batley WF17 9HU
United Kingdom
doghornpublishing.com

ISBN: 978-1-907133-38-1

Cover art by
Vincent Sammy

Typesetting by
Jonathan Penton

UK Distribution: Central Books
99 Wallis Road, London, E9 5LN, United Kingdom
orders@centralbooks.com
Phone:+44 (0) 845 458 9911
Fax: +44 (0) 845 458 9912

Overseas Distribution: Printondemand-worldwide.com
9 Culley Court
Orton Southgate
Peterborough
PE2 6XD
Telephone: 01733 237867
Facsimile: 01733 234309
Email: info@printondemand-worldwide.com

THE
APPRENTICE
JOURNALS

TABLE OF CONTENTS

I
Blitz

Speaking to Fierae Elementals is probably one of the most difficult things I do. I haven't met many other Apprentices, but the few I've found in my travels say the same thing. All I want to do when I've finished one of those momentary conversations is eat and then sleep. I say "momentary," because talking to the Fierae takes exactly as long as a bolt of their light stays in the air before it sounds its thunder and separates. The ancients called those bolts "lightening."

"Blitz" is what they called the Fierae in another of those ancient languages. I like blitz much better than lightening. It's more to the point. To look at the Fierae, in creature time with creature eyes, most people would say they are *very* to the point. If you stand between them when they're joining, the point will be that you don't exist anymore. The Fierae will char you crisp in a nannysecond, and not even notice that you were there. If they *did* notice, they'd fry you anyway.

But I'm getting ahead of myself. The Finished Apprentice who taught me was Thirest. I can't tell you how many times he told me to *explain everything*! He'd say, "You have to remember, Spaul, that the people you keep your journal for will have forgotten the Apprentices and majicking and *everything*. They won't know shite-all about fug-all. Tell them every detail, so they can find an Apprentice again, because if they *don't*, they're fugged."

Thirest had a dirty mouth, but he was right. When the Apprentices are gone, World is fugged. Look what happened to the Ancients. They hadn't talked to the Elementals in so long that the Fierae, the Naiadae, the Terrae and the Zephrae simply forgot they were there. Then something the Ancients were doing with their Teck started warming World and tickling the Elementals, until they began having huge parties all over the place. When the Elementals get together and throw a shindig, watch out! We still get them, but they know we're here now (because of the Apprentices), and try to keep it down. Still, they have trouble understanding our fragility, and if you get caught in one of their hooplas, you can get hurt. Or dead. "Dead," the elementals simply do not understand, so don't expect any sympathy. The best you're likely to get is, "Oops, we didn't see you there."

Of all the Elementals, the Fierae are the most *fun* to talk to. If you take a typical elemental get together, say a hurrakin, the Fierae are going to be the life of that party. They will also be very beautiful and sensuous. How could they *not* be? But, of course, you don't know *anything*, so I guess I'd better explain that, too. Thirest was right when he said this journaling isn't easy. But, who knows, what I'm writing now could save World someday if the Apprentices really do die off. The Fierae, what the ancients called lightening, are nearly asleep most of the time.

The reason they are asleep is that they spread themselves very thin as Charges. When they are Charges, they live in the air and the ground. Even asleep, they are conscious, and manipulate World's elemental flow so that a male Fierae Charge and a female Fierae Charge will meet. Male Charges usually prefer to hang out in Air, and females in Land, but they will change places once in a while. The Fierae you see, that bolt of light, is actually *two* Fierae engaged in love. When I was a New Kid, Thirest used to tell me that thunder is the two of them saying, "Ooey, that feels good!" Of course, that's just a children's story, but if you ever do talk to the Fierae, you'll find that they make a *lot* of very satisfied sounds. The thunder, however, isn't one of them. Thunder is an explosion of sound that occurs when something incompatible with the dimensional fabric of World momentarily exists in it anyway. Actually, the *light* you see, that bolt, is the Fierae expressing physical love. I can't help getting excited every time I see the flash of two Fierae loving. Especially if it's one of those long, drawn out bolts that seems to stand there and pulse. Yowza!

In order to talk to the Fierae you have to speed up, because you can only talk to them just before, and while, they are joined. Remember, when they're Charges they're thin and sleepy. But when they wake up to join, they'll chatter at you, tell you tales, gossip, reveal ancient wisdom from Jess knows when, and all the while they're going at it—sizzling and crackling and totally embraced. Fierae live to love. If you aren't careful when you're talking to them, you'll get caught up in the sheer eroticism of it and join them.

So that you'll get an idea of how to converse with the Fierae,

I'll tell you about the last time I talked to Blitz. I gave them the name Blitz (that Ancient word for Fierae) and they liked it, so it stuck. There's no saying their actual names, you'd have to have fire for vocal chords and smoke for a tongue to be able to say them.

Blitz is only truly Blitz when those two particular Charges join. Fierae will join with *any* Charge that comes along, but often two of them develop an affinity for one another and start manipulating World's flow so they can meet up again. If they get separated into different directions of flow, it can take them decades to arrange another meeting.

The two Charges that are Blitz have managed to stay in one another's vicinity for quite some time now. They've joined half a dozen times in the last couple of years, which is practically monogamy for the Fierae. Don't get me wrong, any female Charge will join with any male Charge if they get close enough. They can't help it. Having joined with them, I know *why* they can't help it. Thirest told me that if I did it once the temptation to do it again would be overwhelming every time I talk to them, and he was right.

He also said creature loving was like pain compared to what the Fierae experience. I can't confirm or deny Thirest on that account, as I have yet to try the creature version. When I do, I know it will be with a girl. Some Apprentices are said to prefer sex with their own gender, but the thought of that doesn't appeal to me. *Girls*, on the other hand, appeal to me very much, but I've avoided it thus far. Thirest said it can be dangerous to do it, but it could also be dangerous to *never* do it. He's dead now, so the next time I visit his bunker I'm going to have to read what he wrote about that in his journal. That's probably the *only* subject he didn't teach me about in *great* detail.

It was about six months ago, during a summer party some Elementals were having, when I last talked to Blitz. Just before dark I heard a distant roll of thunder. I could already smell that a storm-party had started somewhere and was on its way. I had my tent in a pasture by a stream. It was a very beautiful place, and I'd been there for a couple of weeks. You might think that's unusual for an Apprentice, but it really isn't. We travel out of necessity, but sometimes give in to the urge to stay for a little while in a pretty setting.

We travel because we have to find as many Apprentices as

we can, make sure they're journaling, see if they've noticed any New Kids. Thirest said I was the newest Apprentice he knew of, and I was twenty-three at that time. As soon as I became a full Apprentice I quit aging, so I still look twenty-three. Thirest said I'd get tired of it and start to age again, but so far that hasn't happened. Honestly, though, if Thirest said it, it's probably just a matter of time. As for how old I am *actually*, I couldn't tell you. When I stopped aging I stopped keeping track of the years. If I had to guess I'd say I stopped about a decade ago. They say the Ancients gave every year a name or a number, so they could keep track of that sort of thing. I've even heard people say they named and numbered the *days* back then. That's a little far-fetched, but if it *is* true, no wonder the Ancients perished.

Anyway, there I was by the stream, sitting on my little folding stool, when I heard that storm coming. Out in the middle of the field, which was completely flat, stood a huge sycamore tree. It was so big, and so alone in that field, that I had several times gone over and asked it how it came to be there all alone like that. It never did answer me, so I quit asking. But when I heard the storm coming, I marched right back over to that tree. "You'll talk to me *now*, I'll bet," I told it, patting it hard on its trunky flank.

After giving the tree a hug, something the last enlightened Ancients are rumored to have done, I sat against it and began clearing my thoughts. With that party coming, a Land Charge would *surely* climb the sycamore tree looking for an Air Charge to join with. Sure enough, as soon as the waves flattened on the sea of my mind, I could hear a Charge up in the tree, chittering. "They come they come they come," it was saying.

"Do you know of Blitz?" I thought to her. It turned out to be a female Charge, as most ground Charges are.

"They come they come they come they come…"

"DO. YOU. KNOW. BLITZ?" I tried again.

"Spaul!" she said, finally hearing me. "You are in the tree?"

"You're Blitz!" I said, astounded that I had once again found at least half of my old friend.

"Spaul!" she said again. "You are in the tree?" I hadn't answered her question, and until I did, no other communication would occur. Fierae, even when they are Charges, leave *nothing* unfinished. They are *very* linear beings.

"I am in the tree," I answered. "We are both in the tree."

"Tree says, 'I like my lonely meadow. Please don't let this Charge kill me,'" girl Blitz told me.

I laughed at that, and could tell Blitz was laughing also. "Tell tree not to stand tall in a meadow while the Fierae party!" I said, and Blitz laughed so hard I saw sparks on that sycamore's leaves.

Charges are sleepy most of the time, but not when they're aroused by a party. It was a *big* storm that was coming, too. My Charge friend in the sycamore was *very* animated. She'd be jumping the first Air Charge that showed up. "Is Blitz also in Air?" I asked.

"Blitz stretches to me even now," she answered. "You have thrice the time you need to avoid your killing."

That wasn't good. Fierae are notorious for overestimating how fast we humans can move. Somehow, I kept my mind-sea calm long enough to tell her, "I will converse with you!"

"Join!" she invited, as I got up and ran like helluva.

By the time I got seated on my little stool, I figured I had about a minute to speed myself up enough to go speak to Blitz. I calmed my sea again, and felt that little jolt that comes when you disconnect from your body. I have to admit, though, I'm getting very good at it, and almost immediately ramped up my vibration enough to come hurtling out. I was back at the sycamore—minus my gross-body, of course—in a flash. Now I had all the time in World, and took in the beauty of being at this speed. The tree was very alive, pulsing with lines of life flowing up and down it like fast honey filled with shiny metal stars. Blitz was up in it sparking and crackling with intense excitement. "How long since Blitz has joined with Blitz?" I asked her.

"Half a trip around the Ball," she told me.

"That long, eh? You probably can't wait, can you?"

"Of *course* I can," she told me. "How could I *not*?"

Uh oh. I had asked a silly question, and now she'd asked *me* a question *about* my silly question. I needed to extricate myself from this conversation or it would be all we'd talk about throughout their entire joining. "I also can imagine no way in which you could not wait," I said. "Time moves, waiting is inevitable. Upon further pondering, I am sure that you can wait." Hopefully, that would do.

"I can wait. Will you wait also and join with us?"

"I will wait," I told her. "And I will *speak* with you. I am undecided as to whether I will join."

"You will join," she said. "I will bet!"

"You might be right, and I will not bet," I told her.

Thirest had warned me, sternly, not to gamble with the Fierae. There is only one currency that humans possess which interests them, and that is our light-bodies themselves. If you gamble and lose to the Fierae, your body will sit without you wherever you left it until it rots. "All I know is, they'll join with you and take you with them as Charge when they separate. You won't come back," Thirest had told me. "I don't know what it is they do with your light-body, but I don't want to find out."

"Human's never wager anymore," missy Blitz said.

"Have you ever wagered with an Apprentice?" I asked her.

"Oh yes, when the first of you spoke to us, after we'd stepped on the invisible ones. Those who lost are still with us. Those who won are here also."

"You mean, win or lose you take our light-bodies?" I asked, more than a little unsure if I'd understood her correctly. Fierae cannot *cheat*. Everything, for them, must proceed precisely as specified.

Girl Blitz laughed and said, "I love the impossibilities you speak, Spaul. So cute, you human. Those who lose are with us because they lost and their choice was none. Those who won are with us because their choice was two, and they chose us. Their choice is still two, they can coalesce their light bodies again, but they do not. They choose us still."

"Could I speak to one of those who gambled with you?"

Again she laughed. "So cute so cute. We are speaking. I can speak, you can speak, they can speak. Those who lost have no choices, but you could speak to *them*. Those who won have choices, and could choose speech with you. Do you see my answer?"

"I see it," I lied. If I told her I didn't understand, her further explanation could take up most of the joining, and I didn't want that. When Blitz joined, I wanted to hear some stories. I also knew I might join with them. Oh, who am I kidding, my body was sitting right next to a cool stream I could wash in. I'd known all along I was going to join.

It was going to be another short while before the Air Charge Blitz arrived, so I looked out over the meadow. As speeded up as I was, I could see all the life moving in pulsing lines through everything. Even the stones had fingers of light pushing through them, though it was slower than in the growing things. The only lightless thing in the whole panorama was my body, sitting there by the stream. It looked like a cutout in the fabric of light that was everything else. It's actually a little scary to see your body like that, devoid of life and time and connection to everything else. But it would only be that way for a few seconds. For *me*, of course, speeded up in my light-body, those creature seconds were passing incredibly slowly. Then I heard Blitz, up in that sycamore, start chanting almost maniacally, "He comes he comes he comes he comes..."

    I could feel it, too. Suddenly he was close enough, and I watched as those two jumped toward each other. What a magnificent sight! Above us, a glow appeared in a cloud. Then the top of the sycamore seemed to stretch upward in a burst of light and color. A solid line of dense white light ran alongside of the tree to the ground, as if girl Blitz was stretching a foot down the side of the sycamore to touch her toe to the meadow. Even speeded up, those two racing toward each other was quick, and if I'd blinked I'd have missed it.

    There is a moment, just before those two touch—when they are each outstretched, desperately and violently engaged in getting to one another—that you can actually see their faces for just an instant; searingly beautiful faces that are etched with the pain of still being half a nannysecond apart, and the anticipation of their imminent blinding ecstasy. When those two faces met, the kiss that followed produced my old friend Blitz, whole and wide-awake.

    "We are one!" that most beautiful voice cried out.

    Blitz' voice sounds like a billion dragonfly wings humming over a lectric river. It is male and female at once, but it is a single voice speaking in two-part harmony. "You are magnificent," I said, meaning the word "magnificent" with all my heart. I was already being pulled into their joining, but I resisted.

    "You will join, I will bet!" Blitz said, with so much passion and seduction that I had to sail my mind-sea to keep from joining immediately. Finally, I regained control and said, "I promise to join later. If I join now I will miss the radiance of your stories and the intoxicants of your voice."

"So cute, cute, cute. Ahh, we would have you with us, Spaul. Wager with us, we would have you or give you us, either way. So cute cute, human."

"I cannot wager with the likes of the Fierae," I said. It was my standard answer. The Fierae will always offer to wager, at least once, while you're with them. Don't do it. "I am but a puny human," I added.

For some reason Blitz always laughed when I said the "puny human" part. "Cute cute cute, but not puny," they'd say through their laughter.

"Tell me about the Ancients!" I enthused. "Tell me how you *know* about the Ancients!" There were a billion stories I wanted Blitz to tell, but even speeded up, this tryst wouldn't last forever. Also, if I joined with them, as I'd intended to do before all was said and done, it would be at least a month before I could speak with the Fierae again. Even if I *didn't* join, it would take me a week to recover just from the conversation. And on top of all that, the odds of my finding Blitz and Blitz meeting again were not good. How the three of us had managed to meet six times (this was the sixth) in two years was simply unphathomable. Each time we met the ecstasy of being together increased.

"Ahh, Ancients!" the voice of Blitz moaned, filled with crackles and frizzy sounds. "The invisible ones! Tremendous gatherings we arranged over them, never seeing, they were invisible. Over the Great Pool the Zephrae bore us, and the Naiadae jumped up from their heavy depths and joined World's twirl. Even Terrae joined, traveling on the Zephres from the great red desert. The sand the Terrae inhabited frictioned us, and we were so awake, joining from cloud to cloud, from cloud to Water, illuminating the depths.

"This party we took to Land, so we could join with the Terrae in earth and tree. But we found earth where the Terrae would not dwell—hard, angular earth. We found sand broiled into glass, and the metals of Land grown up into dead trees—metal trees that no Elementals would inhabit. These things we crushed as best we could. World had no use for them, and we did our best to wipe them out. It became a game!"

"Where were the Ancients?" I asked.

14

"Invisible!" Blitz replied. "And they were in the dead earth and glass and metal trees. The Naiadae coalesced, and beat at them in rain, but they were like dead granite cliffs. Then the Naiadae swelled the Great Pool, with the Zephres at their backs, and drove it to shore in walls higher than tree upon tree upon tree. It was riotous fun, this game, and we played it all over World while years and years spun around the Ball! They were invisible, and crushed beneath the weight of that game!"

"But how did you find out about the Ancients, the invisible ones, if you never knew they were there?"

"Long, long after the dead earth and metal trees ceased to rise, the first of your kind came—the first Apprentices. When they realized us, they said their kind had once inhabited the dead earth and metal. This we still do not understand. Your kind inhabits creature. 'Yes,' they told us, 'and within creature, we inhabited the dead earth and metal.' So cute cute, human. Creature cannot inhabit! It is *inhabited!*" Blitz laughed at that in almost a scream of ecstasy. "Ahh, Spaul, come to bed," they cooed. "We would share this squeal of passion with you! We would drink yours!"

That was pretty much all I could stand. What happens to me when I join with them doesn't translate into words. But when it was over, I took my weary body and laid it down in the stream.

II
Terrae and Innkeepers

That night, after I finished washing my exhausted body in the stream, I packed up and left my meadow home. I'd intended to sleep first, but I didn't have enough to eat. You need to eat a lot even if you just *converse* with the Fierae. Joining with them completely empties you (in more ways than one). Unfortunately, food wasn't the only thing I was short of. When I had everything rolled into my pack, I checked and found that my little leather aytiem had not so much as one coin or piece of gold in it. Normally, this would not be a problem, and I could just contact the Terrae and have them push me up a little lump of gold or silver from Land. But I was really exhausted, and was going to have to add to that exhaustion by walking two klicks to a little village I knew. Usually, any tiny trick that proves you're an Apprentice will get you anything that's available, free. But I knew my bag of tricks would be as empty as my aytiem by the time I walked two klicks carrying my pack. I didn't even have the energy to float it along beside me on World's mag lines.

There was nothing else for me to do but try and contact the Terrae right then and there, before I left the meadow. I lay down on my stomach (hoping getting close would help me majick in my depleted state,) legs and arms spread wide, and tried to calm my mind-sea. It was choppy in there, and I couldn't seem to tame those whitecaps. Normally, Terrae are the easiest Elementals to contact, because they pack themselves densely into Land. Oh sure, they bubble up into trees and grass, even rocks, anything that grows or is of-Land. But down in the deep dirt they just snuggle up against one another and cuddle. They're so thick down there that they barely need to move to push up a hunk of gold or a precious gem. Of course, a *lot* of them work together to excavate like that. Still, they hardly even know they're doing it.

I could not connect. Sweat was soaking me again, and I wasn't even sure I could get back up off the ground. Then something extraordinary happened. Out near the sycamore, which was still about half-alive, I noticed the crackle and hum of a Charge running across the ground toward me. I could see it like little bolts of Fierae dancing through the grass. When it arrived, I heard it say, above my choppy mind-sea, "So cute cute, human, all love-tired, all Fierae loved. I command these Terrae for my lover cute, little Fierae human."

Almost immediately, two pieces of gold, about the size of robin's eggs, came pushing up out of the ground like shiny boils on the skin of Land. "Thank you," I said aloud, but the Charge was gone and spoke no more to me.

I was absolutely flabbergasted. *Never* had an elemental contacted me. I'd never even *heard* of such a thing. Oh, they'll be happy to communicate if *you* contact *them*, but for a Fierae elemental to actually move toward me and speak, not to mention command the Terrae to scavenge me up a tidy sum of gold, well, it was *beyond* unheard of. How could that Charge even tell I was there? Once I was back in my body, it shouldn't even have been cognizant of me. Could it be The One Certainty?

Oh, that's right, you won't even know about *that*, will you? The One Certainty is the very first thing every Finished Apprentice teaches his New Kid. It goes like this: "Life is in all, power is in life. All power abides by World's rules, except love. Love is above the rules."

That's the long version you learn as a New Kid. If you ask a full Apprentice what The One Certainty is, he'll tell you, simply, "Love is above the rules."

Lying in that meadow, flat on my face, looking at those two little orbs of gold, I was just too exhausted to cogitate on it anymore. After slowly managing to get to my feet, I picked up my little treasures and put them into my aytiem. Then I started the grueling, two-klick walk to Smith's Village, which was actually just an inn and a few outbuildings owned by a man named Smith. The reason he could make a living with his inn, was because it sat very near the Interred State of Ninety-five, which was once a big road for the Ancients to travel up and down the Infinite Eastern Shore. Apparently, they had some kind of Land boats they made with their Teck that they sailed on wheels over their hard seas of road. Here and there you can actually see pieces of the dead, black earth they made that road out of.

At that time, I was probably three quarters of the way down in the South of the Infinite Eastern Shore. Of course, it isn't really *infinite*, it's just called that. It ends way, way up north, and down by the Southern Edge, where it supposedly keeps going right into the swampy mess called the Florida, then into the Atlanta Sea (which the Elementals call The Great Pool).

You have to remember, this was several months ago, almost half a trip around the Ball, and I'd just started my travels north. I'll know when I'm actually in the North because I'll cross Mason Dicksin's Line. The Line is really just a wall of rocks that is almost as ancient as the Ninety-five. Supposedly, somebody (apparently named Mason Dicksin) built it shortly after the Elementals threw their big parties and stepped on the Ancients. It's still there, but it's so low now you can step right over it. Why Mason wanted to build a wall between North and South, once practically everybody was dead, remains a mystery. Maybe he just didn't have anything better to do.

As I walked toward the village of Smith, I tried again to calm my mind-sea. My pack was getting heavy, and if I could just find one little mag line, one tiny thread of World's force, I could let it shoulder my burden. I just couldn't do it. Blitz had simply rode me too hard and wrung out my wet. That's an Ancient saying. Thirest taught me hundreds of them, but I can't recall him ever explaining what they meant. I try not to use the dirty ones, like "Fug you, and the horse on the road to the inn." I know horses don't exist anymore, but Thirest told me what they looked like. "And people fugged them?" I asked him.

"All the time," he told me.

When I finally made it to Smith's Village, I had just enough strength left to plop down at a table and say to Smith, who waited on me himself, "Food!" Then I rolled one of those little gold balls out of my aytiem and handed it to him. "Keep it coming," I added.

"Yes *suh*!" he answered, all big-eyes and smiles. "You gonna want a bed?"

"Think that nugget'll cover me?" I asked, smiling back at him.

"For about a *week*!" he answered absently, ogling the gold he held between his fingers. Then he realized what he'd told me and said, "Well, three days at least. We can haggle it out later. You lookin' hungry."

18

"You have no idea," I answered.

"Got a couple girls for rent if you like. They're in the kitchen, but I can clean 'em up and haul 'em out if you wanna have a look."

"Actually," I told him, "I'm a little oversexed right now. I need some rest."

He laughed at that and said, "Hey, do you know what one Ancient said to the other Ancient?"

"What?" I asked. I must have heard a zillion different punch lines to that joke, but his surprised me.

"There's no rest from the Fierae!" he smiled.

"Don't I know it," I chuckled.

It was actually nice not having Smith know I was an Apprentice. People almost always start falling all over themselves to please you once they find that out. And they'll give you *anything* they have. One time I was at an inn, which was also near the Ninety-five, but way down near the Southern Edge. Forgetting to fill my aytiem isn't something new for me, and as I was finishing my third plate of stew in that inn, it dawned on me that I had nothing to pay with. I walked out into the yard of the place for a quick chat with the Terrae, and just as a fist sized hunk of silver came pushing up out of the ground, I noticed that the innkeeper was watching me out of his kitchen window. "Shite," I said. There's quite a few people holed up down near the Florida at the Southern Edge, and I didn't want to have to go through a bunch of that adoration everybody heaps on an Apprentice. "Keep it quiet!" I said to him, as I walked back into the inn.

Well, no sooner did I sit back down to finish that excellent plate of gator stew, then Mr. Innkeeper comes marching out of his kitchen with a very presentable daughter in tow. "Free for the night," he announces, smiling. "If you like her, you can keep her," he added.

Thirest had given me vague warnings about creature love, and I just wasn't ready to take on anything new right then. Plus, I'd been with Blitz not two weeks earlier, and was still pretty played out. Not wanting to seem rude, or cast aspersions on his daughter's looks, I said, "You know, I was just over in Kingstree, and a set of twins just wore me out."

Without so much as a nod or a wink, he spun around and ran back to his kitchen. One second later he was dragging *another* daughter to my table. "Here," he told me. "Try 'em both."

19

At this point I motioned for him to come close so I could whisper. "Some Apprentices prefer sex with their own gender," I said, which actually wasn't a lie, and was also common knowledge. The *lie* was in the implication that *I* preferred sex with my own gender.

Looking rather downcast, the innkeeper dragged his two girls back to the kitchen. I thanked Jess he didn't have a son.

The fried squirrel and rice at Smith's inn was even better than the gator stew at that inn down near Kingstree. Smith served it with applesauce, and some kind of very doughy bread. "It's tater-bread," he told me, when I asked him about it. His wine was very sweet and fruity, and that, he told me, was made out of something called scupnogs. "Ain't never heared tell of scupnogs nor tater-bread?" Smith asked me. "You comin' from north of the Mason?"

"Nope," I told him. "I'm heading up *to* the Line. I've mostly been living in the Lizzy-Anna Purchase, One-Mizzippi, and along the Southern Edge."

"Ain't no scupnogs in the Purchase?" he asked, as if the very idea was unthinkable.

"Not that I know of," I told him, "and I'd definitely remember drinking wine *this* good."

When I said that he hooked his thumbs through the sospensors he had holding up his pants and said, "Wanna look at them girls, now?"

"I want to look at a bed," I answered, adding, "an *empty* one."

"Suit yerself," he said. "Guess I can give you the room with the *small* bed."

I ate and slept at Smith's inn for three days. I don't know who he had cooking, but Smith's food was some of the best I'd ever eaten. One night he plopped down a plate covered by a huge slab of meat that had been fried hard in a skillet, but was still bloody and red on the inside. "That there come off a *cow*!" he said proudly. I ate the whole thing and was amazed at how much of my energy it seemed to restore. Bloody red meat from a cow! I was going to have to remember that.

On the fourth morning since I'd arrived, after a breakfast of scrabbled eggs and skillet cakes, I announced that I was leaving.

Smith had taken quite a liking to me, probably because I was full of compliments that were all sincere. "Reckon I owe you some change," he said, carrying a sack over to me.

"I think we're even," I told him. "I ate like a pig."

"Yeah, but you never even jazzed up my girls. Take this," he said, thrusting the sack at me.

I looked inside, but wasn't sure what I was seeing. When I gave him a quizzical look, Smith said, "Them's hushpuppies. Cornmeal and milk and onions and eggs, fried in bacon fat. They say the Ancients that lived in these parts couldn't go a day without 'em. Yer headin' into Two Carolines now and the food up there is gonna be a bit strange for a gent like you. Specially if yer hikin' the Ninety-five. Swampy damn place, with blue crabs and mush-rats scuttlin' 'round all over the place. Them hushpups'll stay fresh for a week, and you can still eat 'em for a week after that. So if them Caroline's boys ain't got nothin' looks fit to eat, you just stick with old Smith's pups." Then he gave me a pat on the back, and opened the door for me. "If you make it to the Line," he called after me, as I headed toward the Interred State, "Bring me back a stone off it!"

"Absofugginlutely!" I called back.

III
Two Carolines

How the Ancients came up with the name Interred State of Ninety-five is anybody's guess. "Maybe because it's made out of dead-earth," Thirest had told me once, when I'd asked him about it. "The Ancients put their dead in bunkers and called that 'interred.' I think 'Interred State' just means dead. Maybe the Ninety-five part is some kind of measurement of its length. Or maybe it was the number of their Skyshaper Villages that it passed through."

Thinking of Thirest now, reminds me that I was thinking about him as I started up that long trail north, heading away from Smith's. If I ever do get this journal caught up, and I *will*, I'm never going to let it get behind again. Thirest was right, you forget too much if you don't keep up with it all the time.

I was walking right on top of the Ninety-five, thinking of Thirest, when I found a black chunk of it. Sure enough, no Elementals at all, not so much as one tiny Terrae dwelled in it. You don't see much of that dead, black earth as you walk the Ninety-five. The only way you can really tell you're on it is that things grow differently right over it. Mostly small, hearty things, like weeds, and no trees at all take root there. Why, I wondered, did the Ancients build everything out of dead stuff? Where did they even *get* dead stuff? The Fierae said they had dead metal and dead earth, and sand turned into glass. There's plenty of glass in the windows of inns, and even some people's houses. There are people who know how to make it, but who would ever think to build giant villages of it that reach up toward the sky?

Other than the chunk of black road I was holding, glass was the only other dead thing I'd ever seen. Elementals won't live in glass. Thirest once told me you could actually trap an elemental if you surrounded it with glass. If you kept it in there long enough, it might even die. "Why?" I'd asked him, and I could feel myself tearing up at the thought of trapping or killing an elemental. "Why would anyone *do* that?"

"That's the question, isn't it, Spaul? What were the Ancients thinking?" he said, noticing my tears and showing me the smile he always wore when he wanted to say, "I love you."

Thirest only said those words to me once, the day he died. All the rest of those years, from the time they figured me for a New Kid, and handed me over to him when I was five years old, he used that smile to say it. But as he lay there dying, six weeks before I started up the Ninety-five, he'd said it. For a while after he died I wondered what he'd meant by it. Though he'd only used those three words, I wondered if more words were hiding behind them. I wondered if he was saying, "I have always loved you," and then I started to think he might have been saying "I have always wanted to love you, and now it's safe to say that."

I don't know why I was thinking about Thirest like that. I guess because I'd been with him pretty much all my life, and felt like I deserved to know everything. I never saw him pursuing creature love with anybody, girl or boy, and figured he just considered it too dangerous. He almost never discussed those things with me, either, but when he did that word, 'dangerous' always came up at least once.

Why was I thinking so much about Thirest? Because I was missing him. He'd told me not to. He'd said it was all right to remember him, but missing him was like saying he no longer existed. I promised myself to work harder at stopping those feelings I was getting, those feelings of 'missing.' But right then, I wasn't doing a very good job and tears started crowding my eyes. I looked up, with that black chunk of dead earth still in my hand, and said, "I love you, too, Thirest." I'd always loved him.

I couldn't have hiked more than a dozen klicks that day. Though I was feeling stronger (and I give credit for that to bloody cow meat) I was still weak from that tryst with Blitz. Even so, laying out on my blankets that night (the weather giving me no reason to set my tent) I felt just a little shiver of desire when I heard a distant rumble of thunder. I smiled, and whispered, "Is that you, Blitz? Wait for me." I'm sure it was just my sleepy eyes playing tricks, but I thought I saw a spark or two in the trees above me.

The next day I hiked further than the day before. By the third day I could once again summon a mag line to carry my pack. After that, I was making twenty klicks a day at a leisurely stroll. Apprentices very rarely hurry when traveling. If you see an Apprentice struggling to get somewhere, go the other way, because wherever he is going, some kind of az-kicking majick is likely to occur. Thirest had me hurrying with him once when he heard a rumor that some men in the Purchase had found one of the Ancients' Land boats. He was pretty worked up about it, and sparks were actually flying off of him as he marched, with me following, the twenty klicks or so to where those men were supposed to be. He was also talking to himself, sometimes majicking (I knew because clouds were gathering and following us,) and sometimes just cussing. The only thing he said that I could actually make out was, "I'll gollam *bury* them in it!"

It turned out that Land boat was a toy you could hold in the palm of your hand. Thirest didn't want me to see it, but I did and noticed that it had four little wheels. It was just a toy, and didn't seem dangerous to me, but Thirest held it in his palm, glared at it, and we both watched it melt and drip onto the ground. "Gollam Ancients," he swore, as he started marching back the way we'd come.

By the fifth day since Smith's, I knew I had to be in Two Carolines. It was getting swampy, just like Smith said it would. I even saw a mush-rat, and talked him into letting me eat him. As I sent him away from his flesh, he asked me, "Will I be a mush-rat again?"

"More than likely," I said, which was probably the truth, but who knows. He seemed so dejected by that answer that I called to his light as it left, "But you *could* come back as an eagle!" and, who knows, that might have been true, too.

With one thought to the Fierae, I got a nice fire going. I'd skinned the mush-rat, and skewered him onto a green stick of hickory. Mush-rat isn't bloody red cow, but I was getting tired of Smith's hushpuppies. Don't get me wrong, they were good, and I could also see myself using little pieces of them to catch brimlets and perch, so I wasn't discarding them by any means. But Thirest always said a growing Apprentice needs some meat once in a while, and the mush-rat wasn't going to miss that body. He'd be into something else before he knew it. "Thanks again," I said to his flesh anyway, before I took the first bite. "That was right neighborly of you."

The day after the mush-rat, I met my first fellow travelers coming the other way. It was an old man pushing a little dog in a one-wheeled barrow. "Yowza!" he called, when he saw me coming with my pack floating alongside. Since that surely clued him in that I was an Apprentice, I didn't try to hide it. In fact, I reached out with a little thread of mag line, and plucked the dog out of the barrow. I could see, even from a distance, that its back legs hung limp and useless. Apparently that was why it was being wheeled.

I drew on the line and brought the dog to me. It was a scruffy little mutt, white with black spots, big, soulful eyes, and droopy ears. When the old man got to us I said, "G'morning."

"Yowza!" he repeated. "You a 'Prentice, ain'tcha?"

"Yes," I admitted. "And *as* an Apprentice, I'd advise you against eating this little fella. He could have a disease, which might be why his legs don't work. I could check it for you if you like, but it'll take a few minutes. You'd probably be better off with a nice, fat mush-rat, anyway. They're very accommodating around here." I was being glib, I knew, but I felt good, and for some reason I was happy to see another person.

"Ain't disease, Missuh 'Prentice," he told me, "him got kick by a muley. I don't eat him no how, he a friend. He named Rummy. I named Tool."

"Well," I said, holding out my hand for Tool to touch, "I'm Spaul, and if damage is all that's wrong with Rummy, I'll fix him for you."

"You fix ol' Rummy?" he exclaimed. "Hear that you l'il sheet-eater, Missuh 'Prentice gonna fix yo' feets!"

"C'mon," I told Tool, "we've got to get off top of this Ninety-five before I can fix him."

"Sho 'nuff," Tool replied.

When we were off the dead road, I found a rock and used it to dig a hole big enough to fit the back of Rummy's body. Then I buried him. He looked really funny with his head and front paws sticking up out of the ground. Tool laughed and said, "Look like he just growed there, like a dog-weed"

"Okay," I said. "Now be quiet a minute while I talk to the Terrae."

Tool sat on the ground and closed his mouth tight. I put my hands on either side of Rummy, and calmed my sea. It took less than a minute to explain to the Terrae what I wanted. When I opened my eyes and lifted my hands off the ground, it was starting to shimmer, and a little whirl of Zephrae played around Rummy, kicking up dust. Apparently, they'd heard me talking to the Terrae and had decided they wanted to help. Whatever. I'd let them figure it out. "It's going to take a few minutes," I told Tool, "but you can talk now."

Tool jumped up, went over to his barrow, and returned with an old, brown liter jug he'd had in there with Rummy. "Got corn?" he asked me, holding up the jug.

"No, I don't," I answered him.

"Do now!" he laughed.

Tool's "corn" turned out to be some kind of ethnyl. Smith's scupnog wine carried about fifteen percent ethnyl. Tool's corn carried about ten percent of something other than ethnyl. The first pull I took off the jug stole my breath, and Tool laughed as I tried to start breathing again. "Good, ain't it?" he said.

"*Too* gollam good," I said, surprising myself with my own foul language.

"Come home," Tool told me. "Two klick west. Give you a jug fo' fixin' Rummy."

Speaking of which, I thought, he ought to be done. I looked over to where the little dog was buried, and called, "Hey! Rummy! Get outa that hole!"

Watching the little dog frantically digging and kicking himself out of the ground had me and Tool and the ethnyl inside us laughing to beat all helluva. When he finally got out, Rummy came running, and jumped so high into Tool's arms that he almost went over his shoulder. "He fix!" Tool yelled, with the dog in his arms. "You come home, Missuh 'Prentice. I kill a yard bird, cook him with yam! Give you corn. You sleep in a bed dis night! Ain't dat somethin', Rummy fix!"

"Well," I said, "just keep him away from that muley, and he'll stay that way."

"Thanky, Missuh 'Prentice. Thanky."

"Call me Spaul, and you should really thank Land," I told him, bending down and patting the ground. "Thank Air, too," I said, waving my hand around over my head. "I think it helped."

Tool bent down, with Rummy tucked under one arm, and touched his other hand to Land. "Thanky," he whispered, with his eyes closed. Then he stood and waved at the sky. "Thanky!" he yelled.

Though he couldn't hear it, I could, and was quite surprised when the Elementals said, "Tool is welcome."

IV
Tool's Treasure

I walked with Tool the two klicks west to his home, which turned out to be a well built, little cottage. Chickens scurried around the bare earth, scratching for worms, and behind a rail fence, a muley tore at clumps of grass. In an open shed I could see the device that was probably responsible for Tool's powerful corn. Occasionally it dripped into a large, wide mouthed, earthen jar. After reminding Rummy to stay away from the muley, Tool put him down and snatched up a fat chicken. I watched as he took it by the neck, thanked it, said, "Good-bye," and then spun it once quick, ending its life. "She say she a *real* tasty bird," Tool said, winking at me. The funny thing is, that bird's light *did* say something as it left, though I didn't catch what it was. "Come in de house, set yo'self," Tool said to me. "I dress out dis bird."

As we were walking across the yard, the door to the house opened, and an amazingly beautiful girl stepped out onto the porch. Her beauty was such that I simply could not tell her age. She might have been fifteen and she might have been twenty-five. Her shining, black hair was all plaited into tight rows of braids, and her eyes were so dark they seemed to be all pupil. Her skin was the same glossy brown as Tool's corn jug. "Dis Pearl," Tool told me. "She dis house' treasure. Look jus' like her po' 'parted mama, Pearl does. Lucky don't look like me, huh?" he laughed.

When we got close enough, I held out my hand and said, "I'm Spaul."

Pearl lightly touched my fingers and smiled. "Pearl don't speak," Tool explained. "Red fever stole her words when she five year old. Land and Air won't do no fix for Pearl, huh?"

"No," I told him. "They won't fix illness or what illness has wrought. I can't convince them otherwise. I've tried."

And I *had* tried, though Thirest had warned me against it. "They'll repair damage," he'd told me, "but they see disease as normal. They see it as part of World's rules. If you keep insisting otherwise, you'll anger them, and you'll only anger the Elementals *once!*"

28

He was right, of course. Every time I tried, the Elementals became agitated, and I knew I had to stop. I have no doubt that if you manage to anger them they will snuff you out in a nannysecond.

Some kind of sorrow must have showed on my face at not being able to help this beautiful girl. Pearl came to me, touched my cheek, then smiled hugely and, with her finger, traced a smile onto my lips. "Pearl say ain't no nevermind. You smile. Pearl like you. Never know, might love you dis night," Tool said.

"No," I told him, though I was not yet able to take my eyes off her beautiful, smiling face. Finally, I turned away from her, and faced Tool. "No," I said again. "And you shouldn't be offering people your daughter. Is that all she's worth to you, a dog's hind legs?" I was raising my voice, and it startled me. I shut up.

Tool smiled. "Has a way of makin' you want to protect her, doesn't she," he said to me. "She my treasure. I never give her *no* man! I break Rummy legs my*self* fo' I give Pearl. All I say, Pearl like you, she might come see you dis night. Man might love Air or Fire, think he know love. Treasure come to a man, he find out different."

"You must tell her not to do that," I said. "Apprentice ways... differ."

"Ain't 'cause we *negra* is it?" Tool asked, squinting his eyes at me.

I didn't know the word he used, and asked, "What is 'negra?'"

"Dis," he said, patting his arm. "Dis brown. We earth color, you hay. We negra."

I smiled and shook my head. "That's just something in your skin that you have more of than I do," I told him. "That's all it is. We aren't different colours, we're just different shades of the *same* colour."

"You knows," Tool said, nodding his head. "Some don't, though. You be careful in Two Carolines. Some says they's negra and don't like yo' kind. Some says I's negra, don't like *my* kind. Stay to de old road, you alone in Two Carolines. Two kinds' bad folk been croppin' up like weed. Far as Pearl goes, she come to you, *you* say no. I *dares* you!" Then he started to laugh, as he made his way inside to dress our dinner.

Tool plucked, Pearl cooked. Smith's food had been excellent, Pearl's was majick. Literally. You cannot be an Apprentice and not notice when the Elementals have had a hand in something, no matter how small that hand might be. Sugars can be multiplied or altered in yams. Juices can refuse to leave a cooking bird. These tiny things would be *much* more difficult than fixing Rummy's legs. Basically, the only point I had to get across was *fix legs*. If I said, *fix yams*, I might open the oven door and find them alive and sprouting.

To make fine adjustments like that, an Apprentice would either have to have incredible patience, or a rapport with the Elementals unlike anything I've ever seen. On top of all that, I'd never met a Female Apprentice. Thirest told me they're extremely rare, and might no longer exist. "But they're *very* powerful, especially with Land," he'd said, "because they are more like earth, like Land, than we are. We're stronger with Fire. If you ever do meet one, watch her carefully. Then decide quickly whether to join with her or run like helluva."

The fact that Pearl could not speak perturbed me. Though I could compliment her cooking, I couldn't ask the questions that were roiling the sea of my mind. Finally, almost independent of my intentions, I looked at Pearl, and asked Tool, "How did she learn to cook like this?"

"Pearl mama a 'Shykik,' named Madama Sia. Madama know *all* element, 'cept Fire. Sia say Fire too fast, too jealous. Want all lovin' be *they* lovin'. Sia talk *once* with Fire. When Pearl been dyin' of Red Fever, Sia call Air, call Land, call Water, all laugh and go away. All say good time Pearl leave, come back boy-child, oughta been boy-child, they tellin' Sia.

"One night, I wake up to thunder. Sia not in de bed. I go out, and there Sia, arms out, facin' a storm comin'. I look close, Sia feet ain't touchin' ground. Storm comin' closer, I see little lectrics jumpin' up Sia toes, crawlin' like lit ants up her, out on her arms. Storm closer. I hear Pearl cryin' in de house, screamin' with what li'l life she got left. I gotta go in to Pearl. No sooner I get in there, *big* flash, *big* thunder, shake de house. Now I'm runnin' back out to Sia. She layin' in a heap on de ground.

"Never seen Sia scared of nothin' 'cept Pearl dyin', but whatever she seen or done that night scared sheet right out her. I take her in, clean her up, get her in bed. She never get out dat bed again. Three days she lay there, sometimes eyes open, sometimes shut, not sayin' a word. I feed her broth, but she don't take much.

Third day, her eyes move, she look at me, say, 'Pearl gonna live. Made a deal for her, but I gotta go.' That all she say.

"That night storm come—Sia dead, Pearl alive, no mo' fever. But she never talk. How Pearl cookin' like dis? She 'Shykik,' like her mama. Tell de food what she want. Dat what you wanna know, ain't it? Pearl talk to dis food?"

"Yes," I answered. "That's what I wanted to know."

That evening, Tool pulled from his jug four or five times to my one. Too much ethnyl isn't good for Apprentices. When you can speak with Elementals, you need to know exactly what you're saying.

After his last drink of corn, Tool showed me to a tiny room, like a pantry, that had a cot made up. There was a single window facing west, and it was open. Tool said, "Leave dis door open, breeze come right through. Corn's in de jug, food in de kitchen you get hungry. I gone to bed."

I wasn't sure where Pearl had gotten off to. I hadn't seen her since dinner. I took one more little pull of Tool's corn, closed my eyes, shook my head, and whispered, "Yowza!" Then I put on a pair of thin shorts out of my pack, and lay down on the cot. A cool breeze was coming out of the west, where I could barely hear the carrying on of a storm. Just as I was drifting off, I felt a hand on my cheek. I opened my eyes to see Pearl, dressed in something thin and gauzy. I could tell by the way it lay on certain parts of her body— her hips, the tips of her breasts—that it was all she was wearing. "You're very pretty," I said to her, "but I...we mustn't."

Pearl smiled, took my hand, and pulled me up out of the cot. She motioned with a finger for me to come with her. She led me outside, and stood me to face west, making me understand that she wanted me not to move. Then she stood next to me, her bare right foot touching my left.

I wasn't sure what was going on, but I wanted to find out. I didn't move. Pearl brought her arms up loosely, like a child might do if it wanted you to pick it up. She motioned for me to do the same. Then she closed her eyes.

Immediately I heard the rushing voices of Zephres gathering. Soon they were whirling at incredible speeds all around us, doing figure eights through our legs, under our arms, speeding around our heads. Though the Zephrae never touched us, not once, they were moving so fast that they were doing something to the space between them and us. Pearl slowly moved her hand toward mine, and took it. Then I realized that our feet were no longer on the ground. I was startled, but not afraid. Had Pearl not been smiling at me and holding my hand, I may have had to fight fear on my mind-sea for a moment or two.

We rose about two meters from the ground, and at that height the Zephres that were playing with us floated our bodies parallel to the ground so that we were facing up at the stars. Pearls's mouth was laughing, though no sound came. When I realized she was laughing, I couldn't help but join in. Then the Zephrae stood us back perpendicular to the ground, and brought us around to face one another, very close. For just an instant, Pearl brushed her lips lightly against mine, then pulled her head back and smiled wickedly. Talk about a seduction!

As quickly as the Zephres had arrived, they set us down and left. I was absolutely *floored*! Flummoxed! And the fact that Pearl couldn't speak was now beyond frustrating, it was unbearable. *How*, I wanted to know, had she done that? What, exactly, had she communicated to the Zephrae?

When we were back on our feet, Pearl tapped me on the chest and nodded her head. Somehow, I realized she was saying it was my turn. But how in helluva was I going to top that, or even *equal* it? Oh, sure, I could speak with Fierae, even join with them, and I doubted seriously that Pearl could, but I had no idea how to duplicate what she had just done. Still, I felt a need to take my turn, to do *something*.

Realizing, now, that Pearl *must* be a Female Apprentice—untrained, perhaps, but an Apprentice none-the-less—I tried to remember what Thirest had told me about them. Very good with Land, he'd said, which would also make them good with Air and Water. "They're better with all three," he'd told me, "than we are. But they shun Fire. The Fierae affect them much more than they do us. If they were to speak with the Fierae, as we do, they would immediately join and never return. There's actually a love potion you can do with a sleepy Charge that arouses women. When you're older, and I'm sure you wouldn't misuse it, I'll teach it to you."

I don't know if Thirest forgot, or decided I might misuse it, but he never taught me that majick. Still, it gave me an idea. That storm party off to the west had drifted a little closer. If I listened, I could hear Charges, here and there in the ground, chittering. "Come come come come, here," they were saying sleepily to the revelers in the storm.

Pearl was facing me, so I took both her hands in mine. Then I calmed my sea, and reached out to the nearest Charge. It would be sleepy, but with that storm out there, it would be awake enough for Pearl and me to feel the tingle of it if I called it up onto our bodies. It wouldn't be as spectacular as being lifted off the ground by a chorus of whirling Zephres, but it would dance little sparks on our skin, and make the hairs on our body stand up and tickle us.

The Charge I contacted came faster than I thought it would, wasn't as sleepy as I expected it to be. In fact, it spoke—not that half-asleep chittering, but wide-awake talking! What it said, as I watched little sparks dance on Pearl's cheeks, was, "Spaul!"

It was the lady Blitz, and she was quite lively, causing Pearl's braids to stand up on her head. "How can this be?" I asked Blitz.

"How can it *not?*" she countered.

"It *is*," I said, hoping that would suffice to negate my silly question. Then I noticed that Pearl was moving, squirming, her eyes were up in her head, and her mouth mimed a sensuous moan. She was dripping with sweat. Then she actually *did* moan. It was an eerie, buzzing, humming sound. "Ahh," she said with that voice. "Spaul! This is lovely! Join with this female, I would know creature love."

"Where is Pearl?" I said out loud.

"I am here, also," she said. "Too much love, Spaul. My body screams with it. Blitz wants us to love, *I* want us to love, but it already peaks with me. Ahh! Spaaaul!"

"Leave us," I thought to Blitz.

"Mate!" she insisted.

"It's too much for this girl," I said.

"Then I will send her out."

"NO!" I said aloud.

"Ahhh, yesss!" Pearl said, rolling her head back onto her shoulders.

"NO!" I thought to Blitz. "If you send her out, I will never join with Blitz and Blitz again."

33

That did it, the Charge was gone. Pearl fell into my arms and began kissing me. This was no brush on the lips. This was her tongue in my mouth and her hands caressing and her body pressing. I managed to get her by the shoulders and hold her back from me. Her smile was wide, and her eyes pleaded for love. I managed to whisper, "No."

This time, when she fell into my arms, she went limp. I carried her into the house, and laid her down on the little cot. She was sleeping, with a very satisfied smile on her face, when I left her. I took the blankets from my pack, and lay down on the floor by the door to that little room. I wanted to sleep, but I couldn't. I had a lot to think about.

What Pearl had done that night had been extraordinary, but the idea of Blitz being coincidentally where I was, again, for the seventh time in two years, and the second time in less than two *weeks*, seemed almost impossible. Could she actually be following me? Could she somehow see me, sense me even in my body? Was that actually her I saw sparking up in the trees just a couple of nights ago?

I began to think about things I didn't want to think about. What if I *had* mated with Pearl while a Charge was in her like that? Would they have joined, become one? Would Pearl and the Charge have become permanently fused, or would it have killed her? Blitz, when I took her onto us, was not inhabiting me, but she was definitely inhabiting Pearl. But Fierae do not inhabit! They are the only Elementals that don't. Then I thought of something Thirest told me once. "We are part Fierae," he'd said. "A tiny, tiny part, to be sure, but Charges move within us." Could a Fierae Charge inhabit a human body? It was a silly question, I had just seen one do it.

When I awoke the next morning, Pearl was stepping over me. As she did she looked down and smiled so suggestively, with her eyes locked to mine, that I had to fight the urge to jump up and grab her, drag her back to that cot. Somehow, I let her pass, just as Tool came in with a basket of eggs. As I sat eating the incredible breakfast Pearl cooked, I had a thought that is very uncommon, and disturbing, for an Apprentice. "What will I do now?"

Normally, I would simply do whatever was most obviously next. I had been invited into Tool's house for the night. I had spent the night. Next, I would leave. But how could I leave Pearl? Of course, being an Apprentice pretty much gave me the right to do whatever I saw fit. If I wanted to stay and observe Pearl, I doubted seriously that Tool would object. If I wanted to take her with me, that was my right. Being an Apprentice, I also had the power to do those things by force. I would not. I had never forced anyone to do anything. Even that mush-rat went of his own accord. If he'd wanted to keep that body, I'd have left him in it.

Like a true Apprentice, I admitted who I was and did the equation. My reservations about creature love were still in place. I wanted more information before I risked it. If I were to stay here, I would either succumb to Pearl and love her, or be forced to leave before we did. If I took her with me, I might as well just love her right now, because there would be no leaving her when the temptation grew too strong. I would not take her from her father, then abandon her. Of those two options, staying was the safest. But why put myself through that kind of desire and denial?

If Pearl could speak I'd have felt a responsibility to the Apprentices to question her extensively. But she could *not* speak to me, and I knew what she *could* do to me. I decided to leave. "I want to thank you for the hospitality, Tool," I said. "I guess I'll be leaving now."

"Pearl goin' with you," Tool said around a yolky mouthful of fried eggs.

The matter-of-factness of his statement startled me, but I recovered and said, "I don't think that would be a good idea."

"Don't tell me, tell her," Tool said, still shoveling eggs.

"Pearl, I really don't..." I began, but then I noticed there was a pack sitting against the wall behind her. She smiled hugely as I looked at it.

I turned back to Tool, who started laughing and almost choked on his eggs. "Don't look at me," he said, "she goin', she goin'. Not you, not me, not Ball in sky, not water in sea stop her. 'Cept it. She good cook, good Shykik, good lookin', 'ventually be good love." Then he started laughing again. "I give you three days, you can't resist no mo'. Maybe two. I bet you!"

35

"I *can* stop her, you know," I told Tool, which caused him to laugh even louder. Then he got up from the table, wiped his laughing mouth, and said, "I gone get a little jug of corn, take with you." He laughed all the way out the door.

Pearl was still sitting there smiling at me. I cleared my mind and contacted the Terrae inhabiting the house, the table, the chairs. I wanted them to overwhelm Pearl and put her to sleep. They actually laughed at me. I'd never heard the Terrae laugh before that day. I started to contact the Zephrae, but realized how foolish that was. Pearl had convinced the Zephres to float us around the yard like leaves on a breeze. She obviously had much more influence with them than I did.

The pump at the sink in the kitchen was still primed, so I got up and pressed the handle down to draw up a little water. When it dripped from the spout, I wet my hands. Pearl was watching, smiling the whole time, but I think she thought I was just washing my hands. Then I went behind her, reached around and placed my wet hands over her eyes. The Naiadae knew what I wanted. I caught Pearl by the shoulders, then laid her sleeping head on the table.

Quickly, I stuffed my blankets back in my pack, and hit the front porch at a trot. Tool was coming with a jug. When he saw me coming out of the house on the fly, he started to laugh. "Take this!" he said, holding out the jug. "Better hurry!" he shouted, as I grabbed it and started jogging. "She fast!"

It was hot already that morning, but I jogged for at least three klicks. I was moving pretty fast. Sometimes I had to grab my pack and scoot it along the mag line I was using to carry it, because it wasn't keeping up. Finally, I stopped, slid the line from under my pack and let it drop to the ground. Then I sat with my back against my Worldly belongings. I looked back south, and was just starting to smile at my cleverness and ingenuity, when I saw something that momentarily scared me. It was Pearl. Her outstretched hands were each resting on a mag line. Her feet were off the ground, and stretched out a little behind her. A large chorus of Zephres were directly at her back, pushing her toward me at an incredible clip. Apparently, she'd found time to braid red and gold beads into her hair before she'd come after me. They were blowing and dancing in the breeze of her passing. I had to smile. Pearl was a marvel. While talking about Female Apprentices, Thirest had said, "Watch her

36

closely, then decided whether to join with her or run like helluva." I had run like helluva, but Pearl could *fly!*

When she arrived at where I was sitting, Pearl lifted her hands from those mag lines, and the Zephrae at her back buzzed off in all directions like crazy bees. She sat down next to me, and bumped me playfully with her shoulder. My mind-sea felt hurrakin tossed, as I considered loving her right there and then. I could hear Tool saying, "'Cept it!"

Instead, I took her hands and turned them palms up. Sure enough, they had red lines running down them, but they were nowhere near as bad as I thought they'd be. You might think that's from friction, but it isn't. It's the magnetics drawing at the metals in your body. Pearl's hands should have been bloody and swollen, and she should have been faint with anemia. Mag lines strong enough to hold up a human are powerful enough to tug the iron out of your blood.

When I finished inspecting her hands, Pearl shook them, making a wincing face, and then mouthed the word, "OW!"

"Yes, I'm sure they *do* hurt," I told her. "Don't you ever do that again unless it's an emergency," I scolded.

Pearl pointed to herself, then made a walking motion with two fingers.

"Good," I said.

Then she patted herself on the chest, then me on the chest, then made the walking gesture again.

"It looks that way," I said.

Why is it that I can't seem to remember, when I write in this journal, to tell you *everything?* I never did explain about mag lines! Magnetic lines of force criss-cross World. The mag lines are what their name implies, magnetic, but they are something else, too. They are also hard to explain, and harder to understand. I'll try, but to be honest, I don't *entirely* understand, myself.

Mag lines are like Elementals in as much as you can contact them, and make them more aware (stronger). But the mag lines don't engage themselves in activities the way Elementals do. Basically, they just are there, kind of like World's nervous system. When I get a mag line to carry my pack, I simply choose one thread and make the contact that strengthens it by making it aware. Most mag lines run pretty much straight across World's face, but you can easily bend a thread as you travel. When you are finished with it, and it weakens, it will slowly move back to its original position.

If I wanted to lift something big, say Tool's muley, I would strengthen a thread or two under it, then bulge them up till I'd accomplished the task. But I wouldn't want to hold a muley like that very long. If the muley was a rock, it wouldn't matter, and I could leave it floating on the mag lines all day. But if I left the muley up there, the lines would start drawing on his metals, and before long he'd start bleeding where the lines touched him. If I left him up there all day, it would kill him, bleed him to death or, who knows, maybe cut him in half. Pearl must have traveled two or three klicks with her hands on those lines of force, and all she got was what looked like slightly scalded palms. I really needed to find a way to question her, find out what kind of majick she'd used to protect her hands, find out how she got the Zephrae to float us. I asked her if she could write, but she shook her head, no. I started cogitating on how I could majick a voice for her. I thought about it as Pearl and I started our long walk together.

V
Spaul's Treasure

Tool knew it would happen. Pearl knew it would happen. I kept telling myself it wouldn't, but I knew it would happen, too. I should have bet Tool, though, because I managed to last six days.

On the sixth night, however, I gave in. One of those frequent, summer-night Fierae squalls was taking place somewhere nearby, and had chilled the air after a very hot day. Pearl was lying as close to me as I'd been letting her, and was about a foot to my left. Suddenly, she sat up and looked at me. Then she wrapped her arms around herself, and made a little shivering motion.

"Yes," I said, "it's cooled off nicely."

Then next thing I knew, she'd rolled on top of me. She had my face in her hands and that look in her eyes. "You're so beautiful," I said. She took one hand off my face and patted my chest. "No," I told her, "I'm not beautiful."

But Pearl nodded her head and insisted I was. Then she kissed me. Before I knew it, she'd somehow gotten under me, as the kissing became fierce. But I stopped for a moment, and backed my head up to look at her. "Such a beautiful treasure," I said, knowing I'd surrendered, and would love her. Then I noticed the light in her eyes and the sparks in her hair, and she fell into the same ecstatic state she'd been in that night after we'd floated. "Blitz?" I said.

"It's me, Pearl," she moaned in that frizz-hum voice. "Blitz is here, but stays out of my sea, stays only in my body. Oh! Spaul! Love is melting me, *please* love me."

"But how do I know this is you, Pearl? And what will happen to you if we join? Blitz could fuse with you, or who knows *what* might happen?" Then I thought to Blitz, "You could become forever bound with this female. You may not care about that now, but just think—no more joining from the trees with Air Charges, no more crawling sleepy through World. You will not be free, and will be small, always small."

"Mate!" she insisted. "I take this chance to know creature love with Spaul!"

39

"It's breaking the rules!" I said.

"Love is above rules!"

I had a very bad feeling about this, and Apprentices need to trust their feelings. Usually. But hadn't I just ignored my reservations about creature love? Wasn't I about to surrender, and love Pearl? Who am I kidding, I *had* surrendered. But this was different. I looked at Pearl, felt her squirming under me, heard her moaning and orgasming all over the place with that hot-to-trot Charge coursing through her body. What if they *did* fuse? What if this ecstasy that was having its way with her never ceased? If it didn't it would surely kill her, though I had to admit, I could think of worse ways to go.

And what about me? I was starting to feel something for Pearl that was reinforcing my fears about creature love. It wasn't just the physical part anymore, though her squirming and pressing up against me were certainly not helping that part either. I was starting to feel Binding Love, the kind of love I'd felt for Thirest. Yet I barely *knew* Pearl.

The equation was solved (for the time being), and I rolled off of Pearl and got to my feet. "Get out!" I thought to Blitz. She didn't answer me, nor did she evacuate. If anything, Pearl was even more animated, lying there on the ground moaning her orgasms. That humming voice was eerie, but it was also somehow appealing, even enticing.

"Spaul!" she called to me with it. "Come back. I *need* you!"

Enough was enough. I settled my mind-sea till it was flat, motionless, not a rippled showed. I was engaging myself in the State of Great Purpose. Blitz had angered me—though, of course, that anger did not show as I floated motionless in the sea of my mind. I called out to every elemental of Land and Air and Water that was in range of the State I was in. I made it known that rules were being broken. I let them feel my frustration with Blitz, appealed to their love of innocence, and showed them how Pearl's was being victimized. Then, for good measure, I allowed my anger to peek out at them. That may have been a bit much.

The little clearing we were in started to glow with elemental awareness. Terrae were rising up through the souls of my feet. Zephres tore at the trees, and Naiadae condensed on my flesh till I was dripping. I was aglow, lighting the clearing. Pearl stopped moaning and writhing and sat up, but it was Blitz who spoke. With an astonished look on Pearl's face, she said, "Spaul!"

"GET OUT!" I roared. The percussion of my elemental voice broke several small saplings, and blew birds and insects out of the trees. Blitz departed immediately, but she jumped up and shocked me on the nose as she did. I'm sure she wasn't happy about the chastising she was going to get from the Elementals I'd roused.

When I looked back to Pearl, her eyes were wide, and her hands were over her ears. I was hoping I hadn't damaged her hearing. I hadn't been thinking properly, or I'd have sent Naiadae to fill her ears and protect them before I exploded like that.

I went to Pearl and took her in my arms. She was shaking violently, and I had to struggle to get her to remove her hands from the sides of her head. Finally, I persuaded her to lie back down, and I held her close against me. She made no more advances to love that night, and I wouldn't have done it if she had. I didn't trust Blitz.

Those first six days of our walk together had been happy ones. Whenever we stopped for the day, I would take a "powder nap" (an Ancient term that means a light dusting of sleep lasting half an hour). When I'd wake from it, Pearl would be coming back from gathering. Every evening we ate nuts and grapes and blueberries and strawberries, and a couple of times she caught fish. I had a hook and line in my pack, but she never took it. I could catch fish without it, too, but I often fished with the line because it relaxes me. We also ate Smith's hushpuppies. Pearl obviously knew what they were, because the first time I showed them to her she put her hands up like paws, and panted with her tongue hanging out of her mouth. What a cute puppy she made!

Those first six days were happy and fun, and Pearl and I grew close. Close enough for the events of the sixth night to transpire. But after that night, Pearl was not the same. She tried to hide it from me, but I could tell that sadness was stalking her. One day I caught her crying while we walked. It was only midday, but I took her by the hand and led her off the Ninety-five to a little copse of trees. Once we were in the cool shade, I told her to sit, and sat facing her. "Tell me, Pearl!" I said.

She raised her eyebrows at that, then shrugged her shoulders. "Tell you what, tell you how?" she was asking.

"Tell me why you're so sad. You'll find a way."

Pearl patted herself on the chest, then held out her hand, palm up. "I want." Next she patted me on the chest, then placed both her hands over her heart. "I want your love," she'd said.

"You have it," I told her, "more than you could know. More than our bodies could prove."

She smiled. Making the motions for "I want" again, she then mimicked talking motions with one hand near her mouth, and patted me on the chest again. "I want to talk to you." Or was she saying, "I want to talk *for* you?"

The universal sign for the Fierae is to make a zigzagging, vertical slash with one's left hand. Pearl made that sign, then patted her chest, then made the talking motion. At first I wasn't sure, but then her eyes grew wide and she smiled.

"No!" I said. "It could kill you."

She shook her head.

"How do you know what would happen if you fused with Blitz?" I took her hands in mine. I could feel the expression on my face pleading with her. "I could *lose* you, Pearl, and my heart would shatter! And from that day on I'd battle the Fierae till they killed me!"

Pearl's expression became shocked and frantic, and she shook her head, "No!" until tears flew out of her eyes. Then, all very quickly, she made the sign of the Fierae, patted the ground, placed her hands over her heart, and touched my chest with one finger. "The Fierae in the ground loves you."

"Fierae love is different. Blitz doesn't love me the way you think..." I began.

But Pearl shook her head again, then repeated those signs. This time, while she touched her finger to my chest, she nodded her head and widened her eyes. "Oh yes she does!" she was saying.

I couldn't argue this anymore with Pearl. The truth was I *would not* do it, not with the doubts and reservations I had. I would not expose her to mortal danger, even if she believed that danger did not exist. I took her hands and drew her to me. Then I touched my lips to hers, and let all my love find its way into that kiss. It was a very *long* kiss, but when it was over, I said, "Do you see, now, why I cannot?"

A shy little smile shaped her beautiful mouth, and she nodded her head. Before she folded herself into my arms, she made a series of signs that, as best I could tell, meant, "Satisfy your fears, then three become two, become one."

Though I know Pearl believed we would make that permanent pact with Blitz someday, she'd obviously resigned herself to waiting. She was happy, again, and we were eating well. Her proficiency at gathering seemed directly connected to her degree of happiness. Though I could go without food almost indefinitely (as long as I did no majicking) I loved those little dinners she prepared for me. If you think about it, it's funny, but all Apprentices, as long as they don't majick, can go without food, yet food is one of the things we love best. And good wine, though we're careful with it. It's said that Apprentices are very fond of creature love, too, but you'd have never known that by Thirest, and *I* had *still* never done it. Thirest said it was dangerous, though he never explained why. Could *that* be the reason the Apprentices were dying off, their fondness for loving? But why were no *new* Apprentices being born? Between Pearl and Blitz, and thoughts like those, I often lay awake in Pearl's arms at night, sailing my choppy sea.

One morning, as we prepared to resume our travels, Pearl snatched our packs off the mag line where I'd just placed them. Putting hers on, she indicated that she wanted me to do the same. Pearl was happy, food was tasty, and I saw no reason to mess that up. I put on my pack and waited to see what she had in mind.

Pearl had me stand beside her, facing north, then she laced the fingers of her right hand into those of my left. Between us, she called up a fat line of force. "Oh no!" I said, forgetting the food and happiness.

Pearl brought the thumb and forefinger of her left hand almost together, and showed it to me. "Just for a little bit," she was telling me. Then a mag line appeared to my right and her left.

She placed our laced fingers, palms down, on top of the line between us, then she rested her left palm on the line beside her. I followed her lead, but I was none too happy about where she was going with this, mostly because *I'd* be going, too!

I watched as she closed her eyes momentarily, then felt the

chorus of Zephrae gathering at our backs. They pushed slowly, at first, and I noticed that Pearl was dragging her feet. Then she lifted the mag lines till both our feet were off the ground, just as the Zephres huffed and puffed and blew us down the Ninety-five.

Immediately, I realized why Pearl's hands had not been badly damaged by her flight to catch me. She probably hadn't been on the lines for more than two minutes. We were traveling faster than I'd ever seen anything (other than Fierae) go before. At least three or four times faster than I could flat out sprint.

Pearl was watching me, and smiling the whole time. I have to admit it was fun, *exciting,* but after about a minute, the thought of what it was doing to my hands made me call out to her. "I think that's probably long enough!"

Rather than stop us, she started laughing that soundless laugh of hers, and I think I could hear the wind in her throat. Then she widened her eyes at me, and ramped up the Zephrae that were at our backs. Now we were traveling *frighteningly* fast. The beads in Pearl's hair were clattering like frantic wind chimes. I wanted to yell at her to stop, but all my words blew back into my mouth. Tears were streaming out of the corners of both our eyes. Pearl had her head back and was laughing to beat all helluva. Then, suddenly, the Zephres were gone, and we were coasting to a stop. Pearl lowered the lines until our feet once more touched the ground and we were walking.

I wanted to inspect my palms, and that's when I noticed that I couldn't untangle my fingers from Pearl's. Something from the mag lines (and I suspect there was more to it than that, something Pearl did on purpose) had glued our hands together. "How long?" I asked. She pointed to the blazing Ball, then slowly traced a line down the sky from it to the horizon. "All day?" I asked.

She nodded her head, put on her shy little smile, and looked up at me through her lashes. Great rivers and sea, she was beautiful! Other than the fact that we couldn't take off our packs, I didn't mind walking hand in hand with Pearl all day. In fact, from that day on, we walked that way most of the time.

Our hands came unglued not a minute after we left the Ninety-five to find a place in the trees for the night. Could she have released us any time she'd wanted? I don't know for sure, but if I had to offer

44

an opinion, I'd say, "Absofugginlutely." Something had her in high spirits, and Pearl in high spirits can be a wonderful nuisance.

That night, she found a peahen, and gave it a kiss before scooting it out of its body. Then she cleaned and cooked it for our supper. It had been quite a day, what with flying and all, but I was not used to carrying my pack, and was a little worn out. I was looking forward to lying lazily in Pearl's arms.

Who would hold who was becoming a nightly game with us. I'd say "You hold me," then she would touch my chest, hug herself, then touch her chest. "You hold *me!*" Then I'd say, "Okay, come here, I'll hold you," to which she'd shake her head and sign, "*I'll* hold *you!*"

That night, however, when I said, "You hold me," she held out her arms and smiled. I was much to trusting, and curled up into them. After a minute or two, Pearl made a move to kiss me, and I responded. Instead of kissing my mouth, however, she kissed my eyelids, touching her tongue lightly to each one. Apparently she'd called Naiadae into her mouth, and knocked me out cold with those kisses.

I don't think I was asleep more than a few minutes, but when I awoke I was flat on my back, with a blanket over me. Pearl was sitting on my little stool just a few feet away, with a smile on her face that made me say, "Uh oh!" That's when I realized I was naked, which was also when I realized that the Terrae were holding me fast to the ground. I couldn't move.

Pearl barely blinked and Zephres fluttered up under the blanket with me. Then she licked her lips, which was an extraordinarily sensuous gesture, considering what the Zephrae were doing to me under that blanket. Controlling them carefully, Pearl kept me in a state of severe and lovely agitation for what seemed like hours. The Terrae allowed me enough freedom to squirm, and my moans and exclamations played in the trees.

When I didn't think I could take any more, I said, "Pearl! Please!"

I watched as she made her signing motions, which clearly said, "You've seen me like this *twice!* Now I'll see you!"

Right about then, the blanket blew off me, and all the strength left my body in one tremendous orgasm. The Zephres flew off, the Terrae released me, and Pearl, getting up off my stool,

45

dropped a little, moist washcloth onto my chest. Then she wandered off, leaving me to clean up the mess she'd made.

Pearl had me dead to rights that night, and could have done anything she'd wanted before I could have freed myself from the Terrae she'd had holding me. Thirest said Female Apprentices don't contact Fire, but I'm certain Pearl could call Blitz if she wanted to. She could have easily made us love, with Blitz along for the ride, while her Terrae held me. But she didn't. Instead she played that little game for my ecstasy and her amusement. Though I couldn't trust her not to play that game with me again (and she did, and her variations were endless,) after that night, I trusted her implicitly. Not only did I believe that she loved me as I loved her, I knew I had her respect, as she had mine.

I don't know how many klicks Pearl flew us over, but the following day, we came to a river. Smith had told me, one night, that there is a big river at the beginning of Two Carolines, and another big one almost half way through. We'd crossed a few small ones, but this one looked like the half-way-through one. Some of the smaller rivers had dubious bridges built across them on the rubble piles left by the bridges of the Ancients. To cross the bigger ones that had no bridges, you had to wade, and sometimes swim, over the rubble piles. Of course, having done it now (or, more accurately, having had it done *to* me) I could execute Pearl's flying trick, and would never need to wade or swim again. I still don't like the idea of my metals being tugged at, but I'll do it for the few seconds it takes to cross a river. Anything less than half a minute doesn't seem to hurt your hands at all.

When we arrived at that river, it was blazing hot. The Ball was sizzling in the sky like a fried egg on a blue skillet. Pearl signed to me that she wanted to fly the river to the sea and swim. That sounded good. "How far do you think it is?" I asked her. Though they didn't hurt anymore, my palms were still a little red.

She signed with her fingers, "Just a little bit."

"Okay," I said, "but don't glue our hands. I want to swim."

"Me, too!" she signed, then conjured up lines and Zephres and off we went.

VI
The Coming and Going of Fargus Macreedy

The Atlanta Sea was lazily patting the shore with half-baked waves. The sand was white as fair-weather clouds. Pearl put us down on that shining beach, then tore off her clothes and ran for the water. I started to join her, but something made me wait. I wanted to watch her. Of course, I'd seen her without her clothes before, Pearl is not shy, don't let her smile fool you. But seeing her in The Great Pool, the salty sea clinging in glistening drops to her magnificent, brown body, was like looking at art. I've always thought the Naiadae are the most beautiful of the Elementals, and Pearl wore them well.

I knew that if I watched her much longer, I'd be embarrassed to come out of my clothes. I started walking toward the sea, unbuttoning my pants, when I noticed something floating behind Pearl. It was big, six or seven meters long, and barely rocking on the tiny chop. It was a boat. "Look behind you!" I shouted to Pearl, who was swimming toward me now, about twenty meters off the beach.

The boat was close to her, not thirty meters away. When she saw it, she reached out with a mag line, and drew it toward the beach. I ran to the boat as Pearl came, beautifully dripping, out of the sea.

Apparently, the boat had had a mast, but it was broken off. Much to my surprise, an old man lay in the bottom amidst empty casks floating on water that had invaded the boat. He looked dead.

When Pearl saw the man, concern painted her face. Quickly she went to him and pulled him up by his arms. I helped her, and we got him out and onto the beach. He was grizzled and furry with white hair and beard. His lips were cracked and bleeding, and he was very thin, but, to my surprise, he was alive. Pearl grabbed a cup that was floating in the bottom of the boat, held it up, and had the Naiadae condense water to fill it. Gently, cradling his head, she poured sips into the old man's mouth. It brought him around, and he opened his eyes. Looking up at Pearl, he said in a weak little voice, "Ay've deed'n gone ta hayven."

Pearl smiled, apparently understanding him. "What did he say?" I asked.

The universal sign for "heaven" is to put your right arm straight up and point with one finger. Pearl made the sign.

"Heaven?" I asked. She smiled and looked down at her own naked body. "Oh!" I said. "He thinks he's in heaven. Well, I certainly see his point."

When the old man came to a bit more, I realized he was actually speaking Inglish, but with a very strange and heavy accent. Pearl had found aloe for his lips, and was boiling little clams in the pot she carried in her pack. Once they were cooked, she shucked them back into their broth, and fed it to the old man. When he'd eaten about half, he said, "Thanky, ney more noo. Where em Ay?"

I was getting used to his accent, and answered, "Two Carolines." The look on his face told me that meant nothing to him. "You're about halfway up the Infinite Eastern Shore," I told him.

"Ay've made it, then," he said, and tears welled into his eyes.

Once the old man had eaten, he fell immediately to sleep. Pearl and I found big forked pieces of driftwood, and propped his boat, upside down, over him. Between the shade and the cool, wet sand, we were hoping the obvious exposure he was suffering from would be relieved. Occasionally, Pearl had the Naiadae wet him down with fresh water. Somehow, she could actually explain to them that she wanted the water *chilled*. Something *else* I wanted to learn.

The old man slept the day away while Pearl and I swam. We checked on him regularly, and found his breathing to be steady. That evening, we built a really big fire on the beach, and Pearl cooked more clams and some kind of kelp. She also called a few blue crabs out of the sea and into her pot. I don't like them when they're alive and blue, scuttling around with those nasty claws up, but cooked and red I like them very much.

We were eating our seafood when the old man crawled out from under his boat. Pearl jumped up and helped him over to our fire. I was glad she didn't fetch him with a mag line. You shouldn't do that to people unless they say it's okay. It isn't just that it might startle them, remember, the lines will tug at their blood. Even though those few seconds cause really no harm at all, a true Apprentice will never so much as place an innocent in harms way. "Live not to harm, die not to kill," is what Apprentices say. As a rule, it's an easy code to live by. It would take quite a number of people to hurt an Apprentice if he were well and able to majick. Besides, everyone loves an Apprentice. If nothing else, we always pay our way (when people let us).

The old man dropped off of Pearl's arm and onto the beach by our fire. Pearl offered him food, and he picked a few clams out of the broth, set them on a piece of driftwood to cool. "D'ya have any spirits, lad?" he asked me, his voice sounding much stronger. I fetched the jug out of my pack. The old man's eyes sparkled, and he smiled. "Aye, and yer a treasure, me boy!" he sang.

"Actually, that would be Pearl," I said, touching her arm.

"Aye, and it would," he agreed, smiling at her beauty.

"Pearl's father, Tool, made this," I told him. "It's called 'corn,' be careful."

"Don' worry, lad, I make a respicktable malt me own self."

I handed him the jug, and he took a belt. When he got his breath back, he said, in a very high voice, "None so respicktable as *this*, though. How, be garsh, do ye keep it from 'splodin'?"

He handed me the jug, and I took a little pull. "I don't," I answered, shaking off the sip I'd taken. "I just hope it never decides to."

The old man laughed, and then grew serious. "Ay'm Fargus Macreedy," he said. "Ay thank ye with me heart for savin' me. Ay was a goner."

"I'm Spaul, and this, as you know, is Pearl. How long were you in that boat? Where did you come from?" Then Pearl made signs and I translated. "Did you see a Mer Maiden?"

"Ay will tell ya me story, but first Ay must ask; the ways you've doctored me, that and the *feel* of ye, are ye Apprentice?"

"I am," I said.

"Great rivers and sea! Thank The Lords and The One Who Watches! They've brought me to what I seek!"

"Pearl is an Apprentice, too," I said.

Pearl's eyes widened into a look of surprise, and she signed, "Me?"

"She may not be trained," I said, looking at her, "but she's a very powerful Apprentice none-the-less.

Fargus Macreedy's eyes welled with tears, then he broke down and cried uncontrollably. Pearl went over and comforted him. When he could speak again, he said, "By The Lords, ye must be *swimmin'* in Apprentices over here. I set me boat upon shore, and *two* come to greet me! One with the beauty of Naia, and one with the divil's own whooskey!"

After eating his clams and drinking a little more corn, Fargus told us his story. "Ay've come from across The Great Pool, from the land of Erin that sits on the western shores of the vasty land of Euro. A storm took mast and sail from me a fortnight ago, and me water's been gone fer almost a week.

"Ay belong to an order that's called 'Masons,' and we search the Eurolands for Apprentices. But for twenty years now, we've found none new, and the few we have are many years Finished and dyin'. One day I took it 'pon meself to try and cross the sea, and see if I could find the Untied Estates."

"I've never heard of the Untied Estates," I told him.

"They call it that because, in ancient times, people from my homeland untied their boats and sailed away to never return. On the land they found, they built their great estates, and had nothin' to do with Erin or Angland again."

"I've heard of Angland," I told him. "But that's halfway around World!"

"Aye, and the Erin Isle sits there with it. 'Twas a long and hard journey, but Ay've been rewarded! I've found the land of Apprentices! Now, if Ay can convince some, and we can find a way, Ay'll be wantin' to take a few back with me across The Pool!"

I felt bad about what I was going to say to Fargus, and dropped my eyes when I did. "Other than Pearl, I haven't seen another Apprentice in five years, except for my Finished, who's dead, now. *He* thought we were dying off."

Fargus' face fell, and he said, "'Tis true, then. 'Tis happenin' all over World."

I comforted Fargus with a little more corn, and Pearl made him eat some kelp and broth. Then we gave him my blankets, Pearl and I would sleep in hers. We bid him sleep well, and left him by the fire.

Pearl had dug out a little nest for us in the sand away from the blaze, where we played, "Hold me, no you hold *me*," until we compromised and tangled up tightly. We fell asleep still sharing a kiss.

When the Ball woke us up, rising brilliantly red (a storm sign) over the sea, we noticed Fargus sitting close to the water, looking out over it. Suddenly, a big fish jumped out of the sea onto the beach where Fargus sat. It was flopping around, but he reached over and patted it once, then it lay still.

Pearl and I went over to where he was sitting, and managed to startle him. He was dripping with sweat, and seemed exhausted. "Ay've been coaxin' that beastie to come be breakfast since before the Ball rose," he told us. "'Tis my thanky to ye both, such as it is."

"How did you do it? Are you an Apprentice?" I asked him.

"Nay, lad, but Ay'm touched by the Wee Folk, and know a few tricks. 'Tis called a markaral, this one," he said, patting the meter-long fish. "Ay'll show ye how ta wrap it in kelp and bake it on the coals of our fire."

While Fargus cleaned his markaral, Pearl went off and gathered some blueberries and wild onions. She gave the onions to Fargus, to wrap into the kelp with his fish. "Aye, and ye *are* a treasure," he said, adoring her with his eyes.

The markaral and onions was really a treat. I love fish, and decided right then to pitch my tent and stay on this beach a few days. It wouldn't take me nearly as long as Fargus to call out a fish, if he could tell me the ones to call that were good to eat. I told Pearl about my idea to say a while, and she answered by throwing off her clothes, and running out into the sea. Apparently, we were in agreement.

While Pearl swam, Fargus and I talked. We both had many questions, being from lands so far apart. "Tell me about the 'Masons,'" I said. "Are there very many? Have you ever heard of one called 'Mason Dicksin'?"

"There are nay many of *anybody*," he told me, and that was true. "And Ay has nay heard tell of one called 'Dicksin.' Masons have tended World since time began. Wherever an ill arises, we seek to find its cure. But we've failed the Apprentices, and our people are doomed. We'll go the way of the Ancients, now, only this time the few will not survive, because few is all there is."

51

"I'm afraid we *all* may be fugged," I told him. "I'm the newest Apprentice I know of, and I stopped my aging a decade ago. It may well be twenty trips round the Ball since any New have been born here either."

"Woe to us all," Fargus moaned. "Truly, we are doomed." After a little spell of mourning silence, he said, "Tell me, Spaul, are ye and she marriaged?"

"What is 'marriaged'?" I asked him.

"Bound by The Lords and The One Who Watches. Ye know, hoosband and weef."

"I'm not sure I understand you," I said.

"In Erin, and even Angland, men and women who know the Bindin' Love of each other, stand together, with their friends around them, and give each other a ring, most of the time made of gold. After that, they are marriaged, and nay will love the body of another again. Hoosband and weef, we say, ne'er to part till death."

I had heard of such heathen pacts. Though I knew of many men and women who stayed together, swearing to love no other is an evil thing. It fosters jealousy and greed. Though I'd love nothing more than to spend my life with Pearl, I would never deny her any pleasure, nor would I allow her to deny me mine if I chose to take it with another girl. "So, you can only marriage one person, then?" I asked, making sure I understood this custom correctly.

"Aye, lest one of ye dee, then yer free to marriage another."

"To each his way," I quoted to Fargus, "but I'll have no part in such things. I love Pearl, and would die protecting her, would give her a child if she asked," (and if we could, I thought, remembering Blitz). "But there are others to play at love with. Why would I deny her if one struck her fancy? Nor would she deny me. In fact," I said with a smile, "she wants to invite a Fierae Charge into our bed."

"How's that, noo? Come again," Fargus said.

"A Fierae Charge that I've joined with several times wants to inhabit Pearl while we love."

"How do ye *stop* it?" he asked me.

"I can't, so we don't love. I'm afraid if we did, the Charge and Pearl would fuse."

"Aye," Fargus nodded. "Seems likely. There's a little bit of Fierae in us all, and more in the Wee Folk. Though I have nay the ability, I have the knowledge, Spaul. Ay'm a very high order Mason.

Me instinct and that knowledge warn against doin' such a thing. Women react strongly to the Fierae. So yer sayin' this Charge has inhabited Pearl already?"

"Three times," I answered.

"That's amazin', amazin' she's nay dead! *Three times,* ye say? Amazin'!"

"Pearl wants me to do it because the Charge gives her its voice."

"And she's *spoken* to ye with this voice?"

"Yes."

"But were ye speakin' to Pearl, or the Fierae?"

"I've spoken with both," I told him.

Fargus jumped up when I told him that, and walked around in a circle till he was back facing me. "Laddy," he said, "this is too much for an old man to digest, on top of all that markaral. Might I trouble ye fer a wee pull from yer jug?"

Once Fargus had his "wee pull," he sat back down and asked me, "What does Pearl think would happen if ye two loved with that Fierae in her?"

"I think she knows they'd fuse. She *wants* to fuse with it, so she could speak, and she says the ground Charge loves me."

Fargus laughed. "Fierae love is a far different thing..."

"That's what I told her," I said, interrupting him. "But she insists it isn't, not for Blitz."

"Blitz?"

"It's a name I gave those Charges when I joined with them."

"Aye, 'tis an old Yarmen word. I've heard it. And ye say ye've joined with this Blitz before?"

"I've spoken to Blitz six times, and joined with them four of those."

"*The same Fierae?* How's that possible, Spaul?" Fargus asked, with a look of skepticism etched into the deep lines of his face.

"I don't know. I don't know how lady Blitz follows me."

"*Follows ye?* In yer *body?* 'Tis nay possible, lad. 'Tis tricks in yer mind-sea, serpents and such playin' in there."

"I wish it was," I told him, just as Pearl came to drip on me, and insist I swim with her. I shed my clothes, and let the salty Naiadae sing the troubling thoughts out of my head.

53

Late that same afternoon, I asked Fargus to describe a good fish for me to call. "Ay'll do better," he told me. "Ay'll find one for ye. Ay can nay call up a line of force as ye can, but Ay can make one pulse for an instant. Watch for it and Ay'll point out a good fish."

After about a minute, I saw Fargus' flash, and the fish it was pointing to. "It's beautiful!" I told him, and it was. It was also huge.

"'Tis a Dorado. They'll often come willingly, and had I seen one this mornin', Ay'd have called it instead of the markaral. It would probably take me nay more than an hour to call the one yer lookin' at now"

"Look out!" I yelled to Fargus as the meter and a half long Dorado, all blue and yellow and shining, sailed past his head, and onto the beach.

Fargus laughed and chased the fish, patted it once till it lay still. "Aye, and yer a fishin' machine, Spaul! Aye've never seen any so fast as ye!"

"He was easy," I said, "as if he *wanted* to be caught."

"Wanted to be eaten," Fargus told me. "'Tis their purpose, and they have an inklin' of it. When Ay was starvin' in me boat, Ay was too weak to call a fish, but was tryin' anyway. Ay thought it was hopeless, but a little, schoolie Dorado jumped into me boat squealin', 'Eat me an' live, ye old coot!'"

Fargus was a good storyteller, and had me laughing with his baby Dorado story. I made him tell it to Pearl as she wrapped the fish and nuts and grapes, and some kind of herbs she'd gathered, into long sheets of kelp. Her silent laugh looked more like a squeal when she told her what the baby Dorado had said. I wanted so badly to hear her laughter. There was so much of Pearl that I was missing.

After we'd eaten, Pearl swam again. She was in the water so much I began to call her "Mer Maiden." Every time I did, she'd suck in her cheeks and make her "fish face," which always made Fargus laugh.

"Mer Maidens are beautiful," he'd say. "That face looks like a cod!"

All that day, after the Ball rose red, I'd been getting the sense of a storm out at sea. I could feel the pressure changing as it grew. While Pearl swam, I told Fargus about it, and, as it got darker, we could see lightening far out to the east. "'Tis the syphus that wrecked me boat," Fargus told me.

54

"Syphus?" I asked.

"Aye, 'tis the grandest dance of the Elementals. 'Twas Syphus and similar parties as killed the Ancients."

"We say, hurrakin," I told him.

"Aye, yes, Ay've heard that word. If that is the hurrakin that tore down me mast, Lords help us if it comes ashore."

"It's going north," I told him. "It may come closer before it passes, but the Apprentices make enough contact with the Elementals. They know we are here, and have no cause to harm us. Don't worry, Fargus, if they come too close, I'll go out and warn them away."

"What if they did have cause to harm us?" Fargus said in a small voice, his eyes lowered.

"What do you mean?"

"There's somethin' I should tell ye, Spaul, though 'tis not easy."

Fargus carried a suede aytiem, tied to a belt loop. He took it off, opened it, and pulled out a small bottle. I'd never seen one like it. It was made of clear glass, and had a tight, glass stopper. It was empty, and looked like it could hold no more than twenty or thirty drams. "I've never seen glass carved into a bottle," I said, as he handed it to me.

"'Tis blown, with a pipe," he told me. "'Tis an Ancient craft that very few know, which is good. In the wrong hands, such a thing could be used for terrible ill. 'Tis only the Masons who have this craft, and we use it to stave off great tragedy, or to do a great good."

"What's it for?" I asked.

"This one we used to help me cross the sea. Before I left, our old Mason Apprentice trapped a tiny chorus of Zephres within it. Ye must know that Elementals won't inhabit glass, nor will they pass through it. Of course, ye could nay trap the Fierae with this, but the other three are stymied by it."

As soon as he told me this, I pulled out the stopper and made sure nothing was in it. "You're lucky Thirest, my Finished, isn't here. I think he might bury this, and you along with it," I said, handing him back his vile cage.

"Ay'm surprised ye did nay smash it," Fargus said, seeming genuinely puzzled.

"I'm not Thirest. What became of the Zephres you held in there?"

"We trapped them in case the doldrums befell me crossin'. Our Apprentice made the Zephrae swear to gather and blow me away from Erin when I released them. If they did nay agree, he told them they'd stay trapped forever. Ay'd been on The Pool a month, and me situation was dire. I must have been in the calm precedin' that syphus, which was so' west of me. When I released the Zephres, they kept their promise, but did nay blow me due east. They blew me into that storm. I dunna know if they're holdin' a grudge, but I thought I should tell ye," Fargus finished, lowering his eyes from my gaze.

"The hurrakin won't come ashore," I told him. "And though I am not Thirest, and make no judgment on what men of other lands do, should you use that trap *here*, you will see an Apprentice fill with wrath and loose it upon you. Though you'd still be alive, for I will not kill, I'd then give you to the Fierae, and let them decide your fate. Then I'd quickly bid you farewell, as the Fierae are fast, and very to the point."

"None came to harm," Fargus said in his defense. "But I knew 'twas a grave thing when we did it. We never do such lightly."

"Then the Masons have done this before?"

"Aye. It is done, more now than it used to be. With the Apprentices all but gone, the few who remain grow desperate to control the elements."

"Then your doom may well be by your own hand," I told him. "You cannot control the Elementals, you can only contact and trust them. You can ask them to cooperate, and they usually do, but to force them is, literally, to throw caution to the wind. You may actually have caused the problem you seek to cure. I hope you haven't caused man's doom all across World."

"We've never kept any trapped more than a half-year," he said softly. "'Tis our law. 'Twould be such a short time to an elemental that we thought no harm would be done."

"Maybe none was, who knows, Fargus. But you won't do it here."

"Ay swear. In fact, I give it to you," he said, handing the bottle back to me. "Smash it, if ye will, but I must tell ye first, Ay think ye could use it to give Pearl a voice."

56

I said nothing. I did nothing. I should have told him to shut up, and I should have smashed that bottle. But I stayed silent until he continued. "Have ye ever listened to the Naiadae who inhabit a running brook? Such voices! Were ye to trap a few drams of them, ye could bind them to inhabit Pearl if ye let them go. She'd have to drink them. Her speaking, of course, would occur as they left her body, so she'd only have a score or two of words at most from that spell. But I think it could be done again and again. I can nay see the Naiadae destroyin' mankind over such a thing."

About that time, I built a fire, and Pearl came out of the sea, stood close, and let it dry her. I was thinking about what Fargus had just told me, and feeling ashamed that I'd listened. "Tell Pearl what you just told me about getting her a voice," I said to him.

Pearl stared at Fargus, unmoving, as he told her his idea. When he finished, I held up the little bottle for her to see. She took it from my hand, opened it, and looked inside. Then she replaced the stopper and smashed it on a rock. When she looked to me, she saw I was smiling, and smiled back. Then she scowled at Fargus and shook her finger at him.

"It breaks me heart to disappoint ye so, m'lady," he said. Then he crawled up under his boat, and left us alone.

Pearl and I went off to our "love nest," though the only love it contained was our kissing and holding. Pearl was wearing only a strange little smile, wicked and enchanting, and it made me say, "*You* hold *me!*"

Her smile grew, but she shook her head, no. Then she executed a series of signs that said, "Blitz has gone off to the hurrakin party."

It took me a moment to add the two of her smile to the two of her statement, but when I did a rush of excitement coursed through my body. I moved to take her in my arms, but she stopped me, took me by the hand, and stood. "Come with me," her eyes were saying. Knowing Pearl the way I did, she didn't have to tell me twice.

She led me down to the water's edge, where the sand played with the sea between our toes. Slowly, with love in her smile and eyes, she draped her arms around my neck, and pressed herself close to me. When I put my arms around her, she jumped up and wrapped her legs high around my waist. I ran my fingers down her back, and supported her, taking her beautiful bottom into my hands. Before I knew it was going to happen, she maneuvered one hand down my side, and used it to put us together. The connection was made, and we were joined.

"It's my first time," I whispered in her ear.

"Me, too," she signed.

I was surprised, when she told me that. Surprised that a girl so beautiful was not constantly begged for love. But I was happy, *joyful*, that our first love was with each other.

As we kissed, standing there like that, with Pearl slowly, rhythmically moving up and down in my arms, a tremendous chorus of Zephres began whirring and chasing around us. When our feet left the ground, the weight of Pearl in my hands and on my hips disappeared. We were like two clouds, now, mingling on adjoining breezes, condensing over one another, then evaporating again so that we could rain into each other once more. Our love, which began so gently, became furious. Caresses became desperate clutches, and kisses, attempts to swallow each other whole. Then a howling moan welled up from deep, deep inside my body, and I thought I heard some distant sound accompany Pearl's silent cries and shudders.

The Zephrae holding us didn't so much as disturb the sweat on our bodies, even as they spun their web of wind around us. I looked down, and could no longer see the beach. Above us, the stars were so close that I reached up to try and touch them. Off in the east, a hurrakin party raged, and the rainbow bursts of the Fierae joining in the clouds were spectacular! But they paled in the explosive light of our first creature love. Blitz didn't know what she was missing.

How long we stayed suspended in that embrace, I couldn't tell you, but, eventually, Pearl had the Zephrae put us down in the cool sea. The surf had come up a bit with that storm out there. Pearl and I joined again, and let it lift us up and down, making our love for us. Naiadae sang in their sweet, sea voices, and the luminescence of invisible creatures caused the waves to glow. When love had finally exhausted itself with us, I held Pearl close, and whispered to her, "You truly are my treasure. If I ever lose you, I'll spend my life waiting to die."

"Then live forever," she signed. "I'm staying with you."

Nestled wet in Pearl's blankets, we held each other tight all night, trying to keep even air from coming between us. Eventually, the sky lightened, but the Ball was hidden by the storm that still raged at sea, as if it was watching. As if it refused to move away from the storm of love Pearl and I were sharing. Blitz would still be out there, so we breakfasted on love in our sandy little nest.

When finally we rose, still sleepy and spent, Pearl pointed down the beach, and began to run. I followed, realizing what she'd seen. Fargus and his boat were gone. When we reached the place where it had been, I could see where Fargus had pulled it back into the water. Pearl stood staring out to sea. "Do you think he's gone back to Erin?" I asked her.

Though she didn't turn to face me, but continued to stare out toward the storm, I could see a tear sliding down her cheek as she made the sign for "heaven."

"And then back here," I whispered, "with all his knowledge gone."

I'd wanted to pitch my tent on that beach and stay a while, but Fargus' leaving affected Pearl profoundly. After staring out at the storm he'd gone to join, Pearl found the rock she'd smashed his bottle against. The little glass stopper was still in the broken neck of the vessel. She picked it up, and held it in her palm for me to see, tears still tracing lines down her lovely cheeks, as if she was saying, "See what I've done."

"If you hadn't smashed it, I would have," I told her, but she would not release her guilt. She closed her hand around that shard, and squeezed till it cut her and she bled. Gently I opened her fingers, took the stopper away, and threw it into the sea. Then I held her, and she cried till she shook. I decided to lay her down to sleep for a while. When she woke, we would leave this place of ecstasy and sorrow.

That afternoon, when we left, Pearl was too spent with love or grief or both, to fly us back up the river, so we walked. I simply couldn't bring myself to execute her flying trick, when she could not. I was amazed at the depth of her grieving, and it affected me like something contagious.

VII
Fargus' Gift

What had been a very quick flight to the beach was a long walk back through the forest that lined the river, and we didn't make it to the Ninety-five that day. I could see that Pearl was still fatigued with grief, and insisted we stop. She would have gone to gather a meal, but I wouldn't let her. We still had chunks of Dorado wrapped in kelp, and several of Smith's hushpuppies. I wanted to eat and then make us a bed of pine straw under our blankets. I had a half-selfish notion to love away Pearl's grief. But when she saw the pine straw bed I was making, she started to cry again. Then she knelt down beside me and patted the ground, made the sign of the Fierae. Blitz was following us again.

I thought Pearl might argue to let the three of us join, but instead she curled up into the bed I'd made. I had never seen her so sad, and it hurt me more than I'd have thought possible. I lay down beside her, with her back to me, and caressed her shoulder. Then she rolled over into my arms, and cried herself to sleep. I was more than half tempted to call Blitz to us. Then I thought to myself, "That's great, Spaul! You'd kill her to see her smile!"

As I started to wake the following morning, I thought I was dreaming of Pearl's frantic kisses high above the beach. But it turned out to be far better than a dream, as I opened my eyes and responded in kind to Pearl's hungry mouth. I wanted more, but when she saw I was fully awake, she signed, "Let's go!"

Something was up, I was very sure, but when I asked her what it was she would only sign, "I have an idea."

She insisted on flying us the rest of the way to the Ninety-five. When we reached it, in less than half a minute, she bent the mag lines we were on, hard to the right, and kept us going north on the old, dead road. We were going so fast, not only couldn't I talk, but was finding it hard to breathe. I was glad she hadn't laced our fingers, because we flew at that ferocious speed for at least four minutes. When, finally, she stopped us, my hands felt scalded, and I saw that hers were starting to bleed. Dizzily, I watched as Pearl teetered, then dropped onto her butt. We'd definitely overdone that trick.

"That was too far!" I scolded, as I dropped down to sit beside her. With a drunken little smile on her face, she nodded in agreement. Then she reached in her pack and pulled out a big piece of kelp that she'd wrapped something into. It was the liver of the Dorado, heavily salted by the Naiadae and probably majicked to keep fresh, because it was still raw. She started to eat it, and insisted I do the same. I knew her reasoning was sound, but did not like the taste of it. Strangely, though, as I started to eat, I could tell my body wanted it, and the taste no longer mattered.

If I had to guess, I'd say we'd covered almost ten klicks in those four or so minutes. It didn't seem worth it, considering how far I intended to go. It was then that I realized, for the first time, that I'd never told Pearl where I was going, and she'd never asked. After Pearl had the Naiadae fill her cooking pot with cool water, we took turns with it, washing down the salty liver. I felt much better, though my hands still hurt. Pearl's were worse than mine, and I was working out, in my head, some kind of healing majick to help them. It would be very similar to when I'd fixed Rummy, but I knew it might not work. The Terrae would very likely see the damage to her hands the same way they see disease, normal. We'd interacted with lines of force, what happened to our hands was the result of that interaction. The more I cogitated on it, the less likely it seemed that I could convince the Terrae to alter the condition.

Still, I had it in mind to try, and started to dig two little holes to put Pearl's hands in. She was standing, facing west, when I called her. At first she didn't hear me, and I noticed she was gently swaying back and forth. "Pearl!" I called again. "Come here and let me fix your hands."

She turned for a moment and looked at what I was doing. Quickly, she signed "Won't fix." Then she went back to whatever it was she was up to.

I rose from my digging, and went to her. "Pearl," I said softly into her hear, "let me try."

Her eyes were closed, and she was swaying again. Without opening her eyes, she signed, "I've tried, won't fix. Hush."

I didn't feel like arguing, especially when I knew she was probably right. Instead, I drank some more water, and thought about telling Pearl my intention to go into the North. She would ask me why, and I wanted to be able to answer her. But the fact was my reasons were vague even to me.

Somewhere north of Mason Dicksin's line, lay the vast rubble piles of the great Skyshaper Villages of the Ancients. Of course, my quest is always to seek out other Apprentices, but I also wanted to see what was left of those monstrous places. I'd seen some of the ones in the South; the one at the Southern Edge, which contained the wreckage of many bridges, and there were also several down in the Purchase.

Some say there are more way down into the Florida, but nobody goes there. Why bother? If the insects don't eat you, the giant gators, panthers, and salt-water crocodiles will. Besides, it's almost all swamp. The hurrakin parties that killed off the Ancients are said to have washed away most of the high ground down there. That's why it's called the "Florida." It's supposed to mean "flushed," as in, flushed out to sea.

I've seen some pretty big mounds of stuff in the South, that were once Skyshaper Villages, but the ones in the North are said to be enormous. It's supposed to be forbidden to dig into the rubble, and for a long time it was one of the main tasks of the Apprentices, to discourage such scavenging. But with the Apprentices getting scarce, I'm sure it happens more and more. I remember watching Thirest bind a man to a tree, with growing vines called kazoo, for digging something out of a place that was once called House Town. He left that man tied for three days, and when he did finally let him go, he incited a Fierae Charge to chase and shock him for over a klick. Thirest was actually a very gentle soul, but when it came to the Ancients and their doohickeys and gewgaws, he was fierce. If you didn't like foul language, you wouldn't have wanted to get him started about the Ancients. He called them, "The fug-all, gollammest idiots that ever sucked their mama's teat."

Would I scavenge in the rubble when I found those places in the North? Probably. As an Apprentice, knowledge of the Ancients was important to me. Thirest did it, but he rarely took anything away from those places, and some things he destroyed as soon as he found them. Others he'd study to try and determine their uses. But mostly there was very little to find. The Ancients are long, long gone, and World has reclaimed most of their accoutrements.

One thing Thirest *would* have kept, if he'd found any, were books. But if he did find any, he never showed them to me, and I think, being made of paper, it's highly unlikely that there are any to find. That's why, when we Apprentices die, we put all our journals, and anything we think is important, into a bunker that's been majicked to preserve. Someday, I'll go back and visit Thirest's, if for no other reason than to see him again. We put our bodies in there, too. I left Thirest lying on cedar boughs with gardenia blossoms in his hands. It smelled very nice in there when I majicked it shut. It will smell just like that when I open it again.

I was starting to wonder what Pearl was doing. Some sort of majick, I was sure, but it seemed to be taking a long time. I decided she must be looking for something. It was so frustrating not being able to have her teach me some of the things she did. Her signing was fine for basic communication, but explaining her kind of majicking would need the detail and nuance of precise language. Some things, like flying using the mag lines, was easy once I'd seen it, but I had absolutely no idea how she got the Zephrae to float us the way she did. I asked her, one night, if we couldn't travel that way. Signing, she made me understand that you can only go up and down. As best I could tell from our limited form of conversation, if the Zephrae tried to move you parallel to the ground, you'd be pushed, or pulled, I wasn't sure which, out of the wind-web they create. In other words, you'd fall, but I couldn't understand what she was trying to tell me about why you would fall. It was all very frustrating.

I thought about trying to teach Pearl to write. Though there aren't any Ancient books around that I know of, people do make them (and they're very expensive). The ones Thirest taught me with are in his bunker. Someday, I'm going to take Pearl there, and we'll get them. Ideally, I wanted to think of a way to majick her a voice, but I couldn't eve *begin* to imagine how. Not without a glass bottle, which I wouldn't have used anyway.

I was thinking that I'd never *force* an elemental, and that started giving me an idea. Just as that idea was formulating, and getting me excited, Pearl came over to where I was sitting, and held out her hand to pull me up. She was smiling. "I have an idea," I told her.

"Me, too," she signed. "Hush and stand still."

63

I did, and she wrapped me in her arms. Then the Zephrae arrived, and up we went.

We were quite a ways up, and facing west. The terrain rose steadily, and was very wooded. Pearl pointed to a place that was probably twenty or thirty klicks away. "What?" I asked her.

She made the sign of the Naiadae, a wavy, horizontal motion with her left hand. I still didn't get it. "A river?" I asked.

"Smaller," she signed. Then I knew we both had the same idea. "A brook!"

She smiled.

"Do you think we can?" I asked.

Again she smiled, then nodded her head, then shrugged her shoulders. "I think so, maybe, who knows?"

I had another idea. "Pearl," I said softly, with a smile of my own, "Blitz couldn't reach us up here, could she?" There wasn't a cloud in the sky, and without an Air Charge, Blitz couldn't get off the ground.

But Pearl burst my bubble, making a face that said, "Don't you think I'd have thought of that?" Then she signed that the Zephres were creating a charge all around us. Blitz could be on us in literally a flash, and would probably screw up the majick that was keeping us aloft.

I must have looked pretty dejected, because Pearl gave me a very long kiss, and signed that it was a lovely thought anyway. Then she got the Zephrae to put us down, so we could start our long hike up into those woods. There's no riding mag lines into a forest, but I'd have hiked a lot further than thirty klicks to get Pearl a voice.

Those woods were so thick we had to carry our own packs. Still, I figured we could probably make ten klicks a day without too much exertion, say three days to find Pearl's brook. But on the second day, in the early afternoon, a storm came up out of the east. It was the hurrakin party breaking itself up into little squalls. Before it got to us, I pitched my tent within the protection of a thick stand of hardwoods. Pearl and I got inside. It's a small tent, but Pearl seemed to like being in its cozy confines with me.

A game of "You hold me" had just ended with Pearl in my arms. My sea was extremely calm, and I was suddenly able to hear chittering very near us, saying, "He comes comes comes, he's coming."

"Oh shite," I said. Pearl sat up with a start, just as I did. Apparently she could sense, if not hear, Blitz's excitement.

"Get out and go a hundred meters north," I told her. "And don't argue," I said sternly to her arguing eyes. "They're going to join very close to here, and I want to speak to them. It'll only take a second or two, but don't look. Now go! And cover your ears!"

I went with her for about thirty meters, then made certain she kept going. When I was sure she was obeying me, I sat on a stump and calmed my sea. A few seconds later, I was sped up and out of body. I found Blitz high in a pine, chittering away in her crackling voice, "He's coming he's coming, he comes comes comes."

"Blitz!" I said.

She heard me right away, and answered, "We are fierce with the party still, where is your body?"

"Thirty meters away," I estimated.

"That should do, it will do. This pine will die, its boiling blood will fly, but should not reach your flesh. He's coming is coming. Will you join?"

"I mustn't, and you mustn't tempt me. It hasn't been long enough. But I wish to converse. Even that will be dangerous for me. Do you understand?"

"No danger, little Fierae. He is here!"

All my apprehension about being with Blitz again this soon disappeared when I saw their faces; hers so white, with mother-of-pearl rainbows on her cheeks and strung through lectric-silk hair. Both their features were chiseled, carved from marble moons. I loved them almost to the point of worship, as they met and exploded into that single entity, Blitz.

Immediately, I wanted to join with them, and it took every effort to sail my sea and resist. "You will join, I will bet," Blitz howled.

The strain was so great on me, that I almost agreed to the wager, just to keep me from joining then and there. But I caught myself, and said, "Puny humans must not wager with the mighty Fierae!"

In their ecstasy, Blitz laughed, and screamed, "More and more, you are less and less! Still, so cute, little Fierae human!"

There were things I wanted to ask Blitz, reasons I had risked this conversation, but the overwhelming urge to join, and the strange things they were saying, confused my train of thought. "What do you mean?" was all I could think to ask.

Searing, ecstatic laughter pierced me, and they answered, "We mean fire, we mean love. All we do and all we say, we mean. Life, we mean..."

"All is meant by the Fierae!" I interrupted, hoping to stop their answer to my hastily asked question. "What is meant by 'Fierae human,' when you address me as such?"

"We give you take. Each time you grow more, grow less. Come with us, wager or no, we will bring you, or stay, little Fierae human cute, and we will call you often to play. All choices are yours."

"What about Pearl? Why do you inhabit her?"

"Choices! We come to you to be Fierae human girl-child! Choices! Ah, Spaul! New choices of love! Above all rules is love! Love becomes the rule of rules! Come, stay, choose, choose!"

These are the things they said to me, but you haven't heard them the way I did. Each word, each sound was a sizzling seduction in itself. The very light of Blitz in their ecstasy was blinding every sensory aspect of me. I knew I could not stop myself from joining with them, but I was afraid that, while we were joined, they would convince me to go with. I had never been in such a state of totally oblivious ardor before, and we weren't even joined yet. "Promise you will not take me away if I join!" I begged.

"Would never *take*!" they exclaimed. "But you will come. I bet!"

"Promise you won't allow it! Swear by our love!" It was my last ditch effort. I never heard their reply. I was swept up into their loving as if sifted out of humanity.

I don't know how long it was till I opened my human eyes again. When I did I was in my tent, naked under a blanket, with Pearl bending over me. Her eyes were swollen from crying, but for a moment there was also a startled look on her face. Then she laid her head on my chest and wept. I wanted to comfort her, but I couldn't move, couldn't speak. When Pearl got hold of herself, she sat up and

66

bravely smiled at me. I was trying to talk, but she put her finger to my lips, then signed that she would be back in a moment.

I'm not sure if I passed out again, or if she was back so quickly it only seemed so. The next thing I knew, she was lifting my head, bringing a pot of cool water to my lips. I couldn't feel any of it, and if I swallowed I didn't feel that either.

When she'd finished trying to feed me water, Pearl brought a piece of cloth she had in her hands up to where I could see it. Something was wrapped deep inside. When she'd finished unwrapping it, she held a little mirror, about eight or nine centimeters square. It was a treasure worth a dozen pieces of gold the size of the one I'd given Smith. Where, I wondered, had she gotten it?

Pearl was trying to sign something to me, but I couldn't respond to help her know what I did or didn't understand. As best I could tell she was trying to say, "Don't be afraid, I must show you." Then she held the mirror so I could see my face. My eyes were steadily glowing. The usual brown of my irises had gone amber with that shine, as if candles were lit in my head behind each eye. Pearl signed again, and I believe she was asking me, "What does it mean?"

Even if I'd known I couldn't have told her. I couldn't speak. I couldn't even remain conscious.

I'm sure it was days before I could move at all, though I began feeling and tasting the broth Pearl was feeding me sooner. I could tell it was mostly blood. Then, one morning, I noticed the cuts on her wrist, and spoke my first words since the day the Fierae lit my eyes. "No more," I said in a throaty croak. Then I somehow managed to move enough to take her wrist in my hand and examine it.

Pearl pulled away, then signed, "No more, but this I've already drawn. Don't waste me, my love," and she smiled. I drank that last draught of her, warm and watered.

Though morning shone bright above us, it was still pretty dark in my tent. Pearl pulled me by the shoulders till I was half way out, and into the lighter day beneath the trees. Then she took her little mirror, and held it up for me to see. Though my eyes still bore a very faint glow, it was hard to see in that morning light. Pearl smiled, then signed, "At night, they still glow like a wolf's. I will learn to make hushpuppies."

Pearl was trying to lift my spirits, and I could see that my speaking had lifted hers. Most of her time, now, was being spent trying to make me eat, and I knew her reasoning was sound. Still, I watched her as best I could, and kept an eye on her wrists. At one point, when I wasn't cooperating with her efforts to feed me, she became angry, and signed, "Eat, or I'll cut my throat and bleed myself dry into you!" Then she laid her frustrated head on my chest and cried. After that, I ate everything she brought, even when I saw her catching lizards and frogs.

In about a week, I could sit upright against a tree without fainting. Every morning Pearl dragged me out of the tent, propped me up, fed me, made me raise my hands as high as I could, and massaged my legs and feet till they tingled. Then, one day, I awoke and the tent wasn't over me. I looked around and saw that Pearl had packed everything up, and was finishing weaving a litter with vines between two poles. When she saw me looking, she signed, "Work to do, no more lying around! I would *speak* to you about all this!"

I say "all this," but the sign she made referred to my eyes. If I were going to get a tongue-lashing about my excursion into Fierae love, I would gladly have it if it could come from Pearl's lips. I didn't even *try* to argue about her plan to drag me to that brook.

I don't know who that journey was harder on, Pearl, or me as she pulled me circuitously around and between the trees. At first, the motion drove my consciousness away. When I'd wake, Pearl would be stopped and mopping sweat from my brow. I stayed tied to that litter day and night, except when Pearl washed me. She hadn't dressed me again since that day, which made sense, as I had little control of my body and its functions. Later, I found that she'd discarded the cloths I'd been wearing, as they were not only badly soiled, but bloody. As best I could tell from what she signed to me, I'd sweat blood while the Fierae loved me, and bloody tears had stained my cheeks. Apparently I'd been a sight, and it hurt me that the image of it was in Pearl's thoughts. It was then that I realized what I did to myself I also did to her. Thirest had been right, love is a dangerous thing.

I must have been sleeping when we arrived at the brook. I awoke to hear it speaking to its stones, and gurgling songs into the air. Pearl had something cooking in her pot, which turned out to be

68

fish. Before she fed it to me, she made me eat several tiny fish livers, raw. I thanked her sarcastically, and she laughed in her beautiful and silent way.

We'd been at the brook for three days before Pearl made any attempt to majick. I knew she was regaining the strength she'd taxed dragging me there. She began her majicking early one morning, after propping me up so I could watch. "Do not speak," she signed, as if I was a New Kid and knew nothing at all. I smiled.

Pearl must have thought out her majick carefully as she'd dragged me through the forest. After removing her clothes, she bathed, then sat with her back against the gentle flow of the water. She'd taken her mirror out, and placed it under the water in front of her, on the pebbly bed of the little brook.

I couldn't see as well as I'd have liked, but I believe she swallowed a tiny stone she'd retrieved from under the water. Then she gazed deeply into her submerged mirror, while a chorus of Zephrae played with the braids in her hair. She stayed like that all day, not moving, gazing down, the Zephres cooling her profusely sweating body. Sometime in the late afternoon, she scooped up water into her hands and drank deeply several times. Then her head tilted back, and her body went rigid. A gurgling cry came from her screaming mouth.

I tried to go to her, and ended up flat on my face. I was unable to rectify the now undignified (I was still naked) nature of my position. All I could do was call her name, which blew dirt up my nose and into my eyes.

Before long, Pearl came and set me upright again, wiping dirt off my face. She was smiling, which answered the question I was about to ask. Then she started to sign. "I have two score of words, and cannot do this majick again. I would drown. I will not waste my words, but will give you three right now."

In a voice that, truly, only Mer Maidens own, bubbly and sweet and multi-tonal, Pearl said, "I love you." Though tears streamed down both our faces, she signed, "Now I have thirty-seven left."

At first, Pearl seemed fine, and I thought the majick she'd done to herself was causing no harm. Very soon, I realized it was not the case, and I understood why she couldn't repeat the trick. At night, especially if she lay on her back, she would struggle to breathe, and cough thickly, her chest rattling with congestion. I realized then that she was keeping the Naiadae that had agreed to inhabit her, in her lungs. I knew she'd be fine once her thirty-seven words (and their Naiadae) were spent. But I also knew she bore a great discomfort to house them.

"Let them out," I said to her one night, when the violence of her coughing caused her to vomit. "Come on," I said, "we'll have a nice long conversation, and that will be that." Really, I saw no reason for her to suffer like that. Thirty-seven words would not be enough for her to explain any of her majick to me, although I wondered if, between those words and her signing, she could teach me the floating trick.

"I worked *hard* for these words," she signed. "Wait! They may help us one day."

I wasn't sure what she meant, but suspected she might know some verbal majick. Perhaps something she'd learned from her mother. Other than using an elemental voice, I knew none of that, and neither had Thirest. It was extremely powerful, and supposedly the very first Apprentices used it. If she could do that sort of thing, I could understand her wanting to save her words. Still, I hated that cough and her suffering with it. What I *liked*, very much, were her kisses, which tasted like spring water and honey, now, flavored as they were by the Naiadae.

The brook was a good place for us to camp while I recovered. The water was sweet, and held fish (though tiny) and crawdaddies. Small animals came to drink there, and, though *I* would have asked them first, Pearl was not averse to scooting them out of their bodies. She even made me a pair of rabbit-skin moccasins. "For the cold North," she'd signed.

"How did you know I intend to go into the North?" I'd asked her, a little ashamed of myself for forgetting all about my intentions to tell her.

She tried to sign her answer to me, but I simply could not understand what she was saying. Finally, she pointed to herself and said, "Shykick." As she said it, she showed me the sign for the word; right hand, middle three fingers dragged down her face across her eyes and nose. Then she signed, "Now I have thirty-six," and it

70

suddenly struck me how very precious those words were to her.

"That means you could tell me 'I love you' twelve times," I said, smiling at least twelve 'I love yous' at her.

"Not enough," she signed. "Not nearly enough."

Another week at the brook, and I could stand. Pearl made me two canes out of the poles she'd used for my litter. Though I was still amazingly weak, my standing and taking a few halting steps made Pearl incredibly happy. So much so, that she laughed aloud, a sound that I will never forget as long as I live. It was like a waterfall of little bells trinketing down into an echoing pool. When she realized she'd done it, she covered her mouth, and her eyes grew wide as she tried not to laugh at the fact that she'd laughed. "Thirty-five, thirty-four, thirty-three. Oh well!" she signed, shrugging her shoulders and smiling hugely.

Those three words she'd used to laugh when I walked said, "I love you" to me even clearer than the first time she'd spoken. I wanted to take her in my arms and love her so badly it literally caused me to moan.

As soon as I was able to stand, Pearl wanted to start back for the Ninety-five. I told her I was maybe good for a dozen steps a day and I needed to get a little stronger. "At twelve steps a day, we'll be old farts by the time we get down there," I laughed.

"Stronger every day," she signed. "More walking, more strength."

Then I noticed the troubled look on her face. "What is it, Pearl?" I asked.

"Not a good place," she signed, looking furtively around us. "Evil has been here, will come again."

I'd never seen Pearl make the universal sign for "evil" (showing only the back of the middle finger of your right hand), and it gave me a shiver when she did. Suddenly, I wanted to leave that place, too. "Tomorrow," I said. "If we only get twelve steps away, it'll make me twelve steps happier."

"Me, too," she signed, obviously spooked, and sensing something I couldn't. Pearl was afraid, and that, I knew, was a very bad sign.

VIII
Tool's Warning

I awoke that next morning to Pearl's pleasing, Naiadae kisses. The ball hadn't quite made its way into the sky. Still, as early as it was, Pearl had everything packed up and ready to go. Instead of my tent over me, stars were fading above the trees.

She was keeping a smile, trying to act naturally, but Pearl was nervous, and my physical inability to move faster began to frustrate her. She had her pack on, had fashioned a strap from which to drag mine, and was trying to get those two canes she'd made me into my hands. All the while she was looking around, and jumping at every sound the forest made. Finally, I said, "Pearl, calm down."

"No!" she signed. "Move!"

"What *is* it?" I asked, trying to soothe her with my voice.

Then she made that sign for "evil" again, and it totally unnerved me. All-of-a-sudden I *felt* was she was feeling. "Okay, let's go!"

Once we were moving, Pearl calmed down. I was still in a bad way, and she knew it. She no longer rushed me, made us stop frequently, and, at one point, produced, much to my dismay, more of those fish livers. When, jokingly, I said I'd much rather drink her blood than eat those things, she took out her little knife. "I'm kidding!" I yelled, and she almost laughed out loud at her own joke. I wished she had.

We walked well into late afternoon, and still barely made it a klick away from the brook. Pearl had prepared food in advance, which we ate, and then slept against our packs. I was completely exhausted, and fell asleep before I'd even finished eating. Sometime after dark, Pearl woke me. She wanted to check my eyes. "Am I still a wolf?" I asked her.

She nodded her head, but signed that they seemed a little dimmer. I wanted her to show me with her mirror, but she signed that it was packed up and she didn't want to dig it out.

"Come here, then," I said, "and let me use your eyes for a mirror." I was actually joking, and intended just to steal a kiss, but when she got very close, I could actually see my Fierae light reflected in her eyes. "I don't think they're any dimmer," I said, surprised by what I was seeing.

"No," she signed, "they're not."

When I opened my eyes the following morning, the Ball was fully risen. Pearl was next to me. As soon as she saw I was awake, she placed her hand over my mouth and pointed in the direction from which we'd come. About a hundred or so meters up into the forest, several men were moving through the trees. At least one had a bow slung onto his shoulder.

I reached over and got my arm around Pearl's neck, drew her ear to my mouth. "Can't see us," I whispered. "Just let them pass. We made it."

I was trying to reassure her, but I also believed I was speaking the truth. The men were obviously heading for the brook, away from us. In a minute or two they'd be gone, and we'd be traveling in the opposite direction. We'd also be moving faster. The sight of these men had not only motivated me, but made me think of Tool's warning: "Stay to the old road...bad folk been croppin' up like weed."

The men were almost out of sight. I'd counted five, but noticed that one was tied by the wrists and being led by another. If I weren't incapacitated, I would have investigated that. Fully capable, four or five men, with or without bows, would not have intimidated me. If some injustice was being perpetrated, I would have set it right. But I was *not* fully capable. In fact, I was certain that I could do no majick whatsoever.

Though I wasn't sure what Pearl was capable of (especially after the intense majick she'd done at the brook,) I knew she could probably protect herself. I did not, however, know what she was *willing* to do. I considered her an Apprentice, but would she *kill?* I didn't want to find out. The thought of Pearl scooting someone out of their body like a rabbit, scared me. Whatever she could and would

73

do, I knew she couldn't protect us both, not in the close confines of these woods. But it didn't matter. In another minute those men would be gone. That's what I was thinking when everything went wrong.

Normally she'd have sensed its presence and avoided it. Normally, even if she was distracted and *didn't* sense it, when it stung her she'd have had no voice with which to cry out. But the *not* normal occurrence of a bee stinging Pearl on the cheek, caused the *not* normal sound of her Naiadae voice crying, "Ouch!"

"Thirty-two," I said to her, as those men came running.

Three men, *all* with bows and quivers of arrows, stood around us, still sitting against our packs. Another had stayed behind with the man who was bound. These men were dressed in sturdy clothes and boots, and looked almost what some would call, "Well-to-do." There was *nothing* about them, however, that I'd have called reassuring.

One of them had something in his mouth, pushed out into his cheek. Occasionally, he spit, black and foul. "Good morning," I said to them. "My name is Spaul. And who might you be?"

For answer, all of them laughed. Then the spitting one, who seemed to be the leader, said to the others, in a sinister tone, "And who might we be?" Again, they all laughed. Then the leader spat, and said to me, "This here yer negra?"

Though the idea was appalling to me, I immediately knew what this evil man meant. Anger flashed through me like a Charge. I was about to say, "She is her own!" when Pearl knelt beside me, bowed her head low, and placed my hand on her head.

"Least he got her trained good," one of the other two men guffawed. Then all of them laughed evilly together.

"We're on our way to the Ninety-five," I said, trying to restrain my anger. I understood what Pearl was doing, and tried to play along, but if I'd been able to majick, all three of these men would already be torn and bleeding. As a rule I follow the Apprentice way and live not to harm. Ultimately, I would probably die not to kill. But *these* men I *would* harm. I'd heard of their kind in myths and legends, in stories to scare bad children into their beds. *Slavers!* I felt like I was in someone else's bad dream.

"We were just about to be on our way, so we'll bid you good-day and be off," I said, struggling to my feet.

"Looks like yer legs ain't a-workin' so good," the spitter said, in a way that made me think that somehow pleased him.

"Mayhap you should set a spell longer'n let me borry yer negra," one of the other two said.

"Oh, we *all* gonna borry her," the leader said, unshouldering his bow and quiver, and setting them down.

I already had one of my canes raised up, prepared to offer what resistance I could, but I knew it would be futile. I also knew Pearl would not flee to save herself. She was already on her feet and by my side. I wasn't sure what she would do, but I caught myself hoping she *would* kill that spitting bastard. Perhaps, if she did, the other two would kill us quickly in a rage. It was the only thing "merciful" that my mind could conjure.

As that evil trio started to converge on us, I heard rustling, and the heavy footfalls of a hoofed animal. I looked up, just as a man riding a muley shouted, "Sheeny! Take your men and their foul thinkin' up to the branch to fill our canteens. If you cannot control your disgustin' cravin's, you will at least respect another man's property!"

"Sorry, Mistuh Bowagad, we was jus' funnin'," said Sheeny the spitter.

"Ah'm sure!" Bowagad said from his muley. "Now git!" Then to me, he bowed from his perch and said, "Rufus T. Bowagad, at your service. My apologies for the boorishness of my hired help. Though good workers, men of their lower station must be constantly supervised. Left to their own devices, they quickly revert to their animal natures."

"No harm done," I said, happy to have escaped that dire confrontation. "I'm Spaul, and this..." before I could finish, Pearl was on her knees at my side, once again bowing her head low. I had just about had enough of that, but played along, placing my hand on her head. "This is Pearl."

75

"Are you injured?" Bowagad asked me, pointing to my canes.

"Caught in a storm a couple weeks back. A Fierae bolt almost killed me. Pearl nursed me back to health, and I'll tell you now, your men would have had to kill me before they did any 'borrowing!'" I was losing my composure. I was angry that such men existed. I was angry that I couldn't majick them up a suitable reward for their malevolence. Pearl managed to take my hand and squeeze it, and I knew she was right. Don't exacerbate the situation. Let's just get fugging out of here.

"Loyalty!" Bowagad exclaimed. "You are correct to reward and defend it. For the most part, my negras are loyal, and I treat them well. Unfortunately, some don't know when they are well off, and they run. But, of course, they are ignorant. They go to the branch for water, and we catch them. Then, of course, as I reward the loyal, I must punish the wicked. Usually, they only run once."

Bowagad was a strange looking character, perched on that muley. As hot as it was, he wore a jacket over his shirt, and something tied into a bow around his neck. On his head was a wide-brimmed hat, very finely and expertly made of straw or some such. It was white, and had a shiny, black band around it. His pants were also of a very light color, and his boots were like nothing I'd ever seen; high up his legs, and of very smooth leather. "Well, thank you for intervening on our behalf," I said. "We've a long way to go to the Ninety-five, so I guess we'll be on our way."

"Nonsense," Bowagad said, waving his hand. "Look at you, man, you can barely walk. I insist that you come to my plantation. It is no more than twenty miles west of here, down in a most beautiful valley. You will recover your strength as my guest, and allow me to compensate for the rude behavior of my men. You have my word as a gentleman that there well be no more attempts to harass or molest your Pearl."

"Thank you," I told him, "but we're traveling east, and I'm afraid I would slow you down considerably. Twenty miles is a very long way." I'd heard people measure distance in miles before, but could never remember if they were shorter or longer than klicks.

"Not so far at all," he countered, "for you shall ride. I'm due for a good hike anyway. I really do insist, Master Spaul. I have other men still combing about in these woods, similarly low-class men, and cannot guarantee your safety if you two travel alone. Come and recover at my humble abode, and when you are feeling stouter, I will personally escort you to the old road, with a mount to bear you there. How can you refuse?" I couldn't. I knew a threat when I heard one, even if it was veiled.

Bowagad hopped off his Muley, and Pearl rushed to help me climb aboard. As she did, she looked up at me through her lashes, and almost imperceptibly nodded her head. By that, and the look on her face, I knew what she was saying. "Go along with it, you're getting stronger all the time. Pretty soon they'll get theirs."

She was right. Bowagad had no way of knowing who he was bringing home. But, as it turned out, *I* had no way of knowing that I could come to admire a man whom I also thoroughly despised.

IX
The Tara Road

We caught up quickly with Bowagad's men at the brook. Sheeny immediately fixed Pearl with an evil leer. Bowagad saw it and said, "Sheeny, get these men on their way home. Where are the other horsemen?"

"Horsemen?" I piped up.

Thirest had told me that the horses all died off with the ancients. Killed by some disease borne by mosquitoes. I remembered this well, because he'd often describe horses to me when I was a child. "They were like giant, sleek muleys," he'd say, "of every color imaginable. They could run like Zephres, and carry three or four men apiece while they did. Horses, Spaul, were the grandest animals of all the Ancients tamed. I'd give a good tooth to see one, no shite!"

"A figure of speech," Bowagad explained. "Real horses, alas, have fled to the lands of myth. But I have two men on donkeys out here, whom I call 'horsemen' out of a sense of tradition. Sheeny, gollam it, where are those men?"

"Donkeys?" I asked.

"They comin' now, Mistuh Bowagad," Sweeny said.

"There they come," Bowagad pointed. "Yes, Master Spaul, donkeys, like what you are riding."

"Oh, we call these muleys," I told him.

"I've heard that," he said. "You must be from farther south, from the Purchase, perhaps."

"Yes!" I said, surprised by his knowledge and seeming intelligence. "I've spent most of my life wandering the Purchase, and the Southern Edge, down by the Florida. Have you been there?"

"I've been to the Southern Edge, but have never gone west into the Purchase. I look forward to your stories of that place. Have you seen the House Town pile?"

"Yes, I have," I told him, which lit his eyes (figuratively, of course).

"Grand!" he exclaimed. "Horsemen! Come here! You, Farley, give me your muley!"

"Muley, Mistuh Bowagad?" the confused "horseman" asked.

"Dismount, man!" Bowagad roared happily, obviously in overwhelmingly good spirits.

Once he'd mounted the horseman's muley, he rode up beside me and said, "We can ride on ahead, now. We'll make excellent time."

"What about Pearl?" I asked him.

"She'll be safe with my men, I assure you."

"No fuggin' way!" I answered him, flatly.

"You are overly protective, suh! But, of course, she did save your life. All right then, I understand. Come here, girl, and give me your pack," he hollered at Pearl. Then, back to me, he said, "Surely she can keep up if I carry her load."

Pearl was staring holes in me. She wanted me to shut up. She wanted me to bide my time and get well. But there was something else in those eyes she was using to drill into mine. There was anger. And when she broke our mutual stare, and looked over at the brown man being pulled along by his bound wrists, I knew that anger would eventually have to be paid. "Not yet," her eyes said when they reacquired mine, "but none too soon!"

We rode away from the brook, picking our way through the trees, on our sure-footed muleys, and Pearl had no trouble keeping up. Before long, however, we came to a wide trail, and Bowagad picked up the pace. "This is the Tara Road," he told me, "which will lift us straight into these foothills, until we are looking down into the valley of my home, my Tara."

"Tara?" I asked.

"Yes," he answered. "It is the name I've given my plantation. It comes from a very old book, which I'll be happy to allow you to read while you convalesce. You can read, of course?" he asked.

"Of course," I said, just a little indignantly, because of the way he'd asked.

"Forgive my tone, Master Spaul," he said. Then, in a truly conciliatory voice, "I am surrounded by the uneducated, and sometimes am not fit to converse with the few gentlemen I have the honor to come across. Actually, I took you to be an educated man immediately. Something in your eyes, and about the loyalty of your slave. It *takes* an educated man to inspire loyalty. Will you accept my apology, Master Spaul?"

"Call me Spaul," I told him. "Yes, I do."

"Excellent!" he answered. "And you must call me Rufus. You have no idea what it means to me to have someone to talk to besides these rough men I employ. Someone with a *mind*, instead of a skull full of base instincts. I promise you, Spaul, you will love Tara. It isn't often that I get to show her off."

"Do you have more than the one book?" I asked, trying not to seem as excited about it as I was.

"I've a hundred," he answered.

"Books?" I exclaimed, no longer hiding anything.

Bowagad laughed, and I have to admit, he seemed a very good-natured fellow. Then I remembered, he'd referred to Pearl as "your slave." I resolved to be on my guard against this man's charms. If being a slaver was his only fault, it made him utterly despicable.

Pearl was still keeping up with us easily, she was very hardy, and could probably have outrun a horse, if any were left. Still, she was sweating in the heat. I wanted to give her water, but in order to do that, I'd have to ask *her* to have Naiadae fill her pot. It was a dilemma. There was no way I was going to let Bowagad know she could majick. For a moment I considered just having her take him out in some way, maybe float him up a dozen meters and drop him, or have the Terrae trip his muley. But the only way we could have ridden the lines was up or down this trail, and I was sure his men were already on it.

No, the best course of action would be to recover. Once I could majick again, Pearl and I would be very formidable, and could choose among many possible actions. Besides, there were who-knew-how-many people being held as slaves at Bowagad's "Tara." We were Apprentices, and I more than suspected that the Universe had placed us in this situation to serve it. To set things right. Finally, I said, "Do you have any water?"

"Yes! Of course! How neglectful of me. Here!" Bowagad said, tossing me a canteen. Then, to Pearl, he said, "Come here, girl."

Pearl went and stood beside Rufus' muley. "Open your mouth," he told her. When she did, he poured water down her throat, then splashed some onto her face. When he'd finished, he sat there looking at her. He seemed to be getting angry. Finally, he growled, "Have you no gratitude? Can you not utter a simple 'thank you?'"

"She can't, can't speak!" I said quickly, as I was afraid he was about to slap her. "Red fever took her voice when she was five."

"Were you children together?" Bowagad asked, completely ignoring Pearl, now. "Was her mama your nanny?"

"No," I answered, "but we've been together a very long time." I tried to make myself believe that, as I don't like to lie. But I knew I had better get used to it, if I was to keep up this masquerade. "It seems like Pearl has been with me forever," I said, looking at her, but trying to keep the love I was feeling from showing on my face.

Bowagad saw it, however, and his reaction surprised me. Without looking at Pearl, he let his canteen fall till it hung from his hand by its strap. "Take it, girl," he said. "It is for you to keep, for saving your master's life."

The "Tara Road" rose steadily up, and then, as Bowagad had promised, peaked, and looked out over a magnificent valley. What I saw in that valley caused me almost to faint dead away off my muley. It was the biggest village I'd ever seen, with fields full of crops, and workers in them picking and tending. An enormous white house shone in the afternoon's brilliance; a house with another house atop it. Two massive trees had been shaved into columns holding up a part of the roof that flew out over two porches one right over the other. There must have been a hundred pickets in the railings around those porches.

There were many smaller houses, and barns and wells and something I later discovered was called a "gazebo." Pigs and muleys and chickens and goats, and *cows*, which I'd never seen, but, supposedly, had eaten, were corralled and penned. There was a good size stream running through the valley, into which had been built a waterwheel, which served a mill. There was also a contraption that bellowed smoke, and turned wheels onto which long belts were fastened. I could not even guess at its purpose.

Bowagad sat proudly beside me on his muley, watching my reaction to what I was seeing. Finally, I said, "Which one is Tara?"

Bowagad laughed, and I could tell he was delighted. "All of it," he told me. "All of it is home, my Tara."

As we rode down into the valley, it seemed like Tara was coming up to meet us. It became enormous, until we were surrounded by it, dropped into the pot of it, boiling with activity and sounds and smells. Bowagad called it home, the way Tool might call his cottage home, but this was a village. This was something from the past, or maybe even the future. It excited and frightened me at once. I didn't know why, but I was about to get a terrible education. Right then, however, as we entered Tara, I was ignorant. So ignorant, in fact, that I didn't even know I was still innocent. Perhaps that is something you can't really know until you aren't anymore.

We rode right up to the giant white house. A man stood there dressed in the most magnificent costume. Over a very white shirt, he wore a jacket that sat high on his waste in the front, and came down in the back almost to his knees. It had shiny metal buttons, and he, too, had something tied around his neck into a bow. On his hands he wore perfect white gloves, made of smooth fabric. Dark stripes ran down the sides of his trousers. The only skin showing was the man's brown face. I wondered (because I was innocent) if he was a slave, too.

The man held our muleys bridals as we dismounted, then two boys came and led them away. By the time we walked up the steps to the porch of that unbelievable house, the finely dressed man was holding the door open for us. "Thomas," Bowagad said to him, "take Master Spaul's girl around back and have the kitchen girls clean her up, find her some appropriate attire. She'll be staying in the house."

"Yes, Massah Rufus."

"And tell them to quarter her with Ilsa."

"Suh?"

"Pearl, here, is Master Spaul's personal slave. She will be accustomed to house negra privileges."

"Ilsa, suh?"

"Have I stuttered, Thomas?" Bowagad laughed.

"No, suh. Ilsa, suh."

I looked back to Pearl, and she smiled at me, but I did *not* want us to be separated. Bowagad was a master, already, at reading my face, and said, "She will be treated like royalty, Spaul, like a genuine African princess." Then he laughed and took my arm, leading me into the heart of his demesne.

There were many things inside this house that I'd never seen before. From the high ceilings hung circular tiers of clear jewels, arranged around many, many candles. I found myself wanting night to come so I could see if he'd light them all. The floors were immaculate, and oiled shiny. "I shall put you in a room down here, in deference to your legs," Rufus told me.

"Thank you," I muttered, my wonder at this place sounding in my voice.

Bowagad was delighted by my obvious enchantment, and laughed. "It *is* wonderful, isn't it? I forget sometimes, having no one to remind me. Come on, let's get you settled."

He walked us through another very large room, and I saw something in there that froze me solid. Rufus must have thought it was the size of the room that had stopped me, and said, "Yes, it's grand, isn't it? This is the ballroom."

Then I pointed and said, "*Where* did you *find* it?"

On one of the walls, framed and hung like an enormous work of art, was a mirror at least two meters square. "Lovely, isn't it," Rufus said. "There's only one other like it that I know of, and it's hung in my bedroom. Actually, Spaul, I made them both. I had someone else prepare the glass, but the silverwork I did myself. It was the first thing I learned to do from my Ancient books."

Ancient books? That shut me up and dragged me out of my gawking, childish daze. Suddenly I needed Thirest to be alive, to be here with me, telling me what *he* was going to do, because I was helpless. Even If I'd been able to majick, I don't know what I'd have done. Thirest had always known what to do, had always been decisive. If nothing else, I know he would have wanted those books. I don't know if he'd have smashed another man's handiwork, even if it *had been* made using an Ancient craft. There were mirrors around, I'd seen some, and of course there was Pearl's, but those had all been found, not *made*. And now I'd seen one used to work majick, which made me even less happy that Bowagad had two enormous ones.

I was in over my head. I could feel the crushing weight of just how *far* over my head I was. On top of that, the exhaustion of the long, hot muley ride in my depleted state, chose that moment to catch up with me. I know I was saying something as the light faded and my knees buckled. I think I was saying, "Pearl."

"Pearl," is definitely what I said when I came to. I was lying on a bed, and Rufus and the man called Thomas were standing over me. A wet towel was across my forehead.

"Thomas has sent for her," Bowagad told me. The look of concern in his eyes was so obviously genuine that I relaxed, felt suddenly safe. "She was bathing when you fainted, but she's dressing now. I sent word only that you wanted her. I know her devotion to you, and did not want to drive her to hysteria. I know how easily the negra mind can embrace panic."

I could hear Rufus, but he wasn't making sense to me. I wanted to explain to him that Pearl was capable of floating us both above this house and over the valley. I wanted him to know she could summon the Terrae to drag him down into the molten center

84

of World. I needed him to know that she had fed me her own blood to save me. And I might have tried to tell him those things, had Pearl not walked into the room with another very beautiful lady. Both of them were wearing long, cotton dresses. Pearl's was white with indigo magnolias painted on it. Over it she wore a little white smock with lace trim. I'd never seen such fine things as those dresses.

Quickly she came to me, sat on the edge of the bed and took my hand. She smelled of lilacs, and had rouged her lips. "So beautiful," I started to say, but she put a finger on my lips. Then she turned and looked at Rufus, brought her hand to her lips and pantomimed eating.

"He needs food!" Bowagad said.

Pearl nodded.

"Thomas, have the girls prepare dinner, and bring some soup or broth and bread right now."

Again Pearl turned to Bowagad, this time placing her hand on his arm. At first it startled him, then his eyes widened as a strange smile slowly spread across his face. Pearl made motions again, trying to tell him something. It looked like she was pretending to cut her wrist with her finger. At first Rufus frowned, not understanding. Then he asked, "Blood?"

Pearl nodded, then made the gestures of eating again.

"Is he anemic?" Bowagad asked.

Pearl sighed and smiled and nodded.

Bowagad turned to the beautiful lady who had accompanied Pearl into the room. "Ilsa," he said, and I noticed his voice was not so commanding as it had been with Thomas, "go tell Thomas to have them prepare thick steaks for dinner, very rare."

"Yes," she said. "And I think Jubal knows a tonic to make for that ailment. Shall I ask him, Ruf...Master Rufus?"

"Very good, Ilsa, do that. Master Spaul is our honored guest. We must make him well."

Pearl propped me up in that bed, and fed me soup. It was very good, made with ham and peas. Rufus came into the room, what seemed like every few minutes, to check on my progress. His concern affected me, and I had to keep reminding myself that he was not only a slaver, but a slaver with Ancient and possibly forbidden knowledge. He almost certainly had forbidden artifacts, in the form of Ancient books. Rufus T. Bowagad, who's soup I was eating and bed I was lying in, was my enemy, was the enemy of *everyone*, and World herself. I don't know if Thirest had been capable of hatred, but I suspected it, even when he was alive. I suspected that he'd hated the Ancients. Would he have hated Rufus? Had I hated Sweeny when he'd threatened Pearl?

I finished the soup, and Bowagad brought in a bottle of spirits, mixed me some with cool water. "See if it's too strong," he said, as he handed it to me.

I took a sip of the pale, amber liquid. "It's quite good," I told him. "It reminds me of something called 'corn,' though this is smoother, and tastes of smoke."

"It's what the Ancients called sippin' whiskey, or bourbon. We age it in charred oak casks. Tell me, Spaul, how are you feeling?"

"Better," I told him. "I over did it today, too soon after my accident. I'll be fine, I just need rest."

"I blame myself," Bowagad lamented. "Had I known your fragility, I'd never have insisted we ride all day in that hot sun."

"Pearl *walked* all day," I said. She had taken the tray with my soup bowl to the kitchen. Had she been there, she'd have been annoyed with me, but I couldn't help myself.

Much to my surprise, Bowagad bowed his head, and said softly, "I know, I'm sorry. I didn't understand you two, now I do. But even if I'd known then, I couldn't have let her ride in front of my men."

"What do you mean you understand us now," I asked him.

"I know that the heart will not be constrained by convention or propriety. *That*, I've known for a long time. Still, men of vision must keep a certain face, maintain appearances, and ultimately, be the masters of even what their hearts desire. I quartered Pearl with Ilsa because Ilsa, as head of the household servants, has a room of her own. Pearl will be able to come to you without causing the servant's 'grapevine' to vibrate with rumor and unseemly tales."

"I see," I said, and I did. Ilsa had a room of her own. I'd heard it in both their voices, the slaver was in love with his slave. I wasn't sure whether to be touched or be sick.

In a little room off my bedroom, was a washtub for bathing. I'd seen bathing tubs before, but none so large. Before dinner, Rufus had his servants fill the tub with warm water. I eased myself into it and let it draw the exhaustion out of my bones. I hadn't been wet a minute when Pearl came in. She shut the door behind her and we were alone. Without saying or signing anything, she took a cloth and some soap, and began washing me. "You must be as exhausted as I am," I told her. "I can do this, why don't you go lie down on that bed and rest?"

For an answer she leaned in and kissed me. Then she whispered in my ear, in her enchanted voice, "Touch." After spending that one word, she signed, "I needed to touch you," then she whispered, "I'm scared."

Pearl and I spent the time we had in this little room devising signs for our new circumstances. She still didn't want to use her words, and was now down to twenty-nine. Her sign for Rufus was to touch her head with her right hand at the temple, as she was certain he was insane. That is what frightened her most.

After choosing signs for Ilsa and Thomas, and different rooms in the house, she signed that I'd better get out and dry off. Dinner was ready, and Rufus was having it brought to us. He'd also given me a set of light, cotton sleeping attire, and an incredible robe, long and thick and soft, which had been dyed a deep indigo.

Once I'd put these garments on, Pearl threw her arms around me and buried her head in my chest. "It's going to be alright," I told her. "I'll be well very soon, I can feel it."

"That's good," she signed, but I could see the tears in her eyes.

"We're going to be fine, Pearl," I said. She seemed overly distraught, and it worried me. "What is it?" I asked.

"Nothing here is alright," she signed. "They whipped the man they caught by the brook today."

Pearl and I ate bloody red cow meat in my room. I'm certain, now, that her diagnosis of anemia was correct. I had always known interaction with the mag lines causes this, and had suspected that all forms of majicking produce it to some degree or another. More and more I am coming to realize how little even we Apprentices understand about our interactions with the Elementals.

Rufus had left us to dine alone. When we'd finished, Pearl gathered our plates and trays, and let me know she was going to help the servants in the kitchen. I suspected she had it in mind to reconnoiter as well. Pearl was at war, and grim with it, which concerned me. I'd regain my strength very soon, with this kind of food and pampering and rest. What was she going to expect of me once power flowed into my life again. I knew I was going to want to preserve what was inextricably tangled into what must be destroyed. Pearl, I feared, would not deliberate, but simply act.

As I sailed these thoughts on my mind-sea, Rufus came in with some of his servants, and filled the room with candles and lamps. "Pearl has made me aware of the problem with your eyes," he said, which startled me, and I sat up straight in my bed.

"She has?" I asked.

"Yes, she seems to believe your sight will return to normal as you regain strength. She's quite good at making me understand her. She says, when the sun leaves the sky, you are blind, so we shall imitate the sun for you. I've also brought you a book, but you mustn't read if it hurts your eyes. Wait and read in sunlight."

I knew the word Rufus used for the Ball, but had never heard anyone say it before. During the final days of the Ancients, the "sun" had become scorching, and clawed at the people's flesh. The legend is that the searing sun had been giving birth to the Ball, which was lesser, and did not burn men so. Thirest had told me the Ball had always been the same, but the Skyshaper Villages, and the Ancient's Teck, had skinned the sky and made it thinner, making the Ball seem hotter and starker. I never really understood that, but nobody says "sun." Apparently that time of the Ancients was one of their worst and most trying.

After lighting the candles and lamps, the servants left. I had forgotten all about my eyes, and if Pearl had not been so alert and clever, the dim light of dusk would have given me away. I wondered what Rufus would have made of those wolf eyes, as he fixed us small bourbons, and pulled up a chair.

"I know you need rest, and I shan't stay long," he said. "I just want you to know you are safe here. *Pearl* is safe here. Actually, she's getting on famously with the house girls."

"Pearl will love anyone who gives her the opportunity," I told him.

"I hope I can do that," he said. "She's obviously very intelligent, so of course she is leery of me. How could she *not* be?"

"I can't speak for her," I answered.

"There's no need," he said. "Pearl has obviously never been a slave, though she did fool me at first. If I was her I'd be very leery of me."

A little shock of fear ran through me as Rufus said this, but I sailed it away on my sea, said, "No, Pearl has never been a slave. Yes, Pearl is very intelligent. As for how she feels about you, I will not speak for her, but, as you say, it isn't necessary."

"Can she read and write?" Rufus asked.

"No," I told him, and he seemed relieved by that. For a moment I didn't understand, then it dawned on me. He didn't want her giving his captive workforce any ideas.

"She never needs to know what it's like, Spaul. She'd be as free as she's ever been, *freer*, in fact, with the fineries and luxuries Tara offers. And think of the life an educated man such as you could have here. I almost feel as though I've been waiting for you. In fact, I know I have."

"I don't think I'm following you, Rufus. Pearl and I are traveling on the Ninety-five. Our excursion off the road was frivolous and nearly ended in catastrophe. Our intention is to resume our journey. Is it *your* intention to detain us?"

"No," he answered, looking down into his lap. "You are my guests. I ask only that you observe the conventions of this society, of Tara. Recover your strength, and you are free to leave, as I have promised. But I will not lie to you, I am determined to convince you to stay. Tara can be a paradise, but it is populated only by base and ignorant men, and of course, my slaves, whom, you will find, I treat *well*."

"That may be so, Rufus, but you treat them well against their wills. Your intelligence is obvious to me, and you have created wonders here, but do you honestly see nothing wrong with slavery?"

"Slavery is everywhere, Spaul. Have you never rented a girl at an inn?"

"No," I answered him, "I never have."

"Good. Nor have I, but you've *seen* them there, have you ever accosted an innkeeper for offering to sell you his daughter's body?"

I didn't answer, but he had a point. Had I turned my head to such things because they were *common*? Because they represented *convention*?

When I didn't answer, Rufus said, in an astonished tone, "I have hurt you with that question, haven't I? You search yourself too hard, Spaul. We are but men, beset by hard challenges and hard lives. We do what we can to meet those challenges, and smooth the sharp edges of life, but we cannot task ourselves to right every wrong and cure every ill. Who are we, even, to make such determinations as right and wrong, especially for other men, whose lives and hardships we know nothing about? Perhaps the innkeeper sells his daughter to feed his sons. I know you have traveled, and seen much, Spaul. World is enormous, and lives with no care or thought for men, so we survive the best we can. Who are we to judge the means by which men survive?"

Rufus arguments were roiling my sea, and exhaustion crept back over me like a dark cloud. "I'm sorry," I said, closing my eyes. "I invite this conversation, I really do, but my weakness overwhelms me again."

"No, of course," Rufus said apologetically, "we have plenty of time to talk when you're more rested. I shouldn't have sprung this on you so soon into your convalescence. But do keep an open mind.

I beg you. Don't dismiss my offer out of hand. Hear me out when you are more able."

"I will do that much," I said to him, but I was again growing faint. "Would you ask Pearl to come?" I asked.

"Yes," he told me, obviously able to see now that I was in distress. "I'll fetch her at once, and of course she must remain with you. I have a tonic my herbalist made for your anemia, I'll send it with her. I will instruct the servants to keep this part of the house quiet. Hopefully, you can sleep well into the day tomorrow, and regain some of your strength. I'm sorry to have taxed you. Sleep well."

Rufus had taxed me, indeed, strength and conviction. I felt sick, sick that this slaver had sat there and made so much sense, caused me to doubt. When Pearl came in I could see on her face that I did not look well. As best I could I smiled, and said, "*You* hold *me*."

She was carrying a jar of Rufus' anemia tonic, and spooned some into my mouth. It tasted of molasses. Then she blew out all the candles but one, and took me into her arms. I looked up into her eyes, and she said, in her wonderful, Mer Maiden voice, "Darling wolf."

My days recovering at Tara soothed and aided my Fierae worn body, and troubled my mind with contradictions. I read Rufus' book, *Gone With The Wind*, which was an Ancient artifact. Knowing I could not let Tara stand as it was made me feel like a dastardly Yankee. I did not want to be an evil man doing the right thing.

In the evenings, with candles and lamps ablaze in my room, Rufus and I had long conversations, sometimes into the night. He was ravenous for my tales of the Purchase, and the things I'd seen in my travels. On several occasions, I caught myself starting to tell him stories through Apprentice eyes, and had to rearrange events to circumnavigate the truth. I hated that, and wanted desperately to reveal myself for who I was. I wondered if it would make a difference to him to know that an Apprentice would have him free these people he held as slaves, and make a different start at Tara.

Rufus hid nothing from me, which made me feel like a spy and a traitor. His story was amazing. In his youth (I took him to be in his early forties) Rufus had made an incredible discovery. Though he was less than forthcoming about the exact location of his find, I took it to be somewhere south of us by perhaps a hundred klicks.

This place he'd found, had once been a small, Skyshaper Village. As was the case with all those Villages, it was a rubble pile when he found it. But, apparently, an Ancient named Thomas Cooper had built a library there whose different levels of books went not up, as was the usual configuration of those Skyshaper buildings, but down into the earth. Though the above part was destroyed, and hardly recognizable as anything more than a slight bump in the landscape, beneath it lay a treasure.

Having been built high on a hill, water had only collected in the very bottom levels of Thomas Cooper's trove of books. "The twisted upper frame of the place blocked my entry to the lower levels," Rufus told me, "but I managed to squeeze and shimmy myself in, until it opened up. I had very little light, just candles, and I knew I'd never be able to bring more than myself and those back down through that tight and twisting entranceway I'd found. Nor would I be able to carry out more than four or five books, and still be able to squeeze through. On that first excursion, after several trips down into that dark vault of enlightenment, I retrieved twenty texts. With them, I made my fortune."

Apparently, Rufus sold a couple of his treasured books, and made little mirrors, which would fetch incredible sums. With those funds, he began his work on Tara, in this valley from which he'd originally come. Here, Rufus story became sinister. To the west of the valley, he knew, men lived up in the mountains, rough men, and families betrayed by inbreeding. Humans, as you know, are not abundant in World, and Rufus took what he could get, made them his foremen and, eventually, his slavers. These men were not fond of what they called "negras," and delighted in finding and enslaving them. With these men, and his ill-gotten workforce, Rufus built Tara.

"Several times I journeyed back to Thomas Cooper's library, always going alone, always being sure I wasn't followed. I understand the dangers as well as the benefits of such enlightenment. I believe I have been a good steward."

I did not disagree with Rufus out loud, but his "stewardship," I decided, was anything but beneficent. One night, some days after he'd told me that story, Rufus outlined his "plan," which included Pearl and me. Once I'd heard it, I realized Pearl had underestimated the degree of Rufus' dementia, and I began to share her fear of him.

"What Tara lacks," he'd told me, "is a future, a generation to carry on, and build upon these foundations I've laid. I need heirs, and I need men of similar intelligence, with similar heirs, to begin this new society of betters. These people I've brought down from the mountains are not fit to interact with, much less breed. In fact, I limit their propagation, as best I can, with herbs and additives in their food and drink. It is not one hundred percent effective, but they no longer multiply like vermin.

"Though I would wish for it to be different, I cannot produce my offspring by Ilsa, though I admit, she is intelligent. I have had to forbid her strictly from my books, or I'm sure she'd have taught herself to read by now.

"Through my travels, however, and the travels of horsemen I send out on this specific errand, I know of girls that show signs of intelligence; daughters of innkeepers and farmers and craftsmen. Soon I will contract for several of these to come to Tara and bear my heirs. If one or two of them seem *very* promising, I may even allow them to stay, though this is not necessary. Ilsa craves children of her own, but her maternal instincts, I believe, will cause her to adopt and raise these offspring. She understands the great potential of Tara and my vision.

"Though I understand the irony of her being mother to a new, white society, I embrace it. I truly want these negras treated well, and I think Ilsa's influence will insure that," he said, struggling to read my face. Then he added, "As Pearl's will."

"Pearl's?" I asked. Suddenly, I realized I must be careful of what I said. Insanity is unpredictable.

"Yes. I will fetch similar women for you, Spaul, and build you a mansion, and share the fortunes of Tara with you. Your sons and daughters, raised by Pearl, will marry my own prodigy, and bear the future lords of the manor."

I understood "marry" from Rufus' books. It was the same as Fargus' "marriage." Were the people of Erin also insane? Fargus had certainly made a case for it, admitting, as he did, that they regularly enslaved Elementals. I found myself wondering if evil produces insanity, or if insanity is drawn to it. Either way, I would be compelled to deal with both.

"Will you consider this, Spaul? I know you are a man who will not make such decisions lightly, but I only ask you to *consider* it. Your life, and Pearl's, would be wondrous here. Already, she and Ilsa are best of friends. Why, not an hour ago, they were trying on dresses I've just had made for them. They were happy, and if she could, I know Pearl would have been laughing along with Ilsa. Imagine those two with children to look after. Imagine us schooling our sons and insuring their destinies. We can build a *nation*, Spaul, a confederacy of enlightened men! Will you not join me?"

"I will consider it," I said, hoping to calm him, as he became feverish with this insane vision.

It seemed to work, and he said, "It is all I ask. Pardon my fervor, we must lighten our conversations for your sake, in deference to your recovery. In two days time, I am having a party. Twice a year, once in late summer, and again in late winter, I allow most of the slaves to gather for a barn dance. Our party will coincide with their summer celebration. I want us to have the house to ourselves, without the prying eyes of the servants. I want you to see what life at Tara might truly be like. Allow me to impress you, Spaul. Open your mind to me."

X
Party of Four

When Pearl came to me that night, she was wearing a new dress. It was the color of Tara's manicured lawn, but with tiny, white dots all in perfect rows. The collar was also white, and laced. New beads, made of green gems, which I recognized as emerils, were braded into her hair. Legend has it that if you wear an emeril while you're cooking, the food will taste better. I wasn't sure about the truth of such claims, but Pearl, with her bejeweled hair sparking in all that candlelight, certainly looked good enough to eat. Her darling wolf was growing strong again, and was hungry for her.

Once she'd closed our door, Pearl began blowing out some of the candles, which hid my eyes from Rufus. "Not too many, I want to be able to see you," I said. She was truly stunning. Her demeanor, also, seemed calmer, more relaxed. When she came close, I saw that her lips were rouged, and a thin dusting of silky, green powder adorned her eyelids. "You've been playing dress-up with Ilsa," I said, desire suddenly starting to disturb me.

"Am I pretty?" she signed, turning a pirouette for me.

"I want you so much it hurts," I told her. "I want to love you."

"I think you should," she signed.

"I don't trust Blitz not to be here," I said.

Pearl made the universal sign for the Fierae as if it were a dance, then pointed down, "Blitz is here." Her movement was fluid, making the green gems in her hair seem to orbit her. The powder over her eyes shined in the candlelight.

I felt drugged. "I feel drugged," I said out loud.

Pearl twirled into a little dance of signs again; zigzagging her arm, "Fierae," swooping to pat the floor quick with her left hand, "in the ground," smoothly bringing her palms over her heart, then, dramatically, head down, arm outstretched, pointing her finger sharply at me, "loves you!"

Desire was overwhelming me now. Pearl's exotic dance of words was becoming erotic. Then she froze, posed with her head up and her arms back. A smile of such seduction formed on her lips that I moaned deep in my chest. Her smile formed a word, and it bubbled out in her hypnotic, Naiadae voice, "Mmmate!"

I *burned*! My blood was dragon-breath hot. Pearl was seducing me as a Shykick. This was majick she was doing without the aid of Elementals, except for the Naiadae in her voice. But there was something else, too. As an Apprentice I had used many herbs and drugs to seek knowledge and improve my ability to majick. Things like sybic mushrooms and peyote. Woodrose and beldonae. I knew many compounds and infusions that could be mixed to induce sleep or arousal or stupor. If I'd been able to majick, I could have asked a tiny chorus of Zephrae to sail in my lungs and tell me if something foreign was in my breath and blood. But I really didn't need them. I was drugged. I could feel it.

Deeply, I looked into Pearl's eyes, with my own lit intensely, and could see it there too. Pearl was also under some influence. "Come to me," I said. I could see the drug opening her to suggestion, could feel it doing the same to me.

Pearl danced fluidly into my arms, spun around and leaned her head back onto my shoulder. The drug was taking me, and I would take Pearl, now, Blitz be gollammed. But, somehow, I managed to whisper in her ear, "We are drugged. Have the Naiadae in your lungs remove it from you."

Then I was gone, overwhelmed by the drug. I spun Pearl around to face me, her eyes were focusing, showing fear at the realization that she'd been drugged. All I could see was the incredible beauty I *needed* to partake of. Pearl was backing away now. I must have looked wild, with my amber eyes glowing, trying to devour her, the rumble of a growl sounding in my chest.

She was signing to me, trying to get something between us, the bed, a chair, but I was one-willed and coming for her. Finally, she said sharply, "No!" as if she were scolding a dog.

"Yes," I breathed, and I could see this was still exciting Pearl, too, but she knew she would have to stop it, have to stop me. I, however, was determined.

She may have actually giggled during that chase, but, at some point, she snatched up a glass of wine and emptied it into the air in front of me. Immediately, a chorus of Zephres appeared, caught that liquid cloud of grape, and sent it flying down my throat and into my lungs.

It hurt. It was choking and drowning me in fire. Then, when I thought the sensation would black me out, the Zephrae flew from my mouth with the wine and whatever amount of drug they'd cleared from my system. I dropped to my knees. Pearl knelt to hold me and said, in a giggly, Mer Maiden voice, "I'm sorry."

"Yowza," I breathed, "that hurt!"

Though neither of us was free of the drug completely, we were in control, if barely. We were on the bed, holding each other as if in some magnetic field of tension. Our feelings were too confused. Fear and desire (no, *lust*) and uncertainty and euphoria all blew hurrakins across our seas.

"Why, do you think?" I asked her, noting now that we were both shaking.

"Suggestion," she said, that voice drawing on my desire like a bowstring.

"It is a powerful drug. Look at us, drawing it out abruptly has us trembling. He's trying to make me want to stay. That's the suggestion. This is some sort of hypnotic compound."

Pearl nodded, shook, and produced a semi-sober smile. "Food?" she asked, and I realized she was speaking because her arms were pinned to her, hugging against her shaking. She couldn't sign.

"It could be in anything, food, water, even the rouge on your lips," I said. "It will be hard to search everything. I still can't majick, and we can't let them see you summoning Zephrae to check our food and drink."

"Antidote?" her beautiful voice bubbled.

On a little table Rufus had placed in my room, which held wine and glasses and fruit, was a bowl of peanuts roasted in their shells. I got up and started crumbling their shells off them. "The anemia tonic," I said to Pearl, still clinging to herself on the bed. "Take some of it and eat these. Protein in these goobers should sober us, and that iron tonic might help, too.

Pearl seemed to think my reasoning was sound, though in no way proven. We ate the peanuts and took spoonfuls of the thick, molassesy tonic. If nothing else, we stopped shaking, though I knew we were still fairly drunk with the drug. Somehow, we managed not to risk merging with Blitz, but we kissed and petted like hormone-crazed teenagers all night long.

We slept for perhaps an hour at dawn. The drug was persistent, and Pearl used another three of the Naiadae in her lungs to clear more of it out of her. That made six that she'd used without even speaking. "How many left now?" I asked her.

"Fourteen," she signed.

"Then you *did* giggle while I was chasing you."

"A little, two-Naiadae giggle," she signed, giving me those phony shy eyes.

"You aren't completely free of the drug either, are you?"

She shook her head.

"Can you clear it all out of me?" I asked.

"If you want to breathe wine half a dozen more times," she signed.

I really, really didn't. "Keep an eye on me. Keep an eye on our food and drink, as best you can, but don't give yourself away. Rufus will be with me a lot, he'll want to talk to me while I'm drugged, try to place his suggestion, get me to stay. The day after tomorrow is his party. I must start attempting contact with the Elementals. That party worries me, it's somehow part of his plan, and drugging us has something to do with it. I'm afraid you're right, Pearl, he is dangerously insane."

"Too soon for you to majick," she signed.

"I'm going to have to start pressing it," I told her.

"I think you should love me instead," she signed, folding herself into my arms. "I no longer fear Blitz at all."

"Once we're out of this fix, I promise to listen, and consider it."

"Or consider it now to get us out of this fix," she signed, and I wondered if the drug in her was speaking, or if she had some notion of what that Fierae fusing might produce.

I'd been correct about Rufus focusing his attention more intensely on me. During those two days before his party, he showed me plans for the house he would build Pearl and me. He showed me an earthen jar with something in it that allowed him to jump a spark between two copper threads. He called this a "battry." He talked about the women he would bring to Tara to bear us children, how they'd have to be beautiful as well as intelligent.

It was uncharacteristic of Rufus to talk of loving, but when he spoke of these women he ventured into erotic ground, saying men of our ilk and vision must be free to explore all manner of sexual play. This turned the attention of his monologue to Pearl and Ilsa. Beautiful bookends, he called them, complimenting one another like moonlight and mist, like spring-flower scents mingling in fresh morning air.

I was not immune to his musings and titillations. I had seen Pearl and Ilsa together, seen Ilsa's fingers weaving Pearl's hair, seen her finger lightly correct a faulty line of rouge on Pearl's lips. The drug in me magnified these things in my mind, painted them with vivid colors, and washed them in scents of lilac and gardenia. I fought the desire to have them both, while I smiled for Rufus, allowing the drug to show its musings on my face.

Pearl was busy as I was being tantalized by Rufus. Apparently Ilsa knew we were drugged, and began casting little rose petals of suggestion over Pearl's mind-sea. It was a subtle seduction, and the drug made it hard for her to ignore the compliment of Ilsa's beauty to her own.

But Pearl managed to use these advances to her own advantage, lightly kissing Ilsa's eyes and sending her gently to sleep. During the brief time she had alone, Pearl raided the medicinal pantry of Rufus' Herbologist, Jubal. But she didn't have long enough before Jubal appeared, and managed only to compound a small amount of what she thought *might* be an antidote.

When she told me about all this, it worried me that she had majicked Ilsa. "What if she recognizes what you did to her?" I asked.

"Don't worry," she signed. Apparently I'd given her an idea when I said the drug could be in her rouge, and she used one more of her Naiadae to lace her lips with it. "Ilsa will awaken to a kiss."

Whether Pearl was playing her part, or really as drugged as she seemed, I couldn't tell. Once, when she and Ilsa came into my room, where Rufus and I were conversing, Pearl knelt beside him and took his fingers in hers. Rufus smiled, and placed his hand on her head, ran it down her cheek, and cupped her chin in his palm. "Such a treasure," he said, and those words from his mouth momentarily cleared the drug from my mind.

The girls had come to my room so that Ilsa might discuss some arrangements for the party with Rufus, and the two of them left to attend to some detail. Time was running out. The party was the following day, and I could not connect with even the Terrae. I should have been more worried than I was, but the drug prevented it. Pearl showed me the little jar of antidote she'd concocted. "Shall we share it?" I asked.

"Not enough," she signed. "May not even work for one." Then she turned the jar up to her lips and finished its contents.

"What about me?" I asked her.

"I like you drugged," she signed, smiling wickedly.

If the antidote was working in Pearl, I could not tell it. Again that night, we couldn't keep our hands off one another, and flirted with an encounter with Blitz. Somehow, we avoided it. The following morning, Ilsa brought me a huge breakfast, but took Pearl with her, saying they'd eat together, then start getting ready for the party. "It's barely past dawn," I said.

"We want to be beautiful for you tonight," Ilsa said through a smile obviously meant to cause me some distress. "Don't you want us pretty as we can be?" She had no idea, or perhaps she did, how I wanted them.

I was hungry, but knew my breakfast was probably drugged. I wondered if some cat or dog would eat up the evidence if I dumped it out the window. I decided not to risk it, and to simply feign a lack of appetite. Just then, however, Rufus appeared in a robe very similar to the one he'd given me. He was carrying a tray with his own meal. "Such a morning!" he exclaimed. "Let's breakfast together on the porch."

I began to explain that I had no appetite, but Rufus was having none of it. "All the more reason to eat," he told me. "You'll want your strength for our festivities tonight."

My hunger, and drugged susceptibility to suggestion, made me forget about additives in my food. Everything seemed to taste better than any food I'd ever eaten. Morning light through the trees dappled the porch with fiery gems. My senses were acute, and loving everything that played with them. I could hear myself carrying on at Rufus' little jokes, and feel myself adoring the sound of his voice. Some tiny part of me hoped that Pearl was faring better than I, then it disappeared, leaving me wonderfully and overwhelmingly content.

I saw neither of the girls all that day. Rufus was with me constantly, still clad, as was I, in a robe. "We shall lounge all day in bed-clothes," he sang to me. "I've had you a most wonderful suit of apparel made for the party. You shall be Ashley Wilkes, the most genteel and handsome of southern men-folk, and I shall be that scoundrel Rhett, rakishly handsome, with the magnificent Scarlette draped on my arm. Such a play I shall direct, that will shake you to the core with sensuality. Here, have a drop of bourbon in your tea, drowse the day away, for tonight we will rouse ourselves brilliantly awake!"

At some point, Rufus tried to teach me a game played with cards, but I couldn't follow it. I was deep in the arms of the drug, now, and apologizing to him for my torpor. "I may have to take a nap," I said.

"A nap will serve you well," he told me. "And don't worry, when you awake I have a mild stimulant that will get you in the mood for our party. I can already tell it's going to be a perfect night. Now go to your room and rest. I'll come with Thomas to wake and dress you for our affair."

I'd obviously eaten drugs for breakfast. I barely made it to my bed, before sleep closed around me like a fog. It was a dreamless, oblivious sleep, and when Thomas woke me, I felt as if I'd just closed my eyes. Rufus was also in the room, mixing something into a small glass of lemonade. "This will get you going," he said, handing it to me. "Drink up!"

If he'd told me to stand on my head while I drank it, I'd have tried. I was a puppet hung from his fingers on the strings of the drug. The lemonade potion worked quickly, bringing me fully awake. Bringing my senses to full intensity, making everything appear to be made of frosting that I wanted to eat.

The suit Thomas dressed me in was crisp and new and magnificent. Something like a scarf around my neck felt like silk, which was exceedingly rare. The new clothes felt amazing against my skin, and I couldn't stop touching the fabric of my shirt and jacket and trousers. I have to admit, Rufus combination of drugs would have been perfect for an evening of festival abandon, if the true nature of my predicament were not so malevolent. I was tangled in a spider's web for sure, and waiting for the dark beast to descend and devour me. Feeling absolutely superb in this trap, I accompanied my host, Mr. Butler, to our rendezvous with Miss O'Hara and Mrs. Wilkes.

Rufus' ballroom had been decorated, and looked like a place out of fairae legend come to life. Lamps shown through boxes made of dried leaves, turning the light gold and rusty red. Candles burned whose wicks had been fused with compounds to make them burn green, and some threw tiny silver sparks as they burned. A single table, set for four, was centered in the enormous floor. Behind a cheesecloth screen, four musicians played on a pipe and a flute, some reedy instrument, and a sighing violin.

The music was enchanted and surreal. I found myself floating around the room, looking at everything; pictures on the walls, flowers in vases. Then I came to that incredible mirror, hung facing a wide, low couch that had no back. I saw myself reflected with the earthy light, and fell immediately in love with that image. I looked spectacular! I wanted to give this vision of me to Pearl like a present, like something to unwrap slowly and savor. Where was she? Where were the girls?

"Oh, they'll be here soon," Rufus answered me. "Women must *always* be late, and their lateness is always for our benefit. It enhances their beauty with our anticipation of it."

"Yes!" I agreed enthusiastically. Just then the music seemed to change, grow anxious, as double doors to the room opened, and Thomas appeared, announcing, "The ladies Pearl and Ilsa!"

Their scent came into the room ahead of them on a lukewarm breeze. Then they entered together, and my heart rattled its cage, my viscera went molten. The pastel dresses they wore, one pink, one blue, cascaded out from them in waterfalls of lace and frill. Torqued tight at the waist, the girls seemed to rise delicately up through their skirts into bodices of starched silk flowers and gauzy trim.

I could not yet determine which was Pearl and which, Ilsa. Both were wearing wigs of golden hair woven into identical styles. As they seemed to sail on their skirts across the floor, I saw that they both wore white gloves to their elbows. Finally, I could see their faces clearly, and was shocked by the strange beauty I saw.

Their skins had been faded pale with a silvery powder, even on their arms and shoulders. Pearl was in the pink dress, her lips rouged cherry red, while Ilsa's were darker, like dried blood. Still, they looked very much alike in their illusion of white skin, under their shiny blond hair.

If Pearl's antidote was working, no sign of it showed on her face. Her eyes were sparkling and dilated, as if touched with beldonae. She smiled and signed, "Are we pretty?"

"Angels!" Rufus exclaimed.

"Fairae princesses!" I added. I was alive, now, in a land outside human dimensions. I was swallowed into a mythical tale.

Rufus took Ilsa's arm, and seated her at our table. I followed his lead, and seated Pearl. The music droned softly, as Thomas brought little dishes of delicacies for appetizers: liver pate and quail eggs and mushrooms sautéed in wine and cheese. Then ducks, cooked in sweet and heady bourbon sauce, were set before us, with yams and all manner of vegetables and bread and greens.

The wines we drank kept changing color, from bloody reds to crystal whites to blushing rosés. After dinner, deserts were piled on the table, and Rufus lit little cigars, one for me, one for him. Though some tobacco was in them, they were mostly of an herb called Maria, or ganja, which is a very soothing intoxicant. Rufus filled his lungs with it and blew it into Ilsa through a kiss. Then Ilsa took the cigar, and did the same to Pearl, filling her with smoke, and painting smiles on Rufus face, and mine.

The music became something subliminally on the air. We were breathing it as well as hearing it. When Thomas came in with a fresh pot of tea, Rufus said, "That will be all for tonight. Go to the barn dance now."

Thomas set the pot of tea down, said, "Thank you, suh," then left, closing the double doors behind him.

I sat in a haze of smoke and night and Pearl, as Rufus and Ilsa went around extinguishing lamps. Some they left lit, and set them on small stands near the couch by the mirror. Only that area remained lighted. The rest of the room was dark and cavernous.

Dazed by drugs and wine, now, stunned as if by shock, I let Ilsa lead me, with Pearl, to that couch. Rufus was perched in the dark, watching. When Ilsa left us sitting there, already unable to keep from one another's touch, Rufus said, "You can watch yourselves in my mirror, Spaul. Let love have its way, and in a while, Ilsa and I will join you."

Love was already having its way, but Rufus voice made it a command, a necessity. Nothing was going to stop it from occurring, but somehow, I managed to hear myself say, "Blitz," out loud to Pearl. If she were in any way free of the drug and in control, she would have to act now. Unless Pearl stopped it, the three of us were going to join. "I fear for your life," I managed to say, and was suddenly very aware, though I could not see them, that Rufus and Ilsa were watching.

I think I expected Pearl to somehow stop us right then, but instead she worked at opening my clothes. Then she whispered in my ear, "No fear. Be alone with me now."

XI
Birth of a Wild Thing

I could feel the crawl of Blitz on my skin, which somehow added to the ferocity of my arousal. "You will mate!" she said in my mind.

"We will mate," I said out loud. Pearl heard me, and pushed herself up on her arms to look down at me. She was hovering there, over me, with her eyes lit like a she-wolf in season.

The laughter that sounded from her was blended with fire, and seemed to consume our air, dimming the little lamps around us. As those lamps dimmed, Pearl's eyes grew brighter. Fierae powered, now, she left my clothes in shreds. She was partially in and partially out of her voluminous dress, but at some point she spread her skirts over me, and I felt us joined.

Heat! I don't know how the couch and Pearl's dress didn't burst into flame. So intense was the Fierae fire coming from us, that the mirror warped and distorted, then, finally, cracked. Pearl was screaming a high-pitched moan, and I wasn't sure if I was feeling pain or unbearable pleasure. If you could join with the Fierae while still in your body, perhaps this is what it would feel like, this incredible ecstasy of being fried crisp.

How long that lasted I cannot say, but at some point I wanted to ask Rufus if he and Ilsa still wanted to join us. "How about a little fire, you scarecrow!" I wanted to scream at him.

The drug was gone, vaporized out of me. I was clearer than I'd ever been. Pearl was still on top of me, kissing me now, rising and falling onto me, into her, clawing and frantic to dive down my throat tongue first, to lick the skin right off my bones. "Pearl!" I shouted.

"Mmmate!" she roared, becoming her own storm, raining sweat, cycloning my breath away, sending Fierae bolts into my loins. Suddenly, I was afraid this wouldn't end until both of us were dead, liquefied and spattered across the walls and flowers and mirror and couch. I think I even resigned myself to it, to die in the arms of bliss.

Just as I expected Pearl to rip me open to get to my heart, she calmed, settled into a rhythmic crawl up and down against me. In

105

my mind I could hear the faint voice of Blitz say, "We are one now, we three."

Pearl still had six of her Naiadae words left. Though she shared Blitz' voice, now, she chose to free those last six Naiadae, and say to me, for the last time in that voice I adored, "I love you, my darling wolf!"

In the cracked and wavy mirror, Pearl and I sat up and saw our eyes pulsing with light. "I'm sated, for the time being," she said to me, her voice a hum that vibrated and tickled my ears. "Now I've a taste for something dire, and Blitz joins me. She is angry also. She knows what I know, now!"

Pearl rose off the couch, and a crackle of sparks flew from her fingers. Suddenly, all the lamps and candles in the room grew flames. Rufus and Ilsa sat side by side, as if at a theatre, in the chairs from which they'd been watching. They seemed petrified. In the very center of the room, Pearl stood, raising her arms. Her tattered dress, blowing like confetti around her in the Zephrae wind she'd summoned, was hiding very little of her spark-bejeweled flesh. "Luna Mundisi linea Terren," she chanted, and she was not solely Pearl right then. She and Blitz had become a third personality. I would come to find, later, that she could be Pearl, or she could be Blitz, but when the two combined, which they were doing now, they became the Fierae powered Shykick Pearl would later call Drea (which is short for Dread). If there is a power greater than Drea in World, I never want to meet it.

The vocal majick Pearl and Blitz, now Drea, were loosing was something beyond, I think, the capabilities of man or Fierae alone. Somehow, they had summoned not only World's lines of force, but lines of force between World and the moon. "Linea clipses Vulcana sur!" she cried, and the earth lurched violently, tearing open the walls and floors around us. The house was in half, and I could see out into the star spangled night.

World shook beneath us, as Drea's Zephrae floated her out through the split roof. Lamps and candles toppled, and before long the room was ablaze. "Come out!" I shouted to Ilsa and Rufus, who sat as if stone in their chairs. With a line of force, I blew down the double doors, splintering them. Yes, I could majick again, but was not yet in control of my Fierae heightened ability.

Ilsa rose, as if compelled by my voice to move. She never looked back at Rufus, who remained in his chair. As if somnambulating, she floated, still a picture of perfect beauty, out those doors. "Come on!" I growled at Rufus, my voice gone elemental. The flames were a storm, now, though I knew they'd need to be higher and hotter to get past my majick, enhanced as it was.

Rufus rose and walked farther into the inferno. "You've killed me already!" he cried. "I will burn on the pyre of Tara!"

I could have snatched him out of the house on a whip of mag line force. I could have surrounded him with screaming Zephres to protect him from those flames. Had I chosen to, I could have picked him up and carried him out myself. Instead, I turned my back on him, and walked toward the doors. "It is yours!" my elemental voice bellowed to him as I left. "You have made it!"

On my way out, I stopped and retrieved Pearl's pack. I knew her little mirror was in it, and, believe it or not, amongst all that was happening, saving it for her was on my mind. As I exited the house, I came upon Ilsa, whose dress and makeup and blond hair were not so much as disturbed by the conflagration we'd just escaped. Seeing her like that, beautiful and calmed by shock, cooled my elemental rage. By degrees, I came back to humanity. Then I spun around to see the furnace in which I'd let Rufus die.

Pearl was high above Tara now, and still in the grip of Drea's fury. Fierae bolts flew from her position in the sky, chasing the slavers back into their mountains. Still the earth shook, and then blankets of fire fell onto fields and houses and every building save one barn. Around that, the Zephrae sang, protecting it from the all-consuming burn that was devouring the rest of Tara.

I had Ilsa in my arms, now, trying to protect her, as even the air began to burn. Then a chorus of Zephrae lifted us out of the maelstrom, and we watched from above as every blade of grass and tare burned. Though Ilsa never so much as whimpered, I could feel my own tears falling. "I'm sorry," I whispered.

Ilsa heard me, and said in a tiny voice, "I loved him, but he was mad."

XII
Scorched Dawn

Ilsa and I awoke in each other's arms, still floating over Tara in our Zephre-spun cocoon. Above us, Pearl stood upright on air with her arms out and her eyes closed. She was maintaining the Zephres that had held us all night. Below, dawn was breaking over a scorched black circle, perfectly round, that had once contained Tara. Nothing but the protected barn remained. All else was ash, sparking here and there with left over coals from the blaze. "Pearl!" I called, even though I was almost sure my voice could not escape our Zephrae bubble. "Blitz," I thought, after clearing my mind-sea.

"I hear," rang in my mind as well as my ears. Pearl had combined the two Zephrae choruses, and we were all floating together, now. "Is Ilsa alright?" she asked me, her voice somewhat changed, gone lighter and less humming.

"I think she's in shock. How about you?"

"I'm fine, but I do not recall wreaking this devastation. In fact, I do not think it was me."

"It was you and Blitz," I told her. "You became something to inspire dread even in the Fierae. Ask Blitz."

"I know what Blitz knows, Spaul. Though I am solely myself, now, Blitz sails my mind-sea with me. You may speak with her if you like."

"Okay," I said, "Blitz, are you responsible for this burn? Are you capable of this?"

"Not alone," Blitz said through Pearl's mouth. "I could not call such a thing to ground."

"Well, it's done," I said softly, feeling an open wound where my innocence used to be.

"It was done yesterday," Pearl said, and I could easily tell the difference between her and Blitz when they spoke. "It's time to deal with now."

108

"I'll think about now tomorrow," I said, closing my eyes as the Zephrae gently laid us on the ground.

As the Fierae within us grew calm and sleepy, Pearl and I were overwhelmed with human exhaustion. We found a place outside that circle of ash, and slept among some trees. Pearl recovered more quickly than I, and left me still sleeping. When I finally came around, I saw her standing near the barn. All the slaves were gathered around her and Ilsa. "Just as bad as him!" someone was yelling. "*Lady* of de house!"

Quickly I made my way over to them. Apparently, the slaves had a low opinion of Ilsa.

"Ought to burn her, too!" someone shouted.

"Be *quiet*!" I roared, my voice tinged elemental. It was rising too easily in me, I would have to learn to control it. "What do any of you know of Ilsa's plight? Rufus enslaved your bodies, but he imprisoned Ilsa heart and mind! How dare you fault her for surviving it!" Even as I spoke the words, they stabbed me with memories of Rufus. I hadn't wanted him dead, but I hadn't wanted to save him, either. The wound of what I had and hadn't done that night would be a long time healing.

"Ilsa can help you," I told them. She knows a lot, and if you listen to her you can rebuild this village as your own. Pearl and I are Apprentice, and it is what we'd have you do. Buy your lives are your own, again. Do what you will. Remember, though, slavery is everywhere. You can do it to yourself, and you can turn your head when you see someone do it to others. Then your freedom will leave you, as fear puts its shackles on you."

Pearl spoke next, and her voice alone got everyone's attention. I was hard pressed not to laugh when she said, shaking her finger at them, "Be *good*! Listen to Ilsa! Don't *make* me come back here!"

"Who *are* you?" someone asked. "Who can we say destroyed the slavers and set us free?"

"Something dread," I whispered, remembering what Pearl had become.

She heard me, and showed a sad little smile. Then she told the slaves, "It was Drea, and now she is gone. May such an evil never arise that calls her back."

The newly freed slaves of Tara gave me what clothes they could, a jug of corn, and a makeshift pack to carry them in. I had saved Pearl's pack, and she found that both touching and amusing. "In that terrible inferno, you stopped long enough to save my things!" she exclaimed.

"They were all I saved," I said, feeling my wound again.

"Rufus was dead before we got here," she told me, as we walked away from the people of Tara.

I looked back once more to see Ilsa, still wearing her lovely blue dress. "Maybe we should have taken her with us," I said.

"Blitz would be jealous," Pearl told me, smiling devilishly.

"I know no jealousy," Blitz said in my mind.

XIII
Strangers at the Beach

Pearl and I walked up out of the valley to the Tara Road, and looked down on the black circle. From up there it looked like a huge hole. Pearl and I had hardly spoken on the way up. As we looked at that erased village, she said to me, "We were taken against our wills. Rufus fetched us at the Universe' behest, though he did not know it. To regret is to deny the Universe' plan. I will not regret."

"I have regrets," I said, then I fell to my knees. "I'm an Apprentice, and I let him die."

I was broken, up there on that ridge. I couldn't stop crying. I couldn't stop thinking that, somehow, Thirest would know what I'd done. "He would have been proud of you," Pearl said.

"You can read my thoughts, now?" I asked, feeling even more alienated from her.

"Only when they scream," she told me. Then she knelt beside me, touched herself on the chest, put her hands over her heart, then laid her right hand over mine. "It's me, Spaul. Don't let my voice dissuade you. I would not have done this, not *like* this. But I was Drea the moment we began to love on that couch, and she did not subside until morning, when you called to me. Rufus created what destroyed Tara with his drugs and sick mind games. I will accept no blame, nor can you assign any to yourself. You were gone elemental, and Fierae seared, that night. You, as you are now, might have done things differently. But perhaps what you were that night knew *better* what to do. Who's to say?"

"I don't blame you," I said, grabbing her into a hug.

"If you blame yourself, you blame me," she said. "We are one."

I cried myself out of Pearl's shoulder. I wanted not to blame myself, but my mind kept insisting, "Die not to kill!"

"I thought you said he walked into the flames," Pearl said, obviously hearing my thoughts again.

"He did, but I didn't stop him."

"Then you didn't kill. You allowed him his freedom. Had you stopped him, you would have made him a slave."

111

"Did I tell you how pretty you looked in that dress?" I said to her, trying to smile.

"Like a fairae princess," she reminded me. "Now I'm going to show you how a fairae princess flies."

Pearl asked me to trust her, possibly because she was unsure whether I would. We stood together on that hill, and she had the Zephrae lift us high, facing east. "I want to go back to the sea," she said to me. "And we'll build a little hut and play together and eat fish. It is time for us to rest, Spaul, and determine what we are, for we are changed. The *three* of us are changed. Blitz also needs to discover what she has become. Will you do this with me? I fear there is something between us that we must heal. If not for us, then for our child."

"Child?" I asked.

Pearl laughed. "You should see your face, daddy wolf. Do you know your eyes flashed brightly just now? Do you know who, or even what, you are, you who will be my son's father?"

"Son?"

"I am Shykick, and now have Fierae in my blood. I know every cell in my body, and there are several more than there were yesterday. They will grow a boy child in me, your son, and mine, and Blitzes."

"Will he be...human?" I said softly.

"Are we?" Pearl asked.

As we floated there, facing the distant sea, Pearl's brow furrowed as she searched my face for a reaction to her news. When I smiled for her, I could feel my love going into it. She saw it and showed her relief, falling into my arms and saying, "Are you ready for a swim?"

"It's a long way off," I answered.

"Not so long as you'd think," she said, widening her eyes the way she did when I was about to be surprised.

"Uh oh," I said.

Pearl grabbed three lines of force from World below, and raised them up to meet us. "When I dispatch these Zephrae, we're simply going to slide down the lines to the sea," she told me.

"Shite!" I exclaimed. "How are we going to stop?"

"The Zephrae will slow us at the bottom."

"What about our hands?"

"They will be damaged," she told me matter-of-factly.

"*How* damaged?"

"They won't be pretty, but Blitz can heal them in a day or two, if we eat a big, fat Dorado, liver and all!" Pearl's excitement is always contagious, and in a minute she had me ready and willing to shred my hands, and have the iron sucked out of my blood.

Sliding down the lines was unbelievable. The Zephres holding us let go just over the mag lines Pearl had bulged up, and suddenly we were going as fast as we would have if we'd simply been falling. But instead of falling straight down, we were falling on the lines toward the sea.

Somehow, Pearl had gotten the Zephrae to shield our faces a bit from the wind of our wild ride so we could speak. "I think I can improve this trick," I told her, "if you can get the Zephrae to shield us completely so the air doesn't resist us so."

Pearl smiled, obviously understanding my idea. In a moment we felt no wind against us at all, and the speed at which we fell was uncanny. "The beach is coming up fast," I said to her. "Can you stop us?"

Pearl had been watching my face, adoring my excitement. When she turned back to look where we were going, she let out a little cry. "Oh!" she said. "Too fast!"

Immediately she had the Zephrae begin to slow us, but it was too late. At the last moment, Pearl looped up the lines, where the beach met the water, like ramps. Up and off of them we flew, coming down a hundred meters out in the sea. I couldn't help laughing when we hit the water. "That was *fun!*" Pearl shouted to me, and right then I decided I loved her new voice.

"Where are our packs?" I asked her.

"I dropped them on the beach before we went for our swim!" she said, as if she'd planned the whole thing.

"I hope you didn't break your little mirror," I said.

"Right after you gave it back to me, I encased it in a protecting enchantment. I wasn't all that fond of it until you rescued it for me. Now it is very dear."

Pearl and I swam to the beach, and inspected our hands. Both of us were bleeding and swollen, but the extra speed had shortened our time on the lines. It could have been worse. Still, the damage was enough that I knew we'd been drawn on, and were almost assuredly anemic. I called out a big Dorado, and Pearl and I ate his liver raw. The rest of him we cooked slowly, wrapped in kelp.

As the Ball sank behind us, we looked out over the sea. Sitting in our firelight, full of fish, we held one another as best we could with our injured hands. "They'll heal tomorrow," Pearl told me, when she saw me wince trying to stroke her hair.

"But I wanted to touch you tonight," I said, smiling my thoughts of love. "And I wanted *you* to touch *me*," I added.

"I don't need my hands for that," she told me. "Let's go for a swim."

As we walked toward the water, Pearl said, "When water surrounds us, reach out to the Naiadae if you want to touch me."

"How?" I asked.

"Pay attention when I do it to you, and you'll see."

Easier said than done! I was standing chest deep when Pearl began her Naiadae fondling. "How am I supposed to pay attention when...oh! *Pearl!*" She was mercilessly good at this game.

But I did begin to understand. In my mind, I could hear the Naiadae all around us. They were excited by what Pearl was doing with them. Somehow, she was allowing them to feel my response to it. I reached out to them with my mind, and showed them a picture of hands, had them coalesce around Pearl as a hundred fingers running along every curve and angle of her flesh. Suddenly, she gasped. "You learn quickly!"

Oh yes, I did, till this game became almost a battle. I could tell I was winning by how much her distraction lessened what she was able to concentrate on doing to me. Before long, it was all one sided. The majick I was doing swelled in me, and I could feel myself going elemental. I had Pearl encased in a solid block of probing, caressing hands, and the frantic look on her face excited me more. Then I formed Naiadae as *me*, loving Pearl deeply and fiercely. With my mind, I filled her, emptied her, caused the water around and in her to effervesce and vibrate.

I could only see Naiadae, now, and what they were doing. This majick I'd spawned was all that was left of me. I don't know when I heard her, but even when I did, it took me a while to stop. She must have been screaming it, but by the time I started toward her, she was whimpering, "Please. No more."

The thought that I'd harmed her dragged me back up from the depths of my majick. I floated her on her back in my arms. "Are you alright?" I asked anxiously.

With a weak little smile she looked up at me and said, in a tiny voice, "What did you *do* to me?"

Slowly, I guided her floating body toward shore. When I helped her stand to walk out onto the beach, she said, her voice still quivery, "You're *much* too good at that." Then her body went weak again, and I swept her up into my arms. As I carried her to our fire, she said, "You must never do that to me again." After a moment, she added, "Unless I absolutely *beg* you to."

The Ball was well up and warming our skin, when Pearl and I awoke. My hands had already begun healing, and when I inspected Pearl's, I could find no damage at all. "How is Blitz doing this?" I asked her.

"Our bodies are doing it, but the Fierae in us is speeding it up, sending fast messages from the places in our brains that heal."

"Oh," I said. Now I knew, though, of course, I didn't understand.

"How do you feel?" I asked Pearl. "Did I damage you last night?" I was very concerned about this, as I was finding it hard to remember exactly what I'd done.

She showed me the face that melts me, with its shy little smile and her doe eyes looking up through her lashes. "Yes, I am damaged goods now," she said, her voice gone pouty. "I am spoiled, and will have to cavort with Fierae and the likes to find my pleasure."

"And abandon the poor human who adores you?" I said. It was a jest that would turn out to be prophetic.

"I think there is just enough Fierae in you to sate me, my love," she said with her lips touching mine. "Art thee human?" she added, turning her voice into a fairae song. Though she made light of the question, it worried me. Whatever we were, now, we'd created another one.

I touched my hand to Pearl's belly and remembered what I'd become with her the previous night in the sea. "I don't think so," I said, and her smile grew from shy to wild.

Pearl and I built a lean-to all of driftwood, which opened out toward the sea. I'd managed to salvage a pair of shorts out of the trousers

Pearl had mangled that night on Rufus' couch. For the most part, Pearl wore nothing, which gave her an excuse to be in the water most of the time, "to wash the sand off."

For several days, we played, though all our love was made up of games. Whenever I tried to love her, Pearl would devise some majick and leave me exhausted. Finally, one night by our fire, I said, "I want to *love* you tonight. I want you to love me."

"Don't you like my games, anymore?" she said, trying to conjure her shy smile, but failing.

"There's something you're not telling me, Pearl. If you knew how it hurts me when you keep things from me, you wouldn't do it. It makes me feel like you don't trust me, like you think my love is shallow, and could be swept away."

The smile Pearl was trying to form fell into a frown, and her chin quivered. Tears rushed into her eyes, and fell like rain. "I *don't* think that, and I *do* trust you," she cried, her voice gone little girl scared.

I wiped the tears off her face, and waited for her to tell me. After a long pause, during which she wept, Pearl said, "It will be Drea you join with when we do. I cannot stop it yet, and may never be able to."

I don't know what I expected her to tell me, but her answer shocked me and made me feel queasy. All I could think to say was, "Why?" All through her explanation I wondered, "Why did you keep this pain to yourself?"

"Blitz sails my sea, sleepy and content," she began. "She is not yet ready to rise up and look around from my human eyes. She *could*, she *can*, I could sail my sea and give her control, but it is so foreign to her, being this semblance of human, that she shuns it. She hasn't the human emotion to deal with it. Fierae emotion is *very* different, and if she *did* rise into awareness, I'd need to guide her from my sea.

"But when we love, her Fierae emotion will not be restrained, and she leaps from my ocean, tangling us, becoming Drea. I might be able to convince her to come up alone, trade places with me and love you. Though it would not be Drea, neither would it be me. You can love with Blitz, or you can love with Drea. Perhaps, when Blitz has had some human experience, I will be able to teach her to restrain her Fierae impulse, and leave us to ourselves when we love.

Now, I cannot. I'm sorry," she said, as her tears ran again. "I will never keep anything from you again," she wept, begging me with her eyes to take her into my arms.

I did, and said, "Don't cry. You were scared, I understand. We'll figure this out, I promise. We'll learn to be Fierae human together."

"There's more I must tell you, Spaul," she said softly, her head down and tears falling out of her eyes into the sand. "It's the last thing I've kept from you, I swear, but it terrifies me to tell you."

My heart began pounding to be let out. Her tone scared me, and I wasn't sure I wanted to hear what it worried her so to tell me. I tried to make light of it, and said, "You are really Tool's *son?*"

A choked laugh mixed with her crying, and she looked up at me, her face wet and her eyes swollen, trying to smile. When she spoke it was in a whisper, as if, any louder, her words would burn her. "Have you never wondered why I didn't fix Rummy's legs for Papa?"

I sighed, and a great weight lifted off me. My fear of what she might tell me disappeared. "I understood the day you came after me riding those lines. I knew you'd tell me one day, but with all we've been through, I think I forgot all about it. Or perhaps I simply accepted it."

Pearl's eyes went wide. Very lightly, she slapped my cheek. "You knew!" she said through an angry little smile.

"I may not be the Shykick Apprentice you are, Pearl, but I am well trained, and can cogitate. Of course, I don't know *exactly*, and all the particulars, but you sent Tool out to fetch me that day, didn't you?"

What was that look on her face? I saw love there, and amazement, but something else, respect perhaps. As if she'd just realized exactly who and what she loved, and why. "I saw you in a vision," she said, her voice dreamy and sweet. "It was so *strong*, that vision. I couldn't get your face out of my mind. The very day after I saw you in that dream, the muley kicked poor Rummy. It was a month to the day before you came, as I saw the same moon the night after you arrived.

"Papa brought Rummy to me, held him out in his arms, but I said with my hands, 'Not yet.' It was all I needed to tell him. There had been two Shykicks in Papa's life, Mama, and me. He'd

117

learned to trust even our strangest behavior.

"A month later, I saw you again. The next morning I put Rummy in the barrow, and told Papa to walk him over the Ninety-five from north to south. 'You too smiley, girl,' he said to me. 'You playin' some joke on yo' Papa?' 'On myself, perhaps, but not you,' I explained. Seeing me lightheaded and giddy like that made Papa smile. I was already in love with you, Spaul, before we ever met."

I kept the smile off my face that was trying so hard to form there. Pearl wanted to see it, and said, "You're angry with me? Oh, please, no!"

"I'm *very* angry," I said, my own eyes wide and that smile coming despite my efforts. I jumped up and pulled her to me, then threw her over my shoulder. "And when I get you into that water, I'm going to give you quite a Naiadae spanking!" Though I was careful not to lose control this time, I still had to carry Pearl out of the sea when it was over.

We stayed on that beach for over two weeks, eating seafood and playing, of course, but mostly talking, trying to explain to ourselves what we were, now. Trying to decide what we should do, what our lives meant to us as Fierae humans. "I know what Blitz knows, but there are things I don't understand," Pearl told me. "Things she couches in riddle and Fierae terms I can't begin to translate. There is a word for us that she has, which I thought meant 'Fierae human,' but now I suspect it means more. 'Aneke'lemental-nama' is the best I can say it in Inglish, and I believe, when she says it, there is a question in her voice, as if she's trying to name us, or give us a title. Perhaps even she doesn't truly know what we are. Or perhaps *she* knows, and is simply trying to create new language to describe us."

"Do you *speak* with her?" I asked.

"Yes, but she is lazing on my sea. Call to her, see how sleepy she's gone."

Calming my sea, I called through my thoughts, "Blitz! Are you dreaming of me in there?" For some reason, I found myself feeling playful within my sea.

"I dream of melting mirrors and Fierae eyes," she said sleepily. "Wake me to mate, Spaul. Draw me off this sea to your Charge of Air. Steam and boil...love me...mate," she said, as if drifting off into a slumberland.

"But you become Drea," I thought to her.

"Mmmate..." she sighed, lost in her dreams.

"She's seriously sleepy," I said to Pearl, who was gazing into my eyes with a pretty, craving look on her face.

"I miss you, if you know what I mean," she sighed.

"Oh, I definitely know what you mean, but I don't miss Drea so much. Do you know what she does to me? I don't get to do any loving, you know, I just get seriously loved, much worse than you get from my Naiadae. Is there pain when I touch you like that?"

"Almost," she breathed, "but, no. And I *do* know what she does. Your Naiadae are gentle compared to Drea."

"There may come a time when I'll want you so badly that I'll invite some pain, but please don't ask it of me. If I do it solely for you, there will be at least as much pain as pleasure. Do you understand, Pearl, that I'm keeping nothing from you, now, telling you the truth though it hurts?"

"I love to learn from you," she said. "I'll be diligent in telling you *everything*, now."

I didn't think love could grow so large, but Pearl's and mine became enormous when such understanding flowed between us. For hours we held one another in silence, listening to the little waves patting the shore, and sea birds calling to the sky. Then Pearl said to me, "Call Blitz up to love, while I float on my sea. I'm not sure how she'll be, alone up here, but it's time we found out, time you talked to her. Call her and find out what she's become, and what her understanding is of us."

"It won't be hard for me to love your body, even without you, but are you sure you want to do this?"

Pearl smiled at my honesty, and said, "I will feel the ripples of it on my sea, the same sort of ripples that will wake Blitz. So, in a way, you'll be loving me also. Kiss me and call to her. When I feel her rouse, I'll trade places."

"Will you have any trouble trading back?" I asked.

"That won't be a problem. As long as we aren't Drea, I command my body. And, anyway, I have a strong suspicion that Blitz may not even want to stay when she realizes she's alone. I'll try to reach up and comfort her, but I think it will be up to you to keep her from retreating back into her sleep."

"That doesn't sound like Blitz," I said.

"She isn't Blitz, you know. She is human Fierae, now."

Pearl closed her eyes, and waited for me to kiss her. I thought I felt a little spark jump between our lips when they met. "Blitz," I called. "Come join with your Fierae human lover. So cute you are, all sleepy in that sea of Pearl."

"I would know creature love," she sighed, as she opened Pearl's eyes. Instantly the frightened look of a child stole her face. "I am so small," she squeaked. "The universe swallows me!"

So frightened was her look, that it almost made me want to cry seeing it on Pearl's face. Quickly I took her into my arms, and held her tightly. "I've got you," I said. "I won't let you go."

As I held her, her Fierae ardor seemed to wake just a bit, and she searched for my lips with hers. She was trembling, now, and voicing tiny sighs and exclamations. This was not Pearl, not in any way. Even her body was strange, holding different tensions and postures. She was tentative and unsure under my touch, as if incredibly shy.

This little, shy Pearl began arousing me tremendously, moaning in tiny gasps under my caress. Slowly and gently, I petted and kissed her. So fragile she seemed, so delicate. She was completely mine to love, she did nothing but tremble to what I did to her, as if I were loving a little, shivering human doll.

Only after we were joined did Blitz open herself to me, hugging me close and intensely returning my kisses. Little sparks danced on us as we peaked, and even those seemed to startle her.

As soon as it ended, her eyes rolled up, and I knew she was heading back to Pearl's sea. "Wait," I whispered in her ear. "Stay with me just a bit."

Her eyes came back, though dreamily, and she said, "My fearsome, Fierae lover, I'm all sleepy with your touch, all Fierae loved."

"Blitz," I said, touching her cheek, "will you let Pearl love me alone, as we just loved?"

"I will *always* come to mate when you call," she whispered, drifting away from me, back to Pearl's sea.

"Blitz! Stay and talk," I implored.

"She's gone, but I'll talk to you, my fearsome love," Pearl said, smiling at me. "I felt it, and didn't know you could be so tender."

"I didn't know you could be so shy," I said.

"I *can't*," she told me, "but I felt that shy on my sea while you and Blitz loved. I have to say, Blitz demeanor when human is very un-Fierae."

"It's very un-Pearl, too," I chuckled.

"Oh, *is* it?" Pearl said, feigning (I think) anger. Maybe I should call up Drea, so you'll have *all* the harem to love!"

"Do what you will with me, I'm outnumbered," I said, falling back onto the beach.

"Let's go wash the sand off, then I'll hold you in my blankets," Pearl said. "I think you've had enough love today. It is true, you are very outnumbered."

XIV
Bye-Bye, Love

Pearl and I had decided to leave our seashore and look for a village. I needed some clothes, and a noisy inn with stew and wine also sounded good. After we'd eaten, Pearl packed up what little we were carrying. Then we sat in our lean-to and looked out to sea. Pearl touched our tiny shelter and said, "Do you think our house will still be here if ever we return?"

"If not, I'll build you a bigger one, with bathing tubs and big, down beds!" I told her.

"I would bathe in the ocean, and sleep with you in the sand, with nothing over our heads but Air, and be happy," she said to me, and I knew it was absolutely true.

Out at sea, Fierae flashes told us a storm was carrying on. It was the time of year when the Elementals threw their biggest hurrakin parties, and the pressure in our ears told us one was just offshore. "Blitz is singing in my sea," Pearl told me. "Listen."

I calmed and could hear her. "He comes, come here come here," she was chittering. This startled me, and I looked at Pearl, who seemed unperturbed by that calling.

"Can she call to Blitz?" I asked her. "Is she Charge, still? Could they join?" and fry us to ash? I added in my own thoughts, though I didn't say it aloud.

"Don't worry, no," Pearl said, running her hand up and down my back, as if to reassure me. "We are more Fierae than Fierae Charge, and contained. But I think I could send her call, if I wanted. It might draw the storm near, or right on top of us. Shall I try?"

"I like the storm where it is," I said. "See how pretty the lights are so far away?"

Then Pearl's posture changed, and her hand stopped traveling on my back. She was getting that look on her face. "I don't *even* want to know what you're thinking," I said.

"Of course you do," she purred, snuggling up against me, and running her fingernails down my back.

"Of *course* I do," I said. "What was I thinking about? I'm dying to hear how you want to call up a Fierae bolt and ride it to the moon!"

"You sarcastic shite!" she said, digging into my back with her nails.

"Ouch!" I yelped. "You're hurting!"

"Well, you were trying to make me cry!"

To that I laughed, and had to get out from under her fingernails. "You're *much* more likely to make *me* cry, than visa versa," I said.

"Ooo, you *are* a shite!" she snarled, diving onto me and covering me with playful slaps.

When our little tussle ended, with us in each other's arms, she rested her head on my shoulder and said, "But, seriously, I have an idea."

"I don't even want..."

"Don't start that again," she warned, "or I'll take you out in the water and your Naiadae *won't* overwhelm mine this time."

"If that's supposed to be a threat," I told her, "I don't think you understand the concept."

"Are you going to listen to me or not?" she over exaggeratedly pouted.

"Of course I will, my darling," I said. "Tell me how you'll send a Fierae bolt up my az and ride me to the moon!"

"It's an even better idea that *that*," she assured me, "though I might be inspired to work out the details of that one, someday, too."

"It's okay," I said, pulling her back close to me. "Forget about that one, and tell me yours."

She did, and it wouldn't have worried me if I weren't so sure she'd eventually try it. Then it worried me tremendously, as I realized she intended to try it *tonight*!

Pearl's idea, Pearl's *brilliant* idea, was for me to locate a ground Charge, and then let Blitz call to Blitz from very near it. At the last minute, Pearl and I would run away, jump out of our bodies, stroll back to the Charge minus our flesh, and when it met with the Air Charge, have a nice long conversation to find out what we were. "But what makes you so sure Air Charge Blitz will know what's going on?" I asked her.

"Because they are the same, Spaul, Blitz and Blitz. There is no male and female Charge, there's only Charge. They trade places every time they separate from their joinings."

"But I've seen their faces, always the same, he from above, she from below."

"That's right, but they'd *changed places*! They take turns, they can be either or. There is no male and female, they are each both all the time."

"So they really are..."

"One being that lives in two places. And that is their ecstasy when they join, to be whole again. Within that joining they polarize, and the maleness and the femaleness of them coalesces at either pole. *That's* how they love with themselves, separate but whole while they join in the bolt. When they separate, the gender cohesion dissolves, and they're mixed again and fall away in two directions. The Blitz in my sea and the Blitz in Air were once exactly the same. My Blitz is changed now, and is too sleepy and frightened to converse with us. But we can talk to her as she still exists in air. If we can find her."

"Or *him*," I said.

"*Them*, then, you know what I mean, Spaul."

"Answer me this, if the Blitz you carry was male and female as Charge when you took her, why is she *definitely* a girl, now. She was a very girly, girl when we loved, I assure you."

"I know. I think it's because she loves you, and because *I'm* a girl. Or did you forget that?"

"That, I'll concede. You are most definitely a girl."

"And Blitz sails my sea, shares my body. Who knows, there are probably other reasons, too, like she's *changed*, as I am changed."

"Hey, I've got these candle-lit eyes, too, you know."

"Yes, Fierae runs through you, as if you've been transfused, but you aren't *mixed, combined*. Stir some honey into milk and it won't taste exactly like honey, or exactly like milk. I'm a whole new flavor, Spaul, and I want to know what it is. It's the only way I can learn to *be* what I am to my full potential."

I sighed. I closed my eyes and shook my head. "If you spill the milk and honey," I finally said to her, "Spaul will go without. Then Spaul will die of thirst, and all of us will be gone."

"Only the milk would be going with you to speak with the Fierae," she told me. "Blitz can never leave my body again. When it dies, she will die."

124

"Then she gave up immortality for a taste of creature love."

"Fierae are very long lived, but even the Elementals are not immortal," she told me. "And she gave up what she did because she *loves* you. That is the only part that doesn't make sense."

"Thanks," I said, not laughing.

"That's not what I meant," she smiled. "I meant it is not normal Fierae. Something is happening, maybe some sort of evolution, or maybe something they themselves are doing. The Fierae are very connected, and they're World's worst gossips. If this were something they *didn't* want to occur, they'd never have let Blitz join with me. Something's up, and it's time we found out what."

My head was spinning. Pearl was one serious cogitator. "Could you tell it to me again?" I said.

"Which part?" she asked.

"Start at the beginning."

"SPAUL!"

So that was the plan, which may look very good on the paper over which I've written it, but the best plans are made by mice, not men (and, no, Thirest never did tell me what *that* meant, either).

So we baited our trap (maybe that's the "mice" part) and watched as the storm grew nearer. "Blitz will be alone in your body while were out?" I asked, wanting to be sure I had all the particulars. "It will only be a few seconds to her, she'll still be in creature time. As soon as I return, she'll run right back to my sea."

"And she won't just stay in your sea while you're gone, because?"

"Because we pretty much take it with us, Spaul," she said, in a tone that meant, you should know that.

"I know that," I said. "But I also know we don't take it *all*."

"No, we don't, but the lake we leave behind is shallow, and easily roiled, which usually doesn't matter, because we aren't there to roil it. But Blitz will be there, and she'll have that little lake choppy as helluva in a nannysecond. She won't be able to stay on it, but she'll be alright up here for the moment or two we'll be gone."

"I've changed my mind," I told her.

"What do you mean?"

"I don't want to do this."

"Spaul, you're being silly."

"No! Female Apprentices don't speak with the Fierae. Females react too strongly, will join instantly, will leave and never return. These are things *Thirest* taught me, Thirest the *Finished Apprentice.*"

"It's silly, Spaul."

"Then I'm silly."

"I *am* Fierae, Spaul, and I'm *Shykick* Apprentice."

"And you're *female*. Definitely female. I know a female when I love one, and you are one. That's final!"

"What's final?" she asked, and her tone told me to be careful with my answer.

"That you're a girl."

"And this girl is going to talk to the Fierae, with or without you. Maybe it *would* be better if you stayed behind with Blitz and my body."

"Oh no you don't, I'm going with you!"

"Whatever you say," she demurred.

"And *that* will teach me to try and talk some sense into *you!*"

"Yes, it will," she said, as she touched my cheek and smiled.

The chittering Charge I located was sleepy, but had crawled up into a stingy palm. There are two kinds of stingy palms, and this one was a Palmetto. The other kind is called King, but as I traveled north I saw less and less of those, and *no* generous palms at all, (which I missed, because I like the water in coconuts.)

The Charge was in the Palmetto (which gives nothing but its beauty) and it was saying, "Come come come come come."

I calmed my sea, and thought to it, "Do you know of Blitz?"

"I know Blitz comes comes comes, is coming," she said from her tangle of fronds, just barely aware of me, now. I say *she*, because no matter what Pearl had told me, this Charge seemed female.

"She's sleepy," I told Pearl, who was looking up into the palm.

"I know," she said, "I heard. But she'll be awake soon."

"You said, *she*," I told her. "I thought you said they are both."

"They are, and I understand it, now. The maleness sleeps deeper, cradled in its womb of earth. The femaleness must drag it around to move at all. Maleness wakes easier in Air. That is why they appear as male from above, and female from below."

126

"Is Blitz still calling?" I asked her.

"Oh yes, she's starting to ripple my sea."

"*That's* not good!" I told her. "Innkeepers and farm-girls can float out while they're sleeping, it isn't a *talent*, you know."

"Yes, but do they *know* they're asleep in their beds while they're out?"

"No, they say they've dreamed of floating."

"Well," Pearl told me, perhaps a little defensively, "when I dream of floating, I realize I'm doing it, and can go where I will."

"It's not the same," I told her, shaking my head. "I *really, really* hate this plan."

"You're so cute when you worry about me," she said, changing tactics, and for some reason it made me mad. "But you're right about Blitz rippling my sea. I think we'd better get out now, before it gets worse."

I could see this plan unraveling. Now Blitz would be alone longer in Pearl's body, and if she shut down Blitz' call too soon, we might not attract the other Blitz to join with the Charge in the stingy palm. "Please don't do this," I begged her one last time.

"Tell that Charge to call to Blitz, then, let's go!"

"Can you call to Blitz?" I asked the Charge.

"Blitz calls to me, greatly excited. He will come come come, is coming."

Pearl had raced back to our lean-to, which was no more than a hundred meters away. When I got to her, she was sitting in there with her eyes closed. Without opening them, she said, "I've calmed Blitz down, what do I do to get out?"

"You mean you don't know?" I asked. For a moment, that came as a great relief. I could put a stop to this right now. I'd simply refuse to help her get out. Even before she spoke, however, that bubble burst. I knew her little finger was wrapped around me.

"I'll figure it out, eventually," she warned me in her calm-sea voice. "And I'll make you miserable until I do."

"Feel the lines around you," I said, resigned to it, now. "Let them tug at you from all directions. You'll feel thin, for a moment, like smoke, and your vibration will increase. Then you'll feel a little jolt, as your light-body coalesces. You *might* not be able to do it. I don't think Female Apprentices can." But Pearl said nothing, and I knew she was already out. How I calmed my sea enough to be able to join her, I do not know.

Pearl was at the palm by the time I got out of body. I was at her side before a nannysecond could spit. She looked like an angel in her light-body, and had clad it in a tunic that shimmered its glow over the little bit of Pearl it covered. Looking at me, she said, "You are *so* beautiful!" She was already worrying me.

"You *know* enough not to touch me, right?" I asked.

"Would it be so bad?" she said, and I realized she knew. If we touched, our light would mingle, and we'd stay that way forever. My body would rot under the lean-to, and Pearl's would be inhabited only by Blitz, who would not survive long alone.

"I don't know *what* it would be," I told her, "but this is *dangerous*, what we're doing. *Please* take it seriously!"

"I do, my darling, and if this majick teaches me a way to be alone with you to love, I will show you how serious and intent I can be."

"Okay," I said, "but please pay attention to *now. Please!*"

The top of the palm was brightening. "Will you join with Blitz?" I asked the Charge.

"Blitz stretches, calls the name of Blitz."

"He thinks you are Blitz?" I said, wanting this plan to work, now. I wanted to understand the Fierae. What Pearl had told me answered some questions, but birthed many more.

"He knows I am not Blitz, but comes to join with me, anyway. He heard her call, and knows I heard it, too. We will not be Haetu, but we will be one."

"What is Haetu?" I wondered out loud, looking to Pearl, who shrugged her shoulders.

"Fathermother," the Charge told me. "Two of two can join, but only two of *one* contain Haetu. No Fierae baby will race its little ball through sky tonight, or ever again, for Blitz. He has born enek'lemental, and given her to you."

"Her?" I asked.

"Blitz!" she responded very forcefully. She was fully awake.

"Enek'lemental!" Pearl called to the Charge. "Is that what my son will be?"

"Daughter!" the Charge cried, rising into a state of ecstasy as Blitz was just moments away from her.

"But I carry a *son!*" Pearl said.

"You will bear *both*, the same day, but only daughter will be enek'lemental."

"How do you *know* all of this?" I yelled, as she began to scream and moan and stretch up from her palm.

"We know what we do!" she cried out, as Blitz came down and sizzled the night above us.

As soon as I looked over at Pearl, I knew we were in trouble. She was oblivious of me, and lost in an ardorous state. Her light was already bending toward Blitz. "She will join, I will bet!" The Fierae howled.

"Absolutely no betting!" I yelled. "I *forbid* it!"

The Fierae laughed through the groans of their joining. "So cute, little Fierae human forbids!"

"Pearl!" I screamed. "We've got to go back!"

"She does not hear, is coming to us even now. She is very mighty, you should stand away!"

"NO!" I roared, just as Pearl's light grew blinding and rushed toward the Fierae. When they met, such a pulse of fire and light arose, that it knocked me senseless and back to my body.

"Ic eom anna!" Blitz sobbed from Pearl's quivering lips, as the Fierae bolt disappeared, leaving only the echo of its thunder.

XV
Good-Morning, Starshine

Dawn was just beginning to whisper on the horizon. That is the time when the stars shine brightest, before the Ball comes up to hide them away. I was looking up at their beauty, trying to hear their laughter, stunned and unsure of where I was. Then I heard Blitz weeping and shivering beside me, and it all came back into my mind, as if it were happening again. Tears streamed down my face. I *knew* what had transpired, but still I asked Blitz, "Where is Pearl?"

"Gone!" she wailed. "Gone to be Fierae, now! She lives in Air, she is Charge! I am alone!"

"Where?" I demanded. "Can you see her?"

"She is flying," she whimpered. "She always calls, but can only come down in Fire. I must not listen, she will burn us to ash! Please, Spaul, help me, I cannot return to her sea!"

"You're human, now!" I said fiercely. I was angry. It was Blitz who had started all this, and now Pearl was gone. "You'd better get used to it!"

Instead of getting used to it, Blitz did pretty much the opposite, falling from panic to hysteria, and finally into convulsions. I shouldn't have yelled at her. She was keeping Pearl's body alive. She was my *only* chance of ever finding Pearl and getting her back, if that was even possible. And *beyond* all that, I had loved her shy little self, and already regretted blaming her. The last thing the Charge in the stingy palm had said before it joined was, "We know what we do!" The Fierae were all in this together. It was a prime example of theory conspiracy.

As distraught as I was, I held Pearl's convulsing body tight, with one finger in her mouth, keeping her tongue from going down her throat. "Mate," I whispered in her ear. "Come mate with your Fierae human love."

The first response I noticed was when she wrapped her tongue around my finger. Slowly I removed it, replaced it with a kiss. Some part of me was screaming, "How can you love at a time like this?" but I knew I'd lose Blitz, too, as well as Pearl's body, if I didn't.

A long and lingering love I made, as the stars looked down, and dawn began threatening to chase them away. With that love, I called Blitz back from the abyss. In the afterglow, she was calm. "My fearsome, Fierae lover keeps me from the dark," she whispered up at me.

As I looked into her eyes, I couldn't help feeling love for her. This wasn't love for Pearl, or even love for Blitz. This was someone entirely her own, as I'd know her the first time we'd loved. Then she looked up from my face to the stars, and I thought I saw one reflected in her eye. "Your name is Starshine, now," I told her. "Do you understand?"

"Gesse, min nama is Starshine," she breathed, drifting away into sleep.

I slept for an hour or two, then got up and paced around the beach. I wanted to call a fish and eat, but even that was difficult. My majick was weak with the exhaustion of that very brief conversation, and whatever it was that blasted me back into my body. Finally, I caught one, and ate it's liver raw. I needed strength. I was determined to get Pearl back. The Fierae had told me that the human Apprentices who'd joined and stayed as Charge could coalesce their light bodies again if they wanted to. Obviously it wouldn't do them much good, now, as their bodies were long dead and moldered. Where would they go?

But Pearl's body was alive, and Starshine said she could see her. I'd find her, gollam it, and then I'd unwrap that little finger from around me. I'd *make* her listen the next time I was right and she was wrong. *What* had I been thinking about?

Starshine slept all day. She may have simply *continued* to sleep, but I woke her in the afternoon, and fed her fish. I literally had to feed her, and comfort her as I did. She seemed to be frightened even of eating. "It's like love," I said, coaxing pieces of Dorado into her mouth. "Swallow it like a kiss." Apparently, she misunderstood, and insisted on kissing me after each bite. At least she was initiating those kisses, and I took it for a good sign. For the most part, she initiated *nothing*.

When I finished feeding her, Starshine said, "Now love," and she was actually smiling.

"We need to talk, " I told her.

Immediately, her face became panicked. "*Now*, love," she said, beginning to shake and shiver.

"Okay, okay," I said, throwing my arms around her. She looked so absolutely *pitiful*, that I felt guilty, as if I had somehow caused her distress.

I found it easy to love Star. Though she still did nothing in the form of responding or returning the love I played on her, I loved to watch her face, her little looks of surprise at some touch of mine. I'd always believed Pearl loved me, but never did I see it as intensely as I saw it in Starshine's eyes. With her, it was beyond love, it was adoration.

Again, I'd calmed her, and again, she wanted to fall back into sleep once I had. "Please, Star, talk to me. You must learn to stay awake, now. We must find Pearl, then you can float on her sea again."

"Her sea is shallow, and full of waves."

Other than when I loved her, this was as awake and aware as I'd seen Star yet. Her voice, when she spoke to me, was very soft, and her inflection was sing-songy. It rose into high octaves with some of her words. She spoke like a child, yet I knew she was older than the Ancients. Or was she? *Blitz* certainly was, but I had named this girl Starshine because she was new, different, *her own,* and she was. Now I would have to help her grow accustomed to living awake, in a human body. It wasn't easy, but a lot of pleasure was involved.

It took a week to get Star to walk with me a little ways from the lean-to, and if I didn't love her three times a day, she'd fall back into shaking and convulsing. When I realized she was going to need this, I thought I would grow tired of it, and have to force myself, but I never did. Starshine adored me and every touch I gently bestowed on her. She became, very quickly, precious to me. I was frankly startled by my own need to protect her.

Eventually, Star began making progress. She was sleeping no more than ten or twelve hours a day, and I decided we should try to leave. It was not going to be easy, as everything new frightened Star. One evening, after I'd fed and loved and bathed her in the sea, we lay in Pearl's blankets, and I said, "Where is Pearl, now, Starshine?"

She closed her eyes, and her singing voice said, "The hurrakin party soared to sea, to play on the shores of Angland. But Pearl and Blitz sheared from the storm, and climbed into great heights of sweet, thin Air. She *seeks* us!" she said, looking suddenly surprised. The word "seeks" she spoke so high it was almost a squeak. Her surprise caused her eyes to go wide, which reminded me so much of Pearl that my heart jumped in my chest.

"Where *is* she, Star?" I pleaded.

Her eyes began following something not there, and her mouth was open and smiling, waiting to giggle. "Fleogan an swete Air, Pearl!" she called softly.

That was another problem. Sometimes, and it was happening more and more often, she'd start using what I took to be Fierae words. "Speak Inglish," I'd tell her.

"Gesse, Ic spece Aenglish," was always her answer. When she'd shared her body with Pearl, they'd also shared their knowledge. Now Star had only her *own* knowledge, and sometimes she seemed just too sleepy to search it for proper Inglish words.

"No, no, *Inglish*," I'd tell her, "do you understand?"

"Gesse, min nama is Starshine," and then she would smile, and I'd have to smile, too. If I kept at her when she got like that, she'd only begin to cry.

Though it took a long conversation to discover, it seemed Pearl and Blitz were on a high-pressure ridge someplace north of us and a little inshore. I decided to walk on the beach as long as we could, wanting not to startle Star with every tree and bug and blade of grass we came upon. Once, I had walked her off the beach and into a little copse of palms, where she'd passed out cold from fright. I felt so bad about it that, when she came to, I took her out into the tepid sea, which no longer frightened her as long as it was calm. There, I held her hands while my Naiadae gently fondled her nearly into a stupor. "Better?" I asked, carrying her ashore.

"An *eke* love," she said, with her arms around my neck. "Min heorte is thyn heorte, Spaul."

On the morning we started our search for Pearl, I loved with Starshine, fed her some fish, then took her into the sea and calmed her further. If I'd had access to herbs and medicinals, I'd have made her a potion to dull her senses. Love, however, was all I had, so I gave her a very large dose.

"We're going to Pearl, now, okay?" I asked her.

"Pearl! She soars and seeks, but we are invisible."

"Can you call to her?" I asked.

"Gesse. *Pearl!*" she called in her delightful voice. "Pearl! Come home now! Spaul wants you to!"

I smiled, and wanted to cry. Star was so cute, and no help at all. "Can you call to her as Charges call?" I tried.

"Ooer tima," she answered. "She's too far up! But we travel toward the earth that is under her. When will you feed me fish?"

"I will feed you fish off my tongue, if you'll just walk another hour, first."

"I will walk with you," she agreed.

I had to be careful what I said to Starshine. She took everything I told her literally, and considered anything I said I'd do an absolute promise. But I have to laugh, now, when I think about feeding her fish like that. It was actually pretty erotic, having her take my tongue, with a piece of Dorado on it, into her mouth to slide the fish off with her lips. Every time she did it, she sighed, "Mmm," then grabbed up another piece to place on my tongue. "Open!" she'd say.

Once, when she'd placed the fish there, I swallowed it myself, just as she was getting ready to gobble my tongue. It startled her, but she giggled, and put her fingers to my lips, as if wanting to open them and see if her fish was still there. "That one was for me," I told her, and she laughed.

"Thyn fish!" she squealed. "Thyn fish, min tunge!"

She wouldn't be happy until I did, so I ate a piece of fish off her pretty little tongue, which became the beginning of a long and delightful delay. Fierae live to love, and in that respect, Starshine showed her Fierae ancestry. Still, it amazed me how shy she remained, even when being loved three times a day.

Our progress was very slow, but the weather remained fine, clear-skied and bright, and I hoped that meant Pearl would not have trouble staying put. I knew if she got tangled up in the wrong flow, it could take her anywhere in World.

134

Nights on the beach were usually no problem, as Star loved to look at her namesake in the sky. But a couple of times, when some little thing during the day had made her anxious, she'd long to be under the lean-to. "Build me a house," she'd sob. "I miss my house."

One day, a flock of gulls flew low over us and shat. A big, white shite splattered on Starshine's arm. I'm sure she didn't even know what it was, but the fact that it appeared so suddenly made her frantic. I couldn't calm her till I took her into the sea, washed every inch of her, and then showed her that no more spatters were anywhere on her skin. With her voice still hiccuppy from her hysterics, she said, "What if... it comes... back?"

"I'll watch you all day, and make sure it doesn't."

For the rest of the day, she would not wear any clothes. "The Ball will burn you!" I told her, trying to get at least a shirt on her shoulders.

But every time I tried, she threw the garment off, and said, with her eyes squinted at me like an angry child, "How can you watch? You watch!" She kept an eye on me all that day, making sure I watched. Fortunately, she was very easy to look at.

That night, after the gull shite, Star became very insistent that I build her a house. "I'm scared outside my house," she wept, tugging on my heart with her sad little pleas.

"*I'll* be your house," I finally told her.

I rolled over, onto her, and pulled the blanket up over our heads. I could hear her giggling under me, saying, "Min hus heorte beatanes."

"You must only speak Inglish in this house," I whispered.

"Ic speke Aenglish," she said, her hot, sweet breath on my lips. "Sweve me nu, min hus."

I didn't know those words, but the way she said them made me understand exactly what she wanted.

Every day I pressed Starshine for information about Pearl. When I could get her to concentrate, she could actually see her. "She stays with Blitz on the high, thin air. We are invisible, but she knows I see her, mingling her fire with Blitz. So cute cute, human-Charge."

"So, she's alright, then. She isn't damaged?"

"She is scolinge. Blitz teaches her, and she learns. But she is like me, and needs much love," she told me. Then she began calling sweetly to the sky, "Taecan Pearl, Blitz! Sweve hiere gelic hiere hus!"

As I understood it, Pearl and Blitz were remaining stationary in a persistent high-pressure system. I wanted to get under them faster, but was afraid to ride the lines. Not only would it frighten Star, possibly into some land of catatonia, but she would not react well to damaged hands.

Though I'd resigned myself to our plodding pace, I'd decided to try and wean Star off of so much love. If nothing else, I wanted to limit the number of times we actually joined. Joining in love is a kind of majick, and though it doesn't drain me like conversing with the Fierae, I wanted to keep every bit of my strength to use in getting Pearl back. I had no idea what that was going to entail, though I cogitated on it constantly.

I did my best to calm Star in the sea instead of in Pearl's blankets, but there were times when she refused to go. "No! Sweve me!" she'd say, pulling me back from the water. I tried to explain about wanting to save my strength, but when she was like that, she heard nothing I said. "*Sweve* me, min hus!" She'd absolutely insist.

But she was definitely making progress. One day, we came upon a scuttling blue crab at the water's edge. I myself am not fond of them, as I think I've mentioned, but Star ran over to it. "An Crabba!" she squealed. Then she picked it right up and brought it to me.

"It will *bite* you!" I told her.

"No," she said. "He doth lician me."

For almost half an hour, Starshine carried that "crabba" down the beach with us, occasionally holding it up to my face and saying, "See, nought bitan!"

Of all the things! That crab was scaring *me*, and Star played with it like it was a fuzzy little hamster. Then she said, "Uh oh, he is dryge!" and ran to the water to put him back in. She was all smiles when she came back to me, and said, "Wet again! He was very ald and told me tales. He rode on a terrapin once, and a porpoise almost ate him! You don't like min crabba?"

"I like to eat them," I told her.

"No!" she said, squinting her eyes and scrunching up her face. Then she giggled, and said, "I'll tell him to bite you!" Turning her thumbs and forefingers into pincers, Star started pinching me all over and laughing to beat all helluva. "An crabba is bitan thu!" she squealed.

She was just too much, and was growing less and less timid, except when I loved her. In that respect, she remained as shy as she'd been the first time. But the day she picked up the crab, and then started playing that pinching game with me, was definitely a turning point in her behavior. She was becoming rambunctious, and rather than having to protect her, I had to start keeping *track* of her. I'd turn my head for a moment, and she'd be in the water, or stopped and digging some dead thing out of the sand.

One day she stopped and was playing with the shell of a horseshoe crab. Usually I would either wait for her, or go back and get her. This time I kept walking, occasionally glancing back to see what she'd do. She was watching me, and I could tell by her demeanor that she wasn't going to let me get too far away. Suddenly, I came to a little washout in the beach, and hopped down into it, hiding from Star. I couldn't have been out of her sight for but a few seconds, when I heard her coming, running, sobbing my name. I jumped up from my hiding place and grabbed her into my arms. She was weeping uncontrollably, and buried her head in my chest. "Nought laefan me, Spaul. Nought laefan me," she wept.

I felt like World's biggest shite. She cried for an hour, and would not release me from her arms. Finally, she calmed a bit, as I told her for the hundredth time, "I *promise* not to leave you. I'll never do that again."

Slowly, she released me and looked pitifully up into my eyes. "Sweve me, nu?" she asked, and I certainly couldn't say no.

The night after I'd played my dastardly trick on Starshine, she became uncharacteristically chatty. She seemed a little nervous, too, as if she wanted to tell me something, and was trying to figure out how. Or was she trying to prepare me for unwelcome news? "I was scared when you hid from me," she told me first. "It isn't nice to play tricks, I'm damaged goods."

"Where did you hear that, 'damaged goods?'" I asked her.

"Pearl's words. I *am*, Spaul. You know I am no longer Blitz."

"You're Starshine," I said, taking her face in my hands, "and you are *not* damaged goods. Neither is Pearl. She was joking when she called herself that."

"Not a joke for me. I've slipped along the traces, gone back. Not *enough* of me to be human. Poor Starshine. Poor Spaul, to have to care for me."

"I don't *have* to care for you, Star," I told her. "I *do* care for you. I love you, don't you know that?"

"Love Pearl, sweve Starshine," she whispered.

"No," I said, and smiled. Then I touched my finger to her nose and told her, "*You,* I love. And when I sweve with you, I love you more."

Star looked up at me through her lashes, and gave me Pearl's phony shy smile, except that this one was real. Pearl could pretend it perfectly, but that smile was truly Starshine's. I felt like it had *always* been hers. Then the smile left her face completely, and she closed her eyes, said, "Pearl is going to leave, soon. I don't think we will catch her."

"What do you mean, Star?"

"Another hurrakin comes, all the way from Africa. I hear the Terrae singing in the sand. This is the biggest party, Spaul. Blitz will not resist the call of such a storm. He will go when it comes."

Now I knew why Star had to work herself up to telling me this. It made me want to cry. If Pearl was with Blitz, as Charge, and if they joined the hurrakin party, she'd be swept away from me to the ends of World. "When will it come?" I asked.

"It comes it comes, and will kiss the coast at Ginny's Beach."

"Ginny comes after Two Carolines," I said. "We can't be that far south of it. Concentrate, Star, on where we are, okay?"

"Okay."

"Then concentrate on Ginny's Beach, where the hurrakin will kiss. How much distance is between these places?"

Starshine closed her eyes for a minute, then opened them and said, "This much," holding her thumb and forefinger about five centimeters apart.

"You were very high up just now, weren't you?" I asked.

"Gesse."

"How do you go up?" I asked her.

"Zephyrus, eke, is heah."

138

"Please try to speak Inglish, Star," I said, with a hint of frustration in my voice.

"Ic *speke* aenglish, Spaul!" she cried. Then she wept with her face in her hands, and I could hear her sobbing through them, "Ic spece Aenglish."

I wasn't about to give up. I took Starshine into the sea and calmed her with Naiadae love. It was purely medicinal. Star was my only hope, now, and I had to be able to talk to her. Once we were back on the beach, I built a fire and sat her by it to dry. "Do you feel better, now?" I asked her.

"Nought love, was it?" she asked, though she didn't seem upset.

"No, it wasn't Star. I need to talk to you. I know I upset you sometimes, but I want you to try and stay calm, okay? No more crying, just talking. I don't mean to scold you when I say speak Inglish, but sometimes you say Fierae words I don't understand."

Starshine smiled, then yelped a short little laugh. "Can't say Fierae words with human faces," she said. "Ic spece *Aenglish*! I know all and every Aenglish word. Do *you* know all? I think you don't understand because you are so tiny on the traces, an jot on time."

"So you *have* been speaking Inglish, but you're using words I don't know. Old words? Is that it?"

"Gesse."

"Can't you just concentrate on words we use now?"

"I'm slipped in the traces, and very young. Ic spece hwaet Ic spece. It all sounds the same to me, and I cannot know what you hear. See?"

"Are you saying you might be thinking one word and speaking another?"

"Gesse. Ic spece."

"I'm sorry, Star. Maybe your Inglish is better than mine. I'll just have to understand you the best I can. Now tell me again, how did you see from so high up before?"

"Zephrae," she said, looking intensely at me to see if I understood her.

"You can see what the Zephrae see?"

"Zephrae eyes. I find the Elementals I want, and they show me what they see."

139

This was giving me an idea. "Star, do you remember how Pearl asks the Zephrae to lift her up?"

"Gesse. Pearl is mighty with the Zephrae."

"Do you think you and I could do that trick?"

"Flaegan?" she gasped. "Starshine nought flaegan. Don't scare me, Spaul."

"If I hold you, Star, can you be brave for me?"

"Nought *flaegan*," she whimpered, beginning to lose her composure.

"Do you know that Pearl and I once loved while flying over the beach? You and I could do that."

"Sweve me in Air? I'm scared, Spaul. Nought for love, you sweve me, but for min medicine. Please, don't trick me, Spaul."

"You don't know that I love you, do you?" I asked her, and I could feel the sadness of that thought showing on my face.

"I know, but I am damaged, slipped in the traces. But Ic wille flaege with you. Don't let me fall, or I'll find an crabba to pinch you with," she said, tears rolling from her eyes, and a terrible, sad pout on her face.

"If we can manage to do that majick," I told her, "I'll let you pinch me with a crab."

That made her smile, and she said, with her thumbs and forefingers pretending to be pincers, "An crabba comes on you in min hus to niht."

I took Starshine down to the water's edge, and held her in my arms. "Kiss me, and call to the Zephrae," I told her. "Fetch a big chorus, and I'll try to tell them we want to go up, okay? If you can call them, and hold their attention, I can concentrate on explaining what we want. Are you ready?"

"Sweve me in Air?" she said, trying to smile despite her fear.

"Jump up into my arms, and wrap your legs around my waist," I told her. Star did as I said, then held me so tightly I was afraid she'd break something. "It's going to be okay, Star." I said.

"What will you *do* to me, now?" she whispered.

"Call the Zephrae," I said. Then I kissed her, slid one hand off her bottom, and joined us.

Star breathed a little moan, and kissed me back. I could feel Zephres playing around us. I concentrated on them, tried to see them whirling, making that Air cocoon. Star wasn't moving, had buried her head in my shoulder, and was holding on tight. We were joined, but motionless. Suddenly, I felt us being lifted, and weight disappeared. "Sweve me, nu," Star whispered, and I did.

As soon as I'd made my point with the Zephrae, and we began to float, that majick was mine. I understood it, and could do it again, though I'd probably still need Star's help. She was part of the trick, as I now understood it.

I did not hurry that love I made with her. I'd give her no more medicine. If it was love she needed, I would give it to her. If it was love she *wanted*, I'd give it. I would do everything I could to rescue Pearl, but I would *not* do it at Star's expense.

After our lovely dance, floating over the beach, Starshine said to me, "That was not for medicine."

"You're *my* medicine," I told her. "You make me better."

Though we didn't rush anything, eventually Star and I looked toward the north. "Were you this high before, when you saw Ginny's Beach?"

"Higher," she said. "But I see it. There," she pointed.

"That's a hundred klicks away," I said. When will the hurrakin party come?"

"The day after tomorrow, it comes at night."

Softly, I said to Star, "I think tomorrow, in daylight, we may have to try something desperate."

"Please don't tell me now. Beon min hus to niht, and Ic wille beon thyn crabba."

"Will the crabba bite me?"

"An crabba miht pinch you," she said, taking my nose in her pincer.

As soon as dawn cracked a knuckle, I was up, calling a fish. I'd extricated myself from Star, and left her to sleep. What I had in mind was not going to be easy on either of us. In fact, it was dangerous.

I ended up with a big markarel, whose liver would be oily, but would have to do. I cleaned the fish, and put it in the coals to cook. I also put clams and kelp on to boil in Pearl's little pot. Then I woke Starshine, and started to feed her raw markarel liver. "I don't like it," she said, making faces.

141

"Me either," I told her, "but it will help heal our hands."

"My hands aren't broken, see," she said, holding them up.

"Star, I told you we were going to have to do something desperate. When we do it, it will damage our hands."

"You would cut us with mag lines, wouldn't you?" she asked, her mouth saddening into a frown.

"Do you know of any way to protect our hands from the lines?" I asked her.

Star closed her eyes and thought about that for a very long time, so long that I resumed forcing pieces of liver into her mouth. Finally, her eyes popped open, and she said, "Lodestone gauntlets."

I knew what a gauntlet was, a kind of glove, but I'd never heard of lodestone. "What is lodestone?" I asked her.

"Magnetite," she answered.

That made sense. Magnetite is just what it sounds like, magnetic stone. Magnetite gauntlets *would* probably protect ones hands from the lines, and if we ever got out of this mess, and had Pearl back, I'd be sure to try and make some. But it certainly wasn't going to happen today. "I wish I could make you some lodestone gauntlets, Star, but I can't. Can you be very brave for me today?"

"Flaegan?" she asked.

"Yes, we're going to fly, but we're also going to need to fall.

It took about ten seconds for that to sink in, but when it did Starshine started to cry. "Giefan me min medicine," she sobbed.

My hope was to duplicate Pearl's trick that had brought us from the Tara Road to the sea. I would not try to shield us from the wind of our fall, as Pearl had done, because I didn't want us going that fast. Actually, I wasn't sure how to do that part, anyway. Unfortunately, the other part of the trick I wasn't sure of was getting the Zephrae to stop us. I could cogitate on it all day, but there was no way to practice such a thing except by doing it. I'd get one chance, and if I failed, Starshine and I would become a stain on the shimmering white sand of the beach.

My intention was to do the trick exactly as Pearl had, with three lines of force; one between us, and one on either side. Star and I stood at the water's edge. She was wearing the little, makeshift pack the slaves of Tara had given me, and I was wearing Pearl's larger one.

142

"Call the Zephrae," I said to Star, and I noticed she was shaking. Turning her to face me, I kissed her trembling lips. "It's okay," I told her. "Call them."

"*Nought* okay," she sobbed. It wasn't working. She was simply too afraid.

I must have been thinking of giving up. In my mind I was sitting on this beach, watching the storm go by that would take Pearl away from me forever. But some part of me would not surrender, and I realized I was taking the little pack off of Star, and removing our clothes. I put everything that would fit into Pearl's pack, put it on, and discarded the other. "Hop up into my arms, Star," I said.

When we performed the trick exactly as we had the night before, it worked. Star was clinging to me tightly, and I decided to leave her there. I would ride the lines myself, with the pack on my back, and Star on my front. I picked a spot halfway between us and Ginny's Beach. I thought about doing the entire distance at once, but a lot of weight was going to be on my hands. I also knew that if I managed to do this trick once, I'd be able to do it again. If I *failed* once, it wouldn't matter how far we went.

XVI
Stormy

I drew the lines up beneath my hands, and the Zephrae dropped us onto them. I didn't think Star could hold me any tighter, but when we started to fall, she squeezed out my air. "When I tell you to, Star, ask the Zephres to sing at your back and stop us. Will you ask them?"

"I will *tell!*" she yelled over the howl of our wind.

We were coming down fast, but not nearly so fast as Pearl had us going when she'd made that wind shield. We were about three-quarters of the way down when I said, "Concentrate with me, Star. Make them stop us!"

No sooner had I spoken than we were stopped, hanging on the lines over a hundred meters from the ground. "That was very good," I whispered in Star's ear, "but you must let them ease us down."

We weren't moving. The steady wind of the Zephrae was pillowing Starshine's back, and blowing in my face. "Ease us down, Star," I tried again, but she was unresponsive, and hanging on to me for dear life.

Behind us, the lines were still high where we'd mounted them. I concentrated on bringing them down back there. When I'd done that, and left us on what was now the apex of our mag line hill, I slowly started to flatten the lines and bring us down. We hadn't made the halfway point I'd chosen by maybe a dozen klicks, but I felt good about what we'd accomplished. It would be easier the second time. That's what I was thinking when Starshine screamed, "Thyn hondes!" That's when they started to hurt, and I began to faint, and Star cried out, "Min poor, poor lufu!"

I came to lying on my stomach at the water's edge. Star had buried my hands in the wet sand. "Don't move," she said softly, when she saw I was awake. "Ic murnan thyn hondes."

I wasn't sure exactly what she'd said, but took it to mean she was trying to fix my hands. "It won't work," I said, but I didn't move. The cool, wet sand felt good on what was left of my hands.

I had only seen them for a second before I'd fainted, but I was in no hurry to look at them again.

"The Terrae and Naiadae in the sand hear me mourning," Star whispered. They are angry, and do not want to fix you, but I *compel* them." When she said that, her voice became forceful. It was the first time I'd ever heard confidence sound from her.

"If you make them angry, they may harm you, Star!" I told her.

"Gesse. Thei should lician to hearmian me, nu, but Ic thence Fierae thohtes to theym. Thei durran nought hearmiath an Fierae."

Star made me lie still like that for hours, as she gathered and shucked clams to put in my mouth. "Eat them," she coaxed in her singing little voice. "Or I'll bring an crabba to pinch you."

After a while, Star gently pulled my hands, one at a time, out of the sand, and kissed them. "Call to an fish," she told me, "and I will feed you his bloody liver." My stomach was already queasy, and the thought of that almost caused me to wretch. "Ic cnowe, min lufu, but you *must*." Then her voice went singy again, and she said, as if trying to mollify me, "I will feed it to you with my tongue. Would you like it better that way?"

No trace of damage remained on my hands. Star's fix had been perfect. But even without trying, I could hear the Elementals around us, restless and perturbed. "Gesse, Ic hier theym, eke," Star told me. "I dare not compel them again. Though they will not harm me, I fear they might take their anger out on you."

"Will they fly us again? Will they allow us to do that majick?"

"Gesse, but not today. We must wait till tomorrow, until they calm a bit. But they will remember, and tell this tale at the hurrakin party. They will ask for my destruction."

I was surprised at how calmly she told me this. "Aren't you frightened?" I asked.

Star smiled, then laughed. "No. They will all debate, with great fury, but the Fierae will have the final word. Fierae know that love is above the rules."

Though Star had fixed my hands, the lines had tugged hard on my metals. I was weak with anemia, and knew I couldn't eat enough liver to regain my strength in one day. Sitting by a fire that night, holding Star in my arms, I said, "I won't be able to do that trick by myself, tomorrow. Even if I could, my hands would become the same mess they were today. If we were to ride *three* lines, together, we'd be able to do it and our hands shouldn't be that bad."

I looked into Star's eyes, and saw the fear there. "I will try," she whispered, and I had no doubt that she'd do it despite her terror. I knew her love for me would compel her to do this thing, and that's what made up my mind.

"Star," I said. "I think we have tried our best. You've been very brave, braver than Pearl could ever be. Pearl was fearless, and it's easy to be brave when you don't have fear to fight. Sometimes it wasn't even courage she had, but recklessness. We will not fly tomorrow. We will not fall on the lines. We will watch the storm pass, and say our good-byes to her. You have done enough. I will put you through no more."

Star didn't move as I said this, but a single tear dropped out of her eye. "You love me," she whispered.

"I love you very much," I whispered back.

Star wasn't in my arms when I woke. She was standing at the water's edge, wearing Pearl's pack. She was trying to put courage into her voice, but I could easily hear through it that she was terrified. "We flaegan!" she called to me. "It's time to go!"

The part of me that wanted to jump up and run to her, to do that trick with her and fall to Ginny's Beach, tensed my muscles, but I did not move. I really had made up my mind. I really did love Starshine that much. I can be stubborn, even with myself. I should have said no to Pearl. I shouldn't have helped her come out of body. The love I'd allowed to talk me into recklessness had been flawed. I would love on my *own* terms from now on. I would do what I knew to be right.

I couldn't even bring myself to call to Star. I'd begun mourning Pearl, and was overwhelmed with it. Finally, Starshine came running to me. She threw off the pack, and dropped to her knees in the sand where I lay. "Ic wille flaegan with you!" she said.

"I love you too much," I told her.

"Lufest Pearl, eke," she argued. "You will be sad without her."

"I love you more," I whispered, and though it hurt, it was true.

As the Ball began to set, Star and I, sitting by a fire, saw the storm coming out of the southeast. I could feel, in my ears, the pressure falling, and knew a colossus was twirling out at sea.

Star was very quiet as we watched. Her silence calmed my sea a bit, till I could hear the Elementals, excited and still angry, around us. "I'm scared, Spaul" Star said, turning to me. "If Pearl came back, I'd have to return to her sea. I'm frightened that you let her go for me, to keep me with you." Sometimes I wondered if Star could read my mind.

"That frightens me, too," I told her, "though I do not know if it's true. If it is, then I may be an evil man doing the right thing."

"Nought yfel," she said softly, touching my cheek. "Choices. We must make them. It is the blessing and curse on all of us. Nought yfel, Spaul. Say it to me."

"Not evil," I said, but I wasn't convinced.

As it began to grow dark, and the storm flashed fiercely, coming toward us, I noticed the Elementals grow louder around us. They were excited by the hurrakin, but it was more than that. They were shouting their anger to the storm. "Gesse. I hear them, too," Star said to me, certainly reading my mind, now. "It's good that we didn't fly today. They may not have wanted to stop us falling."

"I thought you said you could compel them."

"I think they might have compelled me back," she said, opening her eyes wide at me. "They are angrier than I thought they could be. They are calling the storm. It will kiss us *here* now, and not go to Ginny's Beach. It will kiss us hard and fiercely, and linger while they debate."

"Where are Pearl and Blitz?" I asked her.

Star closed her eyes and whispered, "They come they come they come."

Yes, we make choices, but sometimes choices are made for us. When the Universe chooses for you, you must abide by that decision. Already the storm's edge tossed the sea and blew sand in our eyes. I took Star away from the beach to a sturdy palm, and tied her to it with many vines of kazoo. "You must compel the Naiadae to hold the sea back from this place," I told her.

"They are very angry," she said.

"*Compel* them, Star. Can you also call to Blitz?"

"Nought do both at once," she answered.

"Then concentrate on the Naiadae."

I kissed her quickly, then ran to the beach to search for a Charge. I found one chittering frantically in the sand. "It comes it comes, let us climb into a tree and join."

"Wait," I said, making contact. "The storm is strong, you can join from here."

"You are *Spaul!*" the Charge exclaimed. "Your aneke'lemental lover has angered the Lesser Three. So cute cute, she becomes."

The Lesser Three are what the Fierae call the other three Elementals. I was happy to hear this Charge taking their anger so lightly. "Will you call to Blitz for me?" I asked.

"Blitz is not in the storm," she told me.

"No, he is riding the thin, high air that is retreating now. He is coming to fall into the storm."

For a minute the Charge was silent. Then she said, "Yes, I see him coming. He is mightily mixed with the Charge of your Female Apprentice. He sails with Pearl of the Fierae!"

"Please, call to them. Tell them I'm here. Tell them I would join."

To this the Charge howled her laughter. "They would boil you away to mist, even in your light-body, so radiant are they together. But shed your flesh, then return. I will call them to join, but you must stand away. Do not venture too close, little Fierae human, this joining will be a hard thing to witness for those whose light is small."

Okay! I ran back to Star, and told her, "You must hold me tightly, now, don't let me blow away."

"I won't let you go," she said.

"Hold the Naiadae back, I must leave my body now."

"Wait!" she called. "Kiss me one last time, my fearsome lover," she pleaded. "When you return, I'll be gone."

With the wind wild around us, I took Star's face in my hands and kissed her. She was right, if I managed to get Pearl back, Star would return to her sea. Tears blew off my face, as Starshine held me with all her strength. I managed to calm my sea, and dashed back to the Charge, leaving Star to hold my vacant body.

It is strange to see and hear such a maelstrom of wind around you and not be able to feel it. In the calm of my light-body, I returned to the Charge. "Not so close!" it warned.

"What's going to happen when you join?" I asked.

"Something!" The Charge howled, stirring the sand as she glowed and rose. Then Blitz came down.

Though I'd heeded the Charge's advice to stand away, I actually felt heat from that joining on my light-body. I'd never felt *anything* before without my flesh.

"Spaul!" a voice screamed through a siren of light.

"Pearl?" I called.

"We are here, stand back, I'm coming out to you!"

I did as I was told. A bolt of Fierae fire leapt out toward where I stood. That fire began to pulse, and bright steam seemed to simmer out of it. Then it coalesced, grew more solid, and became the image of Pearl as I'd last seen her. She was smiling, still wearing that tunic of light. "Let's get back to our bodies," she said to me, her voice gone very Fierae. "I want to touch you."

"Behave yourself, little mother!" the Fierae moaned, still joining, but about to separate. "We must go calm the anger of the Three, that the motherchild has wrought!"

"Motherchild?" I asked Pearl.

"Starshine," she said to me. "Yes, I know what she's become. I could hear her when she was watching Blitz and I soar. I'll tell you everything when we're back in our bodies." Just then the Fierae separated, and she called to them, "Farewell, I'll miss you!"

"We will be in the eyes of your child!" they called back.

I entered my body a second before Pearl did. "Good-bye," Star said in a pitiful little voice. Then her eyes changed, became someone else's. Became Pearl's.

XVII
Motherchild Reunion

I was staring into her eyes as they changed. Somehow, the joy of seeing Pearl made the torment of losing Starshine worse. I was frozen and burning in this contradicted emotion. I was only able to stand because Pearl, still tied to that tree, was holding me up. But my mind was on its knees, broken as if by whip, depleted of all fight and resistance. "As well as you have me tied," Pearl said, "I don't think I could escape if you tried to kiss me."

She was making a joke. I could hear it, but it seemed it was coming from another time, another place. It couldn't be happening *now*. She could not be joking in this hurrakin wind, after all I'd been through to find her, after Star sacrificed herself to save her. "I should leave you tied," I said, backing out of her arms.

To that, she only smiled, as the kazoo vines that held her flashed and fell away as ash. "I'm sorry, Spaul," she said, coming to me. "I know you became very close to Star. You will be reunited with her soon. Because Star was in it, my body suffered no ill effects from that joining, but my mind is cruelly weary. Too much is in it, Spaul, the Fierae taught me too much." She brought her hands to her head, and for a moment, I thought she would cry. But she overcame it, and said, in a steady voice, "I will float on my sea and catalogue it all, store it away where I can find it if need be. It will take me a few days to clear enough out so that it doesn't torment me so. Our minds are small, but the Fierae are big as all of time, and every space in World. Please don't be angry, Spaul. *Please.*"

When she came into my arms, I held her. And I kissed her as well. "Did you find out what we are?" I said in her ear.

"I did," she said. "Then I became something different."

Blitz must have mollified The Lesser Three Elementals, as he said he would, because the storm immediately continued north and turned out to sea. I built a fire on the beach, and sat beside it. I was cold and wet and shaking. Pearl sat beside me, but before she did, she stationed her Zephrae above us, like an inverted bowl, to keep the last of the storm off us. "That's quite a trick, you do it like it's nothing," I said to her.

"It *is* nothing, Spaul. I won't lie, I've passed into realms of knowledge far beyond where any Finished Apprentice has dwelled. I am very nearly aneke'lemental myself."

"What is aneke'lemental?" I asked.

"It means, 'also an elemental.' When I heard Blitz say from my sea, 'aneke'lemental nama,' she was trying to think of a name for our daughter, who will be the first, true aneke'lemental. She will be the mother of a new race, a new *element*. This was the Fierae's plan to counterbalance the dying off of the Apprentices. If the awareness of the Apprentices disappears, the Elementals would be blind again to humanity, and humanity would not survive this time. There are too few of us left.

"The Fierae are tied to us, Spaul. Without humanity, they would lose almost all their awareness. They'd become phenomenal as opposed to sentient. The Lesser Three would follow them into that haze of incognizance. World's mouth would be stopped, and her eyes, closed. They could not allow this to happen. They fused me with Blitz so that I might bear the next element, the *human* element. My fate to become this was sealed when I was five years old. It was the deal Mama made for my life.

"The Fierae realized that I might become a Female Apprentice who could fuse with a Fierae Charge and survive. They'd tried it before, but the very few Female Apprentices they were able to find, died in the attempts. They literally died of ecstasy. I was the last Female Apprentice, Spaul, until I became what I am. Now, I'm far from Apprentice, far, even from human. My daughter will be more human than I."

Pearl talked and talked, telling me everything, as if she had to keep pouring out information to make some room in her mind. Apparently, the Fierae hadn't anticipated Pearl being able to leave her body to converse with them. They hadn't believed it was possible. "If they had, they'd have warned me against it," she told me. "Though I was able to get out of body, no female can resist joining. And I wouldn't have been able to tear myself away from them again, if Blitz hadn't educated me. *And,* loved me. I am very much Fierae, now, and I am dedicated to our plan. I came back to save mankind, and World herself, though I'd be a liar if I tell you I hadn't wanted to say, stay with the Fierae. Please forgive me, Spaul. I should have listened to you. I want so badly to be what I was for you."

Pearl lost her composure, then, and lay in my arms, weeping. I could hear in her voice some strain that had gone beyond endurance. I knew she was right, she needed to float on her sea. When an Apprentice heals his mind in his sea, his body goes comatose. Pearl's would not, as she would trade places with Star. It would be the best thing for all of us, I thought. Pearl needed rest and healing, I needed to see Star, and I believed Star needed to see me. "Yes, she does," Pearl told me.

"Reading my thoughts, again?" I asked. "I really wish you wouldn't."

"There are actually very few that I can hear," she said. "She'll be a little different, I suspect, when we trade places this time. My words will be fresh for her again, so she won't speak that forgotten Inglish. Or, who knows, maybe she will. That time is still closer to her than this."

"What do you mean?" I asked.

"When I left my body, it tore Blitz from my sea so abruptly, that she began to regress along the traces, along time. You see, Spaul, the Fierae don't only live here and now, they exist as trace everywhere and every when they've ever been. That's how they can remember everything so perfectly.

Blitz was born long before the masses of Ancients came, when men were few and still had some small contact with the Elementals. When she regressed, that time became the locus of her memory, it is more *now* to her than the present. It is where she is in the traces. Everything that has happened to her since then is a farther memory. That's why her Inglish mixes with the old words.

"When I tore her from my sea like that, she became the Fierae child she'd been all those years ago. Her Fierae age is probably no more than a thousand years."

"You're telling me she's a thousand year old child?" I said.

"I'm not sure," Pearl answered. "She may be as young as eight or nine hundred. The Fierae know that Blitz has regressed, and has taken the name Starshine. They don't see it as a problem, since she was meant to remain in my sea except when we love. I don't think the Fierae anticipated the creation of Drea, though. When my child, or rather, children, were conceived, Blitz and I were joined, and she was still her fully Fierae self. Our daughter will be aneke'lemental, though her Fierae-side mother is now a child."

"Motherchild," I said.

"Yes. Now I must trade places with the motherchild before my head explodes. Will you kiss me good-bye, will you talk Star into letting us love, alone, when I return? I can't go without knowing you forgive me, Spaul, or at least that you'll try to."

"There's nothing to forgive. The Universe plots and schemes, and we are, both of us, caught up in it like specks of dust in a cyclone. Can you read my mind now?" I asked her.

"Yes," she said. "You love me."

I took her in my arms and kissed her, then held her as she drifted away to her sea.

Starshine bubbled up to the surface like a cork, and locked our mouths into a kiss. Then she said, with her little voice shaking, "We must never let her out again! She becomes an wicce deorce." When she saw that I didn't understand her, she thought for a moment, then said, "A dark witch."

I'd heard of witches, or wiccans. They'd been the last among the Ancients to try and keep contact with the Elementals. But the Ancients persecuted them out of existence. Star must have been using the word "witch" in some archaic sense, because we Apprentices are, all of us, wiccans of a sort. "I didn't want to leave you," she went on, curling herself into my lap like a cat. "Sadly, I floated in the sea of Pearl. I wanted to cry, but dared not, lest she hear me. I could tell she'd need her sea for healing when we passed, when she came back into her body. Oh, Spaul! I saw all when we passed, and again just now when we traded. She is not the Pearl you love. She is wicce deorc, ond Ic faer we must never let her out!"

"Even if that's true, Star, I don't think we could stop her rising. She controls her body."

"It *is* true! We must think of a way!"

"Star, I want you up here with me as much as you want to be here, but taking Pearl's body by force isn't the answer."

"You think I'm lying!" she cried, tears rushing into her eyes.

"No, Star, I just don't know what to think right now."

"She believes herself to be a queen," she continued. "She is too much Fierae for a human mind. She is *damaged.* She practically

153

told you that herself. She will compel men to obey her and her children. She will be queen, and all will despair in her light. You must believe me, Spaul!"

"Let me rest my own mind, Star, then we'll talk about this some more. Okay? It's too much. It's overwhelming me."

"Gesse," Star said, calming some. "Though I no longer need medicine, now that Pearl is back in her sea, Ic should nought beon saed to habban thu sweve me, nu."

I smiled and said, "I know you can also speak my Inglish, now that Pearl is on her sea."

"Gesse, but my Aenglish says my love better. I speak it for you."

When I loved Star that night, she was different, calmer, of course, but her shyness had also changed. In fact, she touched me back for the first time. But she was as shy with that touch as she'd been under mind. I wondered how I'd react to loving Pearl again, who was so much the opposite: confident and daring and fierce. Then I started thinking about what Star had said. It was true that Pearl had come back changed. Even she'd admitted that. But she'd also said her Fierae knowledge tormented her. And she wasn't shy of telling me she was *beyond* Apprentice, now, beyond *Finished Apprentice*. She'd been impatient to go to her sea to heal. How badly was she damaged? I said to Star, "If I wanted to, how could I keep Pearl on her sea?"

"You believe me?" Star whispered.

"I don't know. But until I *do* know, it couldn't hurt Pearl to stay where she is for a while. Actually, she *should* be *hearing* us now, though it would take a little time to sink in. Why hasn't she come up to defend herself against your accusations?"

"She is damaged. She is far too lost in her schemes of power and security. She cannot hear," Star said in a hushed voice.

"She certainly *should* be able to hear," I told her. "If she *is* that damaged, her sea is the best place for her. But we'd have to think of a way to keep her there."

"An potion, Ic wille macian! A strong potion to deepen her sleep. Maybe, someday, her sea will heal her. I will listen, always, for her sane voice to return.

It was something to see Star so confident. In all respects, except loving, she was no longer shy. All the next day, she had me hunting far and wide with her for plants she knew of with which to make her potion. "A mushroom with a tan spot on top of its cap, when you break the stem, it will bleed blue. Go look!" she said, shooing me away with her hands. "And from morning glory, I need the seeds!" she called after me.

When we had everything Star wanted, she boiled it in fresh water in Pearl's pot. Then she strained it through a cloth into the corn jug the slaves had given me. The sad part was, I had nowhere to put the corn, and ended up dumping it out (and a little bit, into me.)

It was a dark concoction, thick and noxious, that Star brewed. "What will that do to *you*?" I asked her.

"Nothing much, min lufu. I will channel it, nearly all, to her sea, and it will make her heavy. She'll sink. It could make me a little drowsy for a day, but nothing more. *Swimman deop!*" she called in her sing-songy voice. "*Swimman deop ond Feorr, Pearl!*"

When her potion cooled, Star swallowed one good mouthful out of the jug, then made a face. "It is worse than markarel liver," she told me.

"How long will that keep her on her sea?"

"Every three days, I must take one swallow to keep her there."

"When you *stop* taking it, how long till she'll be able to come back up?" I asked.

"Nought long. That's why I must drink it every third day. While Pearl is sleeping, can we go somewhere, Spaul? An village, perhaps? We've a want of clothes, don't you think? And I've eaten nought but fish, I'd like to try some other food. Will you take me, Spaul?"

"Why not!" I told her. "I've heard there are quite a few villages in Ginny. Let's find one. We'll go to the Ninety-five, float up, and look around. It's time I started going north again, anyway. When I began this journey, I had no idea what a long, strange trip it would be.

Before we left the beach, I casually mentioned to Star that we'd need to have the Terrae excavate us some small bit of wealth to use when we found a village. Immediately, she crouched, floated her hand over the beach, palm down, and I watched as strange little coins of gold popped up all over the place. "Genog sceatt, min lufu?" she asked, though I had no idea what she was asking. "See, I make you a wealthy prince, and I am your Princess Starshine, who carries your eyres in min belly!"

Yes, somehow that fact always wanted to slip my mind. Pearl, I mean Star, well, I mean both of them, *the girls,* were pregnant. They had been for over a month. I went to Star, put my arm around her and my other hand on her stomach. "Not yet," she said. "But soon my tummy will grow like a watermelon!" Then she whispered, with her lips brushing my ear, "You were my house when I needed shelter. Nu, Ic wille beon an hus for thyn eyres."

At the Ninety-five, Starshine floated us up with her Zephres as easily as Pearl would have. Frankly, it surprised me, and she either read that on my face, or was reading my mind. "I am an element, eke," she said, smiling. "Pearl is like a potion in suspension, she is Fierae-mixed, but does not dissolve into solution. But I'm a fair combination. I am aneke'lemental. It is my spirit, min zje-hyzid, that is joined in your daughter-to-come. I am her true mother, true mother of the first-born aneke'lemental."

"But, she's born of Pearl's body," I told her.

"Gesse," she said, her voice gone sad. Then she looked into my eyes, with tears in her own, and said, as we floated high in the clear, blue morning, "Please try to see me as one with this body while I'm here. It's the only body I've ever known, so it's really very much mine. It *feels* like mine. When you love this body, Spaul, please let it be min bodig that you love."

Star and I located what seemed to be a settlement that was near the Ninety-five, and thirty or forty klicks to the north. It appeared as a fairly large, rectangular clearing in the forest. I thought I could make out a cottage or two. "Many buildings are there," Star told me, apparently seeing through the eyes of Elementals closer to the village. "It is a place of great wealth. All manner of goods are there. Your coins will trade well."

"I guess you should put us down so we can get started, then," I said. "It's a two day walk, at least."

"Nought walk," Star said. "We will ride the lines down."

"Honestly, Star, I'd rather walk than damage my hands

again," I said. "I can feel that I'm still anemic, too. I'd like to find some bloody red cow meat."

"I will ride us down so quickly, it will not cut us. You'll see. Come along, now, take my hand," she said in that singy voice. She was so very cute to be so very powerful.

The ride down was a blur. Star completely shielded us, and there was no resistance at all. With Pearl on her sea, Star was totally in control of her aneke'lemental ability. She was as strong as she'd warned me Pearl had become. This should have been a cause for concern, but I was exhausted, mind and body. Though Fierae influenced my blood, I was still a mere human. The girls were each beings unto themselves, unique in World. Not only was I outnumbered, I was also out-powered.

Star landed us on the Ninety-five. The village was about five klicks to the west, and we found a little trail that had obviously been cut between there and the road. "It's very straight," Star said, referring to the path. "We can ride all the way."

"No," I insisted. "Let's walk. I don't want them knowing we're Apprentice. I don't need all that fawning."

"You are right, min lufu. We should nought want to scare them."

"People aren't scared of Apprentices," I told her, as if she were a silly child. I should have been paying attention. Star was no child in the human sense. She was a thousand year old *Fierae* child, cast in the body of a very well grown girl.

XVIII
The First Queen of Ginny
(a very witchy woman)

Star had been right about this village. Though it wasn't Tara, it was almost as large, and had many bobarkers hawking their wares. Starshine was as happy as I'd ever seen her. Watching her shop at the little booths set up all over the place, made me laugh. As easily as she could have the earth cough up any number of fortunes, she haggled furiously with these bobs. When she'd finally get the price down where she wanted it, she'd hold out her palm to me and say, "Sceatt, plese, min cyning," which I understood to mean she wanted some coins. When I asked her what "cyning" meant, she would only say, "*You* eart min cyning."

Before long Star had a croaker-sack, which she'd also purchased, full of all sorts of things. From balls of soap and little brushes for teeth, to soft undergarments and tiny jars of perfume. She handed me the sack, and held her palm out. It was full of little pieces of silver, the change she'd insisted on in her haggling. "Take some of these," she said. "Our coins are far too much for what they're selling here. Go buy some clothes for you, and I will buy some for me, and we'll surprise each other with them. Okay?"

She was in such a wonderfully gay mood, that I kissed her on the forehead and said, "Go shop, pretty princess, but buy my clothes, too." Then I took a couple of small pieces of silver from her hand, dropped my aytiem full of gold coins onto her palm, and said, "I'll be in that inn over there, drinking scupnog wine."

Ah, to be at an inn, again, behind a mug of wine (though it turned out not to be scupnog.) This one was crowded, but not overly so. It was still afternoon, and people wanting dinner were yet to arrive. When the barmaid brought me my wine, I asked her, "What is this village called?"

"Ginny," she told me, "same as the Place. You from Two Carolines?"

"No, but I did pass through it," I said.

"You seem like a nice feller," she told me. "I'm glad you made it through there safely. Ugly rumors come out of that Place. Did you stay to the road?"

"For the most part, and the beach," I answered.

"Good. It's up in them mountains that the bad ones are. Deliverance Billies, they're called around here, though I don't know what they'd be deliverin', 'cept badness," she told me.

I found out from the barmaid, that the specialty of the house at "The Ginny Stud Inn," was cow meat. "Bring me a big steak of it," I told her.

"Cooked all through, or do you like it rare?"

"Bloody and red," I answered. "And if you make hushpuppies here, bring me some of those, too."

When I'd finished that meal, and washed it down with two mugs of wine, I sat back in my chair and folded my hands over my stomach. The barmaid brought me a toothpick, and said, "Would you like something sweet?"

"I think she's coming, now," I said, as Starshine walked in through the door.

"She's *precious*," the barmaid cooed, seeing where I was looking. "Do you think she'll want to eat?"

"Are there stars in the sky at night?" I answered.

"There usually are," the barmaid chuckled, touching my arm. "I'll go fetch her a mug of wine."

Star was carrying another croaker-sack, and when she saw me, her face exploded into a grin. Hurrying to me, she sat herself, and pushed her sack under the table. "Wait till you see our new clothes!" she said, as the barmaid set a mug of wine in front of her. "Thank you!" she exclaimed. "My name is Starshine!"

"Well, I'm Rosemary, Starshine, but you call me Rosie. I'm bettin' you'd like something to eat."

"You would win, so I will not bet," Star said.

"Would you like to try bloody cow meat?" I asked her. "And applesauce and hushpuppies?"

"Yes!" she answered excitedly. "And you must eat some, too."

"I've already eaten. See how fat I am?" I told her, patting my stomach.

Star turned to our barmaid and said, "You must bring him

159

some more. His metals have gone anemic, so I must make him eat till he's well."

"But, Star, I'm really full!" I insisted.

Letting her voice go sing-songy again, she said, "I will feed you off of my tongue!"

"I'd like to see *that*," the barmaid said, and then she blushed. "Sorry," she giggled. "Your voice is kind-of hypnotic," she said to Star.

"She was grazed by a Fierae bolt, and it's been that way ever since," I told Rosie.

"None of my business," she said. "Two steaks, bloody rare, and all the fixins?"

"Why not?" I answered, untying my belt. Then to Star, I said, "I hope you bought me *big* new clothes."

After we ate (in my case, again,) Star got up and said, "You stay and guard my sacks. I'll go haggle for a room."

"Star," I said, grabbing her hand and stopping her, "It isn't like we can't fill my aytiem whenever we want. You don't need to haggle."

But she smiled at me, and said, "We don't want to make them rich!" Then she pulled her hand from mine, blew me a kiss, and went off to haggle."

Our upstairs room was cozy and nice. There was one bathing tub at the inn, which sat in a room on the ground floor. One fill of the tub was included, along with a towel, in the cost of the room, so I'd paid for another fill and towel. I told Star to take her bath first. "If the tub was bigger, we could have our bath together," she told me.

"It's tiny. Come get me when they've refilled it for me," I said, lying down on the unusually comfortable bed.

"Don't look at my new clothes, when I'm gone!" she sang.

"Aren't you taking them with you, to put on after your bath?" I asked.

"No. I'll put them on up here, while you take *your* bath."

"Whatever. But at least wrap the towel around you on your way back up, or I'll have people asking me to rent you."

"They miht asciath, butan Ic eom thyn," she said, tossing her towel over her shoulder and going for her bath.

I must have fallen asleep. I awoke to a wonderful smell, like oranges and fresh cut wood, with maybe just a hint of vanilla. Pearl was still in her towel, fiddling with the perfumes in one of her sacks. "Go take your bath," she told me, "and when you come back, I'll be all dressed in my new clothes."

"Give me mine," I said.

"No. I will dress you when you return." Then she sing-songed to me, "Wrap your towel around you, lest I have to fend off renters."

I laughed. "I don't think anybody'd want to rent *me*, Star."

"Gode! Ic should *morthor* hire hwa dyde."

"You'll have to tell me what that means later," I said as I left.

"Nought tellan!" she called after me.

A warm bath, with soap and a scratchy old cloth, is a very wonderful thing. When I'd dried off a bit, I wrapped the skimpy towel around me, and was ready to scurry back to the room. Through a big archway, I could see the dining room. It had gotten full. "Hey, honey," a very large woman, smoking a pipe, called to me. "How about rentin' me what's in that towel!"

Her fellow diners laughed, and I along with them. "I'm with a very dangerous girl," I called back. "I'm afraid she'd whip us both!"

The diners and the large lady laughed harder. But the big lady must have sucked some food down her windpipe, because she began to choke. For a minute, it looked pretty serious, and I was afraid I was going to have to give myself up as an Apprentice to save her. Just as I was starting toward her, she stopped her choking, and shouted, "Gollam! Felt like a hand about my throat!" Then she started to laugh again, and I made my escape to the stairs.

For some reason, I couldn't stop thinking about what the large lady said. "Like a hand about my throat." It so distracted me that I failed to notice Starshine standing demurely for me in her new clothes. Then I heard her stomp her foot.

"Look!" she insisted.

"Yowza!" I said. Star was wearing a little yellow summer-dress made of some flimsy fabric. Around her neck was a string of tiny, white shells, and a thin snake of gold wrapped three times around her upper right arm. On her feet she wore sandals, adorned with the same shells as her necklace. On her left ankle, she wore a very fine chain of gold, exquisitely made. She'd probably had to give two or three of our coins for it. "You are a princess, aren't you?" I said, becoming physically impressed by her beauty.

"Thyn," she said, coming into my arms.

"I might be wet," I warned her.

"Ic miht beon, eke," she purred. "Sweve me in min lufuc gowne."

I never did get to try on my new clothes till the following morning, as Starshine and sleep, in that order, occupied me that night. When I awoke, Star was already up and gone. I wasn't sure if I liked the idea of her wandering around by herself. I hadn't gotten it into my mind, yet, that she was dangerous, but I must have been premonitating a bit. Occasionally, Apprentices do that, though I think it might really just be subconscious cogitating. I think my mind was adding things up, and one of those things was that big lady choking, and something Star had said in her archaic Inglish. There was something about the sound of the word "morthor" that I didn't like.

Unfortunately, I was more in the mood for breakfast than cogitation. I expected to find Starshine in the dining room, with a face full of skillet cakes and syrup, but she wasn't there.

Rosie the barmaid was working again, and saw me sit down at a table. "Have a good sleep?" she asked me.

"Yes, thanks. How about *you*? You worked last night, now you're back again for breakfast?"

"I own the place, darlin'. Just between me and you, *I'm* The Ginny Stud."

I had to laugh. "I thought you had a little twinkle in your eye for Star!" I said.

"I never mess with another feller's girl. If I did, I'd steal them away and lose all my costumers," she laughed. Then she added, more seriously, "I don't think I could steal Starshine, though, she's seriously set on *you*. I'll bet you've got her wrapped in your little finger, don't you?"

"The other way around," I assured her.

"Ain't it always so!" she laughed. "What'll you have for breakfast?"

I ordered cow steak and skillet cakes, and then asked Rosie if she'd seen Star.

"She beat you down by an hour. I don't know where she's gone, but I can tell she's a shopper. She'll probably wander in with a croaker-sack before you're done eatin'. If not, just sit back and drink some wine. She'll run out of coin eventually."

"Thanks, Stud," I said, as she went to fetch my breakfast.

"Hush," she called back to me. "Now don't let that get around."

Somehow, I was sure that *everybody* knew Rosie was The Ginny Stud. It's the way of village life, everybody knows everything. Sooner or later, they'd find out Star and I were Apprentice. I hoped it would be later. In fact, I hoped we'd be gone before that happened. If Rosie had known I was an Apprentice, she'd never have spoken so casually with me. I *like* people, and want them to be at ease with me, though sometimes, I'd like to tell them a tale or two. You have to admit, I've *got* some tales!

I took Rosie's advice, and had a small cup of wine after breakfast. She even slipped me a little cigar, and said, "On the house. It's just tobaccy."

I expected Star any minute for about an hour. Then I got up and headed for the door. "Good luck!" Rosie called as I left.

"See you for dinner," I called back.

I hadn't realized it was dim in the inn till I stepped out into broad daylight. It was already hot, though I thought I could detect just a hint of seasons changing. I would welcome cooler weather.

Wherever Star had gotten to, I couldn't find her. Apprentices aren't supposed to panic, so I kept it down to extreme anxiety. Though most men I come across are reasonably good, there are bad ones, and Starshine was extremely pretty. She was also dressed in fine clothes, and was wearing expensive jewelry. This is what I was thinking about, and it wasn't helping, when I heard her, clear as a bell, in my mind. "Do not worry so, min lufu. I will join you for dinner, and will be your dessert. Now go play in the village," she said, her voice going singy. "Your princess is very busy."

"Star?" I called in my thoughts. "Starshine?" but she didn't answer. "Well," I thought, "I've got all day to work myself up into giving her a good scolding. What I *ought* to do is give her a *spanking!*" but the more I thought about *that*, the less my mind could concentrate on scolding.

How I went from spanking Star, to buying her a present, was beyond me, but it shouldn't have been. I'd just said it to Rosie; she had me wrapped in her little finger. Then I started thinking about Pearl. Eventually, I was going to have to deal with that problem, but it had only been three days. She probably wouldn't have come up yet, anyway. Originally, I had thought to let her sleep on her sea for a week or two. That would be a good bit of healing. In a week or two, I'd check on her, and that mollified the guilt I was just beginning to feel.

I was starting to feel that guilt, because I knew I was becoming quite addicted to Star. Yes, that's right, people can become addicted to one another, and Star was such a *lovely* little pill. Rosie had been right about her voice, too, it *could* be hypnotizing, when she wanted it to be. And to prove it, there I was, wondering where the helluva she was, as I searched for a present to buy her. I was beginning to wonder if Thirest had really known just how dangerous love could be.

I was sitting in The Stud, drinking wine, with a present for Star in the pocket of the new shirt she'd bought me. I'd never purchased anything for a girl before, and was honestly excited to see if she'd like it. I'd surprised myself, buying such an expensive thing.

The dinner crowd was filling the place. I was starting to hope nobody would want Star's chair, when in she walked, resplendent in her new outfit, but looking a little weak and thin. Still, she was a gorgeous waif, and turned heads as she made her way to me. "I must eat eat eat!" she said, sitting down. Then she looked in my eyes and smiled. "What *is* it?" she asked, excitedly.

"What is *what*?" I said.

"You've bought me a present, haven't you?" she cooed.

"Now you've spoiled the surprise," I told her, "so I might as well not give it to you!"

She scooted her chair around beside me, and leaned her head on my shoulder. "But I *don't* know what it *is*," she pouted. "And I'm *sure* I'll be surprised."

"Reach in my pocket, and we'll see," I told her.

Gently, she slipped her fingers down my chest and into my pocket. She withdrew them, pulling out a braided silver chain. On it, hung a striking emeril, as big as a cat's eye, held in a little silver hand. "Tis min heorte in thyn hond!" she cried.

"I don't think your heart is green," I told her, beginning to understand her "Aenglish" more and more.

"Ah, but it is," she said. "Tis a *jealous* heart, and very greedy for you! Put it on me, min lufu," she said. Then she looked across the dining room, and called out, waving, "Hello Rosie! I'm very hungry! Come and see my present!"

I could hear a little laughter from some of the male patrons when Star called to Rosie. It was *nervous* laughter. Star's beauty made them nervous, and something else, something she radiated. Or maybe they just understood how dangerous love could be with someone like her.

Rosie and Starshine gushed and cooed over my present. Then Rosie gave me a wink, and said, "I don't know, though, it looks awfully expensive. Do you think she's worth it?"

"I'm not sure, Rosie, what do *you* think?"

"I *am*!" Star insisted, pouting her face.

"She's probably right," Rosie conceded. "But it *really* depends on how well she *thanks* you."

Then Star's face mellowed into a smile, and she said, "He will be *very* well thanked. Don't you think you'll be very well thanked, Spaul?"

"She's a very good little thanker," I told Rosie.

"Yes, I am. But I need a lot of food to give me strength. Do you have the cow's liver?" she asked.

"Sure do," Rosie said.

"And lots of applesauce. And some of that green, like that man has," she said, pointing.

"Them's collards, hon."

"And goat's milk."

"Got cow's milk, sugar."

"Okay. Do you have any oysters?"

"First batch of the year come up today, as a matter of fact."

"Good, bring them for my lover. He's going to need them."

"Medicinal oysters, comin' up!" Rosie laughed. "Now you two kids be good till I get back with your food."

"I'll try," Star said, and I wondered if she would.

"So, tell me," I said when Rosie left for the kitchen, "where *were* you all day?"

"*That's* a surprise for *you*."

"What do you mean?" I asked.

"If I tell you what I mean, it won't be a surprise."

"Well, when do I find out what the surprise is?" I chuckled.

"I will take you there tomorrow. It isn't quite finished, but it's close enough. I love your present so much, Spaul," she said, fingering her emeril, "that I can't wait to show you mine. Now ask me no more, or I'll give you the spanking you thought to give to me, today."

"It isn't nice to read my mind," I told her.

"But I *had* to read *those* thoughts. They were keeping me company."

"Maybe I *will* spank you," I said, trying to keep that image out of my mind.

"I wouldn't stop you, you know," she purred. "You can always do what you will with me. I ceom thyn for plagan. Plagan in me."

That night, after Star was so pliant in play, I dreamed of Pearl wearing the emeril. It was definitely Pearl. Though it may be hard to imagine, Pearl and Star look very different to me, even wearing the same body, and it was Pearl in my dream. She was crying, her tears falling on that little green gem. "Don't cry," I was telling her, but she had no voice to speak back. Then she placed her hands over her heart and faded away. I woke with a start, to find myself covered in sweat. Starshine was smiling in her sleep, with one hand touching the emeril. She'd worn it to bed. "I'm in big trouble," I whispered. "Really, really big trouble."

Vague dreams of Pearl tormented my sleep all that night. Finally, before dawn, they ceased, and I fell into an oblivious sleep. When I woke from it, morning was several hours old, and Star was not in bed. "Shite!" I said, jumping up and into my clothes. I hurried downstairs to the dining room, hoping to find her at a table covered with breakfast. She was turning into an award-winning eater.

As soon as I got down there, Rosie came up to me. "Starshine said for you to eat breakfast," she told me matter-of-factly.

166

"You don't happen to know where she went, do you?" I asked.

"She's working on your surprise."

"*What* surprise?" I really wanted to know.

"Come on, now, honey. You'll feel a lot better with skillet cakes and eggs and bacon in you." Then she raised her eyebrows, smiled hugely, and said, "And some nice hot chocolate!"

"Where'd you get chocolate?" I asked, momentarily distracted by the oddity she'd mentioned.

Rosie went conspiratorial, whispering to me, "Star left it for you, but don't tell her I told you. It's our little secret."

"When's she coming back?" I also really wanted to know.

"Relax, Spaul, Starshine knows what she's doing. You just listen to her, okay?" Then, believe it or not, Rosie's voice went sing-songy just like Stars. "Now sit in this chair while Rosie fixes your breakfast, okay?"

"What the helluva was that?" I was thinking, as Rosie wandered slowly back to her kitchen. "Starshine knows what she's doing?" I knew Rosie liked Star, was maybe even attracted to her, but Rosie had believed her to be what she *appeared* to be, a shoppy little scatterbrain. Which she *was*, but she was also, of course, a *lot* more.

Rosie wasn't sounding like Rosie this morning, Star was gone again, and *where* had Star gotten *chocolate?* Gold and silver and old coins and jewels she could raise from the ground, but you don't mine chocolate. Suddenly I wished I could talk to Pearl, but Pearl was asleep in that scatterbrained cutie-pie. I had my elbows on the table and my head in my hands, when Rosie arrived singing, "Who wants hot chocolate?" I was *seriously* in trouble.

I sat at that table until Star came back. It was at least noon, and the place was packed with lunch customers. Starshine actually made an "entrance." She was gorgeous, of course, and I noticed right away that she'd acquired new bangles, including gold rings in her ears. "Hello everybody!" she sang to the crowded room, and I could hear happy voices saying "Hello," and "How are you?" and some where even saying her name, "Nice to see you, Starshine!" Our girl was getting mighty popular.

As soon as Star entered, I noticed Rosie rushing to her kitchen. By the time Star sat down, Rosie was setting a plate of liver and applesauce in front of her. "Thank you, Rosie," she purred like a kitten. "I'm *very* hungry. Bring Spaul a cow steak, okay?"

"Where have you been?" I insisted.

"Spaul, don't yell at her while she's eating!" Rosie scolded.

"I'm not yelling!" I pretty much yelled.

"You've upset poor Rosemary, Spaul. You must learn to be nice to her," Starshine told me. "Now give me a kiss, or I'll eat three desserts and make you wait longer for your surprise."

Believe it or not, I gave her a kiss, and sat there, dumb, while she ate and ate. I was getting a very bad feeling. Starshine fingered that emeril I'd given her all the while. It sparkled in her fingers, as she gazed at me with adoring eyes.

After lunch, we started our trek toward Star's surprise. We left the village to the west, and set off down a newly cut road. I was wondering why Star hadn't wanted to use the lines to travel this very straight trail, when she said, "There are still workmen about. They don't know we're Apprentice, yet, and I see no reason to tell them."

"You know I don't like you reading my mind," I said.

"Oh, did I? I thought you spoke!" Then she giggled and kissed me on the cheek.

When we'd walked about a kilometer, Starshine said, "Okay, now close your eyes."

"Do I have to?" I asked, not as happy as I might have been.

"Yes," she insisted. "Don't worry, I'll hold your hand. I promise not to walk you into a tree," which was precisely what I felt was happening to me.

After walking a little farther, Star stopped us and said, "Okay! Open them!"

Her surprise was very surprising. "What's this?" I asked her.

"Our cottage!" she announced. And what a cottage it was. I have to admit, it was the most beautiful dwelling I'd ever seen.

On a freshly cleared half-acre or so, sat this wonderful house. It was built with white logs, and roofed with green sod, and had morning glories, jasmine, and honeysuckle growing all the way up its sides. The windows, all of them, had panes of glass. Though it certainly wasn't Rufus' house at Tara, it was very large, and centered in the newly cleared lot. Though there weren't any stumps directly around the house, I noticed some around the perimeter of the clearing. Apparently, the trees hadn't been sawed or chopped down, but *broken off* very near the ground. "You built this, didn't you? That's why you've been eating so much!" I said.

"Gesse, min lufu. I built it for you and our children. Pretty soon I will have a *very* big belly. And *winter* will come. We need a place to be, and I think we should make Ginny ours. Wait till you see the inside!"

As she started pulling me toward the house, two men with a muley pulling a cart wandered up the road. "Oh look, it's our bathing tub!" Star squealed. "I had them find one big enough for *two*!"

"Stove's comin' too, right behind us," one of the men yelled to her.

"Stove?" I asked. "Can you cook?"

"I could if I wanted to," she said, pretending to pout. "But I won't need to. Just wait. There are *lots* of surprises, and you can't have them all at once!"

Inside, Star dragged me from room to room to room. In the back of the house, in a corner bedroom, was an *enormous*, eiderdown bed covered with pillows. Everywhere in the house shelves where hung, and lamps and knickknacks of every description adorned them. On the mantle, over a huge, stone fireplace, hung a portrait of Star, wearing her emeril. "I had an artist do that just for you," she told me.

"In a day!" I exclaimed.

"I speeded her up, a bit, but she never even noticed," Star whispered.

"You're not supposed to do that to people!" I admonished.

"I know," she said, pretending contrition, "but I wanted it *now*!"

"And how did you *build* this so quickly? Did you get Zephrae to lift for you? I thought they can only lift *up*, not sideways. And how did you make *glass*?"

"That's Fierae glass, see how green and thick it is! I had them make it on Ginny's Beach, then I got craftsmen to polish and cut it for me."

"But how did you get from here to the beach, and back? Did you fall down the lines that far?"

169

"I didn't go to the beach, silly, I was working on our cottage. Now stop asking so many questions. I built it, and that's enough! There are *many* things I can do that you don't know about. If you're very good, I'll teach them to you."

"Star, I need to talk to you," I said, just as one of the men with the donkey cart stuck his head in the door.

"Where do you want this bathing tub, lady!" he hollered.

"If you call me 'lady,' you must call me 'Lady Starshine,'" she told him, her voice gone so soothing I actually felt my muscles relax.

"Yes, Lady Starshine. Where shall we put your tub?"

After the men with the tub, came the men with the stove, the men with the furniture, the men with the trunk full of clothes, a butcher, a baker, and someone Star hadn't bought anything from, who felt slighted and made the trip to see if he could correct the oversight. I believe he was selling candles.

By the time this procession of merchants ended, it was early evening. I wanted to talk to Star, but I was hungry. "Let's catch a ride on that last muley cart," I told her, "and go to The Stud for dinner."

"No! You're going to spoil my next surprise!" she told me.

"But I'm *hungry!*" I said.

"Come have a piece of cheese and some wine till my surprise gets here. You can tell me how much you love our new home."

Thirest had told me an Apprentices home is World. It was what I was thinking when Starshine said, as if to herself, "And so it shall be. Just wait."

As wine and cheese settled my grumbling stomach, I said to Star, "We have got to talk."

"I love to talk with you," she said, plopping down into my lap. "Spekan, min lufu, tellan me Ic eom faeger ond lufuc."

I knew this was not going to be an easy conversation, and I didn't really know where to begin. Star solved the problem for me. "We can't let her out," she said, in a very final tone. "She's an evil, dark witch, as I've told you. If you let her out, she'll steal you away from me, she'll enchant you, and you won't want to love me! Pretty soon, she'll be so deep we won't have to worry about her anymore.

"What do you mean, she'll be so deep?" I asked. I was getting a little scared, now.

"Never you mind. Here comes your next surprise, up the road. Wait till you see who's here!"

Starshine hopped off my lap, and ran to the door, throwing it open. Then she called to whoever was coming, "Hello! Hurry, come quick! You're just what I need to pacify my hungry king!"

A few seconds later, *Rosie* entered the house, followed by two very fine looking girls. All *three* of them wore new dresses, in pretty pastels. At the inn, Rosie had always worn trousers under her big, white apron. I'd never seen her in a dress, and I really didn't think it suited her.

"Rosie can wear trousers if she pleases," Star told me, "but she *likes* the dress I bought her."

"I *like* the dress," Rosie echoed.

"Rosemary is going to cook and keep our house, and these two girls will be her helpers. She picked them out herself." To this Rosie, The Ginny Stud, smiled immensely. "Their room is the one with the great big bed. Our room is on *this* side of the house."

"There's no bed in there," I said, wondering why I was even discussing beds. This whole thing was absurd! Pearl was coming back! And even if she wasn't, Star was definitely abusing her Apprentice gift! *How* had she built this house in a day? Could she really compel the Elementals? *Was* she compelling them? "What about your inn, Rosie," I asked.

"I sold it," she told me.

"You *sold* it?"

"Gesse, she sold it to me for a goodly sum, didn't you?" Starshine said. "And *I* sold it to a man from Rolly, and took quite a loss on the deal. See what I do for my friends!"

"You're a darlin', Starshine," Rosie said, coming over and pecking Star with a kiss.

"And they're all staying in that back room?" I asked, looking the lovely girls over again."

"Girls *always* like someone to sleep with, Spaul. They'll be very comfy in that great big bed," Star told me.

"I'd imagine," I said, still looking at the girls, and noticing Rosie's cheeks blushing out like apples.

"Nought don folgian theos lasses, min cyning," Star said, squinting her eyes at me, "or Ic wille tige thyn wesule to min bedd!"

"I don't know what that means," I told her.

"It means, don't touch!"

Rosie and her assistants went off toward the kitchen. "Oh wait, let me get the stove going for you," Star called after them. "Okay," she said, half a moment later, "it's ready!"

"*Star!*" I said. "We need to have a long discussion, *alone,* do you understand?"

"We shall be alone in bed as soon as we've had our dinner," she said, her voice soothing my muscles again.

"There's no bed in that room," I told her again.

"It's on its way. I hear them coming now. Wait till you see it. It's made all of brass and silver, and ninety-two bushels of eiderdown fill the mattress. Sweve me deop in the down to niht, min lufu, Ic eom thyn cwen!"

Rosie and her girls were over an hour preparing dinner. Starshine kept pouring me wine and cooing to me, in her soothing voice, about getting a kitty, growing a garden, the possible future dimensions of her belly, our children's names, trips to the beach, me taking a bath with her after dinner (and particulars that she mostly spoke in her Aenglish,) getting a puppy, candles she'd bought that smelled of perfume, building a barn for her mulies and goats, having a bamboo cage made, getting a birdie to put in her cage, and probably two dozen more things that I'd drunk enough wine (by that time) not to hear. I was going to have to save our conversation for bed, if for no other reason than I couldn't get a word in edgewise. Starshine was excited, and full of plans. I was going to have to pull out her plug, or plug up her pulleys, or however that saying goes.

After dinner, once Rosie and the girls had finished cleaning up, Starshine took out three cups and filled them with wine. From the bottom cabinet of a china closet she'd purchased for the dining room, she fetched the jug the slaves had given me, the jug that held her potion. Into two of the cups of wine, she poured one drop of the elixir. After stowing the potion back in the cabinet, she picked up the cup she *hadn't* spiked, and called to the kitchen, "Rosie, you and the girls come and have some wine."

172

"You know, I don't even know those girl's names," I said.

"Good," she told me.

When Rosie came into the room, Star handed her the wine she was holding. "There are cups for the girls on the table," she said. "Take the girls, and another bottle of wine, and play in your room. Spaul and I may want to frolic in our new house. I'll see you all in the morning."

The two girls picked up their fortified wine, and said, in unison, "Good-night, Lady Starshine."

"Good-night, girls."

"Good-night, darlin'," Rosie said, kissing Star's cheek.

"Be *comfy* in your nice new bed," Starshine sang to them all. Then, turning to me, "And we shall be comfy, too. Our bathing tub is full!"

I went with her, and didn't say a word. At least I knew where her potion was. I hated the fact that she trusted me, though she may have simply thought she had no need to. Her majick was so fug-all powerful, she may have thought she had her thumb under me.

While we were in our bath, and she was washing my back, I decided to try and talk to her again. "Star," I said, "don't you know we can't just leave Pearl in her sea? Think of all we went through to get her back. We're going to have to think of a way for you two to share, take turns up here. Don't you think that's a good idea?"

"Now, Spaul," she said, as if talking to a child, "you know she'd leave *me* on her sea. Besides, I told you, she's evil, an wicce deorce. She doesn't love you like I do, or *need* you like I do. And she certainly wouldn't take *care* of you. She's caused you nothing but trouble. You've said yourself, she is reckless. We will speak of this no more."

"We have to talk about it, Star..." I was starting to say, when she giggled and her Naiadae in the tub did a number on me that I couldn't even *begin* to describe. At some point, she got out of the bath, and wrapped herself in a fluffy robe. "Are you going to be good, or should I keep you in there for a while longer?" she asked.

I was so in the grip of this ecstasy she was inflicting on me that I barely managed to say, "I will."

"I'll come and get you in an hour, then," she smiled, "just to make sure."

173

I was really scared when she finally let me out of that tub (though it was very hard to be scared while I was in it). She could probably incapacitate me anytime and anywhere with her elemental love games. Star could turn me into an orgy of one whenever she wanted. I couldn't help wondering how many other men would be scared by that.

I climbed into the eiderdown, worn to a frazzle by that extra-long bath. Star had candles burning that smelled of jasmine. She was wearing a tiny gown that seemed to be made of opaque Air, and actually was. As she came toward the bed, it dissipated and flew away. "I'm ready for you, my precious king," she sang, crawling onto me.

"You did me in with your Naiadae," I told her, thinking maybe that would restrain her next time.

"You must sweve me eafre niht, min cyning. That is all I ask."

"That is *not* all you ask, Star. You ask me to abandon Pearl. You ask me to live in this fairae tale with you. You don't even ask, you tell!"

She'd backed off and was sitting beside me, looking down into my eyes, fingering her emeril, which was all she was wearing. The candlelight danced on it like sparks, as she said, in her pretty voice, "Do you want to make me cry, Spaul? I'll cry for you if you like."

I looked up at her eyes, and could see the tears falling down her cheeks toward the smile on her face. "Sweve me, nu," she sang, and it became my only thought.

The smell of the air in the room was intoxicating. Star looked much too good, even for her. I knew she was working a spell on me, even as I moved toward her. "Is this how you want me to love you," I managed to say, "majicked and coerced?"

Then her smile faded, and her tears disappeared. "No," she said, releasing me from whatever spell I was under. "If you won't love me, I'll love you, till you're ready to take your turn, of your own accord. Until then, it gives me pleasure to give it to you."

When she said that, her Zephrae cocooned me, and floated me just above the eiderdown. It was worse (better?) than the bath had been. At some point I started wondering if she'd ever get tired and go to sleep. Finally, she did, and an hour later her Zephres stopped playing with me. Until I could stop her and rescue Pearl, I would have to love Star as she wanted me to. I would not survive much more elemental love.

It was probably past the thirteenth hour when the Zephrae ungently dropped me into the down. It ended as if someone had blown out a candle. There's really no way to think while that's being done to you, and since you've almost assuredly never experienced it, well, you'll just never know. But, believe me, you *can't*, so I decided to try and to do some thinking then, while Star was asleep, and my body wasn't being so pleasantly tortured.

To get Pearl back, I was going to have to majick the intoxicants out of Star's potion, which is not so easy as it is to say. I had some idea of what was in it, but I'd probably have to take some, then figure out what it was in my body. I'd have to neutralize it inside me to know how to do it while it slept in its jug. The problem was, what I could do in my body, I might or night not be able to do outside it. Apprentices are taught to transmute poisons in ourselves. Even ethnyl can be neutraled, but it's a hard one because you're usually drinking it on purpose. By the time you decide you'd like to neutralize it, you're too buzzed up to be able to do it. That would be one of the problems with Star's potion. I had no idea what it would do to me, or how quickly it would do it. I'd have to work fast. Once it took me over, I might not be able to cogitate.

That's what I was thinking about when I fell asleep, and Pearl came to me in a dream so clear it was more like a vision. She wasn't crying this time, nor was she wearing the emeril. In this vision, she appeared as I'd seen her last in her light-body, wearing the glowing little tunic. The expression on her face seemed sad, but also resolute. I found myself wanting to touch her cheek, when she said, "You know enough not to *touch* me, don't you?"

"I don't blame you for being mad," I said.

"There *is* that, too," she told me, "but we're in our light-bodies. Don't you see it?"

"Yes," I said, feeling (or *not* feeling) it now. "But how...where are we?"

"I've linked our seas for a moment, built a bridge between them, and we're standing on it. I won't be able to do this again, so we must devise our strategy now. Star will drink the potion again tomorrow. She's delayed taking it by a day in order to do all this majick you're only just learning about."

"So the potion affects her, too?" I asked.

"It is *very* strong. She mostly channels it to my sea, but right after she takes it, for about a day, she's limited, can't do the kind of extreme majick she's been doing here in Ginny. She's sending me deep into my sea with the potion, Spaul. After she takes it tomorrow, I may not even be able to call to you in dream, as I did last night. I certainly won't be able to build this bridge again."

"What must we do?" I said.

"I am doing all I'll be able to do right now. If you can't transmute her potion without her realizing it's neutralized, she'll send me so deep I'll never be able to rise. Then she won't need the potion any longer, and all is lost."

"Is there some way I could imprison her, keep her from drinking that stuff until you can rise?"

"I don't think you realize how powerful she is," Pearl told me.

"I'm getting a fair idea," I assured her.

"Your best chance for success, I believe, is to change the potion, neutralize it without her knowing it. But if worse comes to worse, you must somehow give her more of it, more than she can channel. That would send her here, to the depths of my sea."

"*Then* what would happen?" I asked.

"Then you would have two choices, let my body die, or try to keep it alive until our children are born. Either way, both Star and I are lost, and I fear our children would be damaged."

"Is there any scenario that isn't quite so *dire*?" I said. "Because what you're saying is, I've pretty much killed you, and our children as well." I could feel myself falling into despair.

"Remember where you are, Spaul. Dispel your anguish *now*, or you will not awaken sane in the morning."

"Sorry," I said, calming my sea beneath me. "I will rescue you!" I said resolutely. "I'll get you back!"

"You didn't send me here, Spaul, I want you to remember that. I came of my own accord. You were tricked into keeping me here by a majick far greater than yours, and the siren song of a very convincing false love. Even Starshine must not be blamed. She was never meant to inhabit a human body, except during love. When I left her alone in it all that time, she changed, though her love was still true, then. Had I not come back, I think you two would have done just fine. It was my return that drove her beyond her emotional capacities. Being torn from you, and the love between you, was too much for her to bear."

"So there's no way to talk her out of this," I said, with no question in my voice.

"No, and you must not try again. From here on it must be subterfuge. You must make her believe you're succumbed to her, and that won't be easy, she's shrewd, and hides it in cuteness and false innocence. She is everything she's told you I would become. In her mind, she is the white witch foiling the dark. If all else fails, you must give her the potion. The Fierae plan will be ruined, of course, but things will be much worse if Star is allowed to establish her reign."

"Her reign?" I asked.

"She will subjugate World, Spaul. And with our daughter as her ally, she could compel *all* the Elementals, and World herself. She would *become* World, and humans would not even engage her as playthings anymore. It was I who fugged things up, Spaul, not you. I should have listened to you, my love, when you warned me against conversing with the Fierae. I *was* reckless. Please find a way to forgive me."

"Now don't you despair," I told her. "Buck up! You don't think I'd take you *away* from your father, then abandon you, do you?"

"You didn't take me, Spaul."

"But I *did*," I told her. "I was on my way back to get you when you showed up riding those lines."

"Of course you were. I should have known and waited. Our moment is almost over, Spaul. Now listen, don't take the potion if you can help it. It's too strong. It's a psychotropic infusion with hypnotic properties. Place my little mirror in a bowl and fill it with water, then sprinkle vinegar into it. The potion is very alkaline, and vinegar will give the Naiadae an idea of what you want to do. Then you must peer into the mirror, and find them in your eyes, tell them what you want them to do. I know you think that's beyond you, but have faith in yourself. Pour the water into her potion. If you succeed, I'll be able to rise in no less than three days, perhaps four or five. You won't be able to stop her taking that dose tomorrow, so don't even try. She'll be weak for a day after taking it, and that is when you must act."

"I understand," I assured her.

"I have no regrets about our time together, Spaul, except that I did not heed your love and its warning. Do your best, or do your worst. One way or the other, you must stop her."

I was telling her I loved her and trying not to despair as she faded away into her sea. Then I was wide-awake in the eiderdown, watching the last little perfumed candle sputter and go out.

I did sleep that night, and much more soundly than I'd have thought possible. Being with Pearl must have calmed my sea. I awoke to breakfast smells, alone in bed. I was just about to get up, when one of the pretty girls tapped on the door, then came into the room with a tray. "Breakfast, my lord," she said.

"Call me Spaul," I told her.

"Oh no, my lord. Lady Starshine wouldn't like it. She's very clear about things like that. I must do exactly as she tells me."

"What about what *I* tell you?" I asked, curious to see if there was a flaw in the spell this girl was obviously under. There was.

A little giggle escaped her lips, and the pretty girl said to me, "I don't *know*. What would you have me do?"

Just then, Star came into the room, the expression on her face less than cheery. "Go to your room," she told the girl, taking the tray from her. "I'll be in to speak with you in a minute."

"She didn't do anything," I said to Star when the girl was gone.

"Nor will she," Star muttered. Then her expression changed, and she was her perky self again. "Sit up and let me feed you, min cyning. I've little strawberries here that will sit sweetly on my tongue."

I looked at the tray full of food, and said, "No hot chocolate?"

"Oh!" she squealed. "You *liked* it, then? I will bring more today, I promise."

"Where did you *get* it?" I asked.

"I tasted it far to the south, in a place called Mec Seco. I have my Terrae swallow it up and bring it to me, just like my Fierae glass from the beach. But there's really no reason for you to learn this majick. I will fetch you whatever you want, from anywhere in World."

"You wouldn't hurt that girl, would you?" I asked, as off-handedly as I could.

"I hurt *no* one. I ceom hire cwen!"

"Come here, my pretty love," I said, "and feed me a strawberry." I was getting ready for some subterfuge.

Several strawberries later, I had to start trying to remember what I was doing. Star's beauty and playfulness did something to me, even without the addition of her majick. But I steeled myself, and said as innocently as possible, "Have you taken your potion again yet? It's been at least three days, hasn't it?"

"Gesse, min lufu, you are right, I must take it today, right after I bring you chocolate from Mec Seco. I think you are feeling better this morning, are you not?"

"I feel like I missed loving you last night," I said.

"Did my Zephrae not satisfy?"

"I'd rather love you," I said, taking her into my arms.

"Then perhaps you should sweve me, nu," she whispered.

"I will," I said.

I was surprised at how shy she still went under my touch. It was as if she became, once again, the Star I'd known on the beach. My subterfuge always failed when I loved her like that. It was always sincere. I knew she could feel it, and it became the basis for her trust. To say I was conflicted in love would be true, but in purpose I was resolute. I knew what was at stake. I would kill everything I loved, including my children, whom I'd never known, to avoid the catastrophe Pearl had foreseen. My life had gone dire with ominous happenings. I had always believed being Apprentice was the greatest, most noble and powerful thing one could be. Now I knew I was *just* an Apprentice, aligned against powers that dwarfed me, and threatened to steal my World.

When Star had recovered from my love, something she always needed to do, she went to the bedroom door and called out, in a happy, singy voice, "Rosie, there's chocolate coming! Run out and fetch it, it will be on the ground by the front stoop." Then to me, she said, "Shall I have her make you a cup, min lufu?"

"I just had all the sweetness I'll need for a while," I told her, watching how ready she was to believe what was once again subterfuge.

"You make me so happy, min cyning," she said, fingering her emeril in the morning light. It was hard for me to look away when she did that, and harder to concentrate afterward. I was beginning to wonder about that gift. While the emeril itself might have been my choice, I was pretty sure the idea to buy her a present had not been. She was forming some kind of majick with that jewel. It probably didn't matter what I'd bought her, she was making a power over me out of the connection made by the *giving* of it. She also seemed to be using the gem itself to influence others, but it was a different majick than she was using on me.

As soon as I realized this, I also knew that kind of majick could work both ways. I would cogitate on it later. I hadn't even gotten out of bed yet that morning, and I was ready for a nap. I was already drowsy when Star came back to me and sat on the bed. "Sleep more, min lufu, I will go take my potion, now. Soon we'll nought need to worry about the dark queen. But first I must go have a little talk with Rosemary's girl, Lily. She will make no more advances toward you, I promise. She's really a good girl, she was just a little confused."

"Be gentle," I said, still worried about what she might do to that girl.

"I'll let my Zephrae be gentle, and send Rosie to comfort her after they're done. I'm still Apprentice, you know, Spaul, I do not *harm*. I give only pleasure, and seek only loyalty in return. Lily will be loyal to me, and loyal to you, and to Rosie, who takes such good care of min cyning and me. Everyone must be happy, I absolutely insist."

I awoke again just before noon, and felt very refreshed and confident. I was going to rescue Pearl, and stop all this craziness. Then I noticed Pearl's old pack sitting in a corner of the room. Good! Step one, liberate her little mirror. I found it wrapped in its cloth, and protected by majick that was nearly faded away. I reinforced it, and slid the mirror under the mattress. The next time I was sure I could be alone, I'd bring a bowl of water and vinegar into the bedroom, and try to commune with the Naiadae.

180

Star was eating cows liver when I came out of our room. I noticed it was very rare. She was eating liver three times a day, now, and I began to realize that, though her majick was very powerful, it took quite a toll on her physically. She seemed thinner, and her complexion had dulled. This gave me an idea. It might not help much, but a lot of littles can make a big. "Liver again?" I asked her.

"Gesse," she said, sounding a little disgusted, "and I do not like it. Rosie! Bring some more applesauce!" Then, back to me, she said, "It is a sacrifice I make to secure our future. I have many things still to do, and many that I am maintaining. Sometimes my Elementals are uncooperative, and then it takes so much more of my strength to make them...to have them perform as I desire." Suddenly her face developed a very real pout, which turned into tears and sobs. "It is *so* very hard, being queen. I have to give so *much!*"

I sat and told her to come to me, then I put her in my lap and wrapped my arms around her. "*And* you're *pregnant*," I told her. "I don't want you doing so much. I don't want you eating raw liver all the time. I want you to eat *oysters* so you'll be anxious for me at night. I want you to each chocolate pie with cream."

"You're so good to me, Spaul," she wept on my shoulder. "I haven't appreciated you enough." Then she sat up with a start, stopped her sobbing, and said, "I wonder if I drank the cow's blood?"

"You'll do no such thing," I told her. "You must teach me enough to be able to help you. I don't want all this majick your doing to hurt you *or* our children."

"So cute, min lufu, but I would *never* hurt our children. I will teach you whatever you'd like to learn, but it will be a long time before you can help me. No, I'm afraid it's going to be cow's blood for me, but I'll have Rosie make us a chocolate pie, and we'll eat it together after our love."

"Still," I told her, "teach me. I want to help, even if only in a small way. Teach me to be better with the Naiadae, I've always had trouble with them."

"They're easy," she told me. "On our wedding day, I'll teach you a grand trick with them."

"Wedding day?" I asked, not sure what that meant.

"In three days time, we're to be married. It's what keeps me so very *busy*, silly. Preparations! And on that day, when we're husband and wife, we shall also have our coronation. Though I know I am already queen, and you are my king, it won't be official till then. And I'll teach you that Naiadae trick right after." Then she giggled, and added, "We're going to need *lots* of subjects."

I knew Star was unbalanced, but it seemed to me to be getting worse. Wedding days and coronations? I was beginning to understand that getting her back to Pearl's sea was not only for the good of World, but for Star's own good as well. But sometimes, and I've hated myself for this, I wondered what life would have been like with Star if Pearl had never come back. I really had loved her, and still did, and to show my love now, I'd have to put her away from me forever.

When Star "had time" that day, she gave me a lesson in Naiadae Majick. But mostly she sat, glassy-eyed, in a chair she'd had made that rocked. I'd seen one like it in Rufus' home at Tara, but never did get around to sitting in it. It looked very comfortable and soothing.

Sometimes Star rocked gently, sometimes furiously, but often she sat stone still and wide-eyed. She was working Lords only knew what kind of majick. Sometimes, as she sat with those far away eyes, inky black clouds would start to gather, then her eyes would come back from wherever they'd been, and she'd look out a window and say, "Stop that!" and the clouds would disappear.

I knew she was compelling the elements, and wondered how angry she could make them and still maintain control. If it weren't for her having to take that potion, I think her powers would have grown much faster. Just a few more times and she wouldn't need it anymore to keep Pearl imprisoned. Time was on her side, unless I worked quickly. I was hoping her teaching me with the Naiadae would give me a better chance to do the trick with Pearl's mirror. But there just wasn't time for more lessons. I needed to get Star out of the house. I needed the time, and time was running out, but I had an idea.

Activity at the house began to increase the following day. Muley carts loaded with tables and chairs and casks of wine were constantly arriving, unloading, and leaving again. Rosie seemed unperturbed by it all, and glided around directing the confusion as if it was what she most loved to do. The other two girls helped her, though the one called Lily seemed a bit listless and wan. The other one, whose name, I'd discovered, was Tamlyn, bounced around quite excited by it all, and paid particular attention to the boys who unloaded the carts. Lily stayed very close to Rosie.

I found Star in her rocking chair. When I walked in she was drinking out of a large mug. At first, she didn't see me. When the mug came away from her lips, they were red, and a little line of blood dripped down her chin. "That does it," I announced, startling her. Quickly she wiped her mouth. "It's too late for that," I told her. "You're drinking cow's blood, aren't you?"

"Well..." she began, but I stopped her.

"No more!" I insisted. "I want you to rest. Didn't you say our wedding day would make us King and Queen?"

"*That* will make us husband and wife. Our *coronation* will make us king and queen."

"But it's all on the same day, right?" I asked. "Have you gotten us suitable crowns?" I had to keep from laughing at how ridiculous that sounded.

"Why, *no*! I've forgotten all about it! I must start searching," she said, sitting back in her chair and closing her eyes.

"No!" I insisted louder. "No more majick today. I want you to take Rosie and go into the village. No using the lines, either. Catch a ride on one of the muley carts. Find a good craftsman and have him make our crowns. And no speeding him up. He has two days left to do it, okay? Will you do that for me, for thyn cyning?"

"Gesse," Starshine answered, getting up and throwing her arms around me. "Gesse, min cyning, I will do as you command. You are *right*, I need a diversion. And it will be good for me to walk amongst our people once more before I'm officially queen. I shall take Rosemary and Tamlyn with me. Lily I'll leave to serve you while we're gone."

"Take all three with you," I said, walking her to the door to look out at the confusion in the yard. "I'll be fine alone. I have this endless procession of carts to amuse me."

"No," she said. "I will not leave you without a servant. I absolutely trust Lily, now, though I shall have to keep an eye on Tamlyn. *Look!* I believe she's flirting with that boy!"

"That's what girls do, sometimes," I said.

"Not *Rosie's* girls. If she isn't careful, she's going to get a talking to, which would be a shame, Rosie likes her the way she is."

"What?" I asked, a little confused.

"Rosie!" Star called. "Tell the man with that cart to wait, we're riding with him into Ginny. And bring Tamlyn along. You must keep an eye on that girl!"

I watched and waved and smiled as Star rode away with Tamlyn and Rosie on the back of a muley cart. As soon as they were out of sight, and I started to close the door, Lily came up the stairs. "How can I serve you, my lord," she said, sounding tired and looking drawn.

"I want you to sit in Star's chair that rocks, and keep it warm for her. Can you do that for me?"

"Yes, my lord."

I guided Lily to the chair, and sat her in it. When I did, I noticed she'd somehow cut herself on the wrist. It seemed to be a deep, nasty gash. "I'll come get you in a while, and fix this cut," I told her.

When I mentioned her wound, Lily looked at it as if she hadn't known it was there. Then a tear fell out of her eye. She looked so pitiful, that I took her behind the house right then and put her arm into the ground. "It'll only take a minute," I told her, "then you'll be good as new."

"Rosie didn't take me with her," she said, starting to sob a little.

"She'll be back for dinner," I told her.

"Promise?" she said, so pitifully I didn't know whether to laugh or cry.

"I promise," I told her. "There, now, look, your arm is all healed. Go wash the dirt off and then sit in Lady Starshine's chair, okay?"

"Yes, my lord."

That hadn't taken long, but I found myself hurrying, and had to stop to calm my sea. I had plenty of time. I found a large bowl, and half filled it with water, then sprinkled vinegar into it. I came out of the kitchen and saw that Lily was sitting very still in Starshine's chair. Good. It was time to be an Apprentice, though I knew the majick I needed to work was very deep.

I must have been at it five or six hours. Finally, I had to stop, and hope I'd gotten my point across to the Naiadae. I couldn't trust Star to be gone much longer. If she caught me doing this I was truly fugged. If I lost her trust, she could keep me Zephrae cocooned or soaking in the tub until Pearl was too deep to rise again. I took my majicked water, poured some into the jug, and shook it up. "Please work!" I said out loud.

I'd forgotten about Lily in the other room, who must have heard me, and said, "What work shall I do, my lord?"

"Is the chair nice and warm?" I called to her.

"Oh, yes!"

"Good, then go to your room and take a nap. You've had a very long day."

That night, after dinner and endless descriptions of what our crowns were going to look like, Pearl got out her cups and poured three full of wine for the girls. Then she got her jug, and dribbled a drop into only one of them. She saw me watching, and said, "A single drop will soothe the rambunctious, and make them, well, more agreeable." Apparently Star trusted me completely, now, to the point of believing me complicit. I definitely needed that trust, as she was quite insane.

"Who's the rambunctious one?" I asked.

"Tamlyn. She's not so obedient as Lily. But Rosie likes her, and this will make her quite compliant."

When the cups had been distributed, Tamlyn getting the spiked one, Starshine bid the girls sleep-well, and fetched a chocolate pie from the kitchen. "This is for after you love me," she said. "I feel so much better! I must listen to you more often. You are, after all, my king."

Love had made Star playful, and chocolate pie was all over both of us. I was licking some off her ear, when, through her squeals and giggles, I heard a ruckus out in the house. The girls, it seemed, were having a row. "*What* in *World!*" Star said, jumping up and throwing on her robe.

She was out of the room like an arrow loosed. I almost didn't follow, but curiosity, and need of a napkin, got the better of me. What I saw and heard would give me hope, then take it away again.

It was Tamlyn who was most upset, and making the lion's share of noise. "I don't *want* to, anymore," she was shouting at Rosie, onto whom Lily was clinging. "I don't *like* it! I want to go home!"

185

"What's going on?" Starshine demanded, stomping her little bare foot.

"Tamlyn won't play," Lily said softly, hanging on tighter to Rosie.

Starshine spun around to face me, and whispered, "I *saw* her drink that wine." Then she spun back around to the girls, stomped her foot again, and said, "Hush! Tamlyn, would you like a nice cup of wine?"

"No! I want to go home!"

Once again, Starshine spun and whispered, "Pay attention. Here's some Naiadae majick for you to learn." Then she actually winked and blew me a kiss.

By the time Star spun back around to the girls, Tamlyn was soaking wet, condensed all over by the Naiadae. Star turned her head to me and said, "See how I had them make the water warm? Now, listen to their singing, hear the song I teach them."

Suddenly, Tamlyn went quiet, then her body twitched and she started to moan. "She'll be good, now, Rosie," Star said. "Tomorrow I'll have a little talk with her, or find you a different one, whatever you like. Run along now, you three. Be comfy!"

Back in our room, I said to Star, "What was that all about?"

"Oh, silly girl games. They'll disturb us no more tonight. What I *don't* understand is how that drop of potion didn't work. I *saw* her drink it."

"Maybe you got the cups switched around," I said, realizing, now, that my majick must have worked.

"No, I didn't. I suppose it *could* be fading, but it *shouldn't*, not so soon. It's a very powerful draught. None-the-less, I shouldn't take chances. I should brew a new batch."

"There's no hurry," I told her. "You just took some yesterday."

"Yes, and it was working quite well, then, too. I could feel it. Could that silly girl have grown immune?"

"I'll bet that's it," I said.

"It's curious and curious," Star said to herself. "But I'll know for sure the day of our wedding. I'll know if it's any good the minute I take it again. Now come and feed me pie. I want chocolate pie kisses to put me to sleep."

Star would be paying strict attention when she took that potion again. She'd know it was no longer potent. I'd managed the majick, but hadn't counted on Tamlyn the flirt to give it away. It might have worked, but who knew. She might have detected my tampering anyway. Things were looking grim.

I was sure, now, that Star was abusing people. Everyone in this house (possibly even me) was under her majick to some degree. I didn't realize how bad it had become until the following morning, when I saw how quiet and docile Tamlyn had turned. Later that day, a shock of fear ran through me, when I saw the cut on her wrist, right where Lily's had been. Not only was Star taming these girls for Rosie, she was drinking them as well. There was no confronting her, she was far more blind to her megalomania than even Rufus had been. Soon, she'd no longer pretend to be doing no harm, or perhaps that day had already dawned. She wasn't even healing the girls' wrists. Her insanity seemed to be growing with her majick.

The night Star Quieted Tamlyn, after she'd fallen asleep with chocolate pie on her lips, I tried to call to Pearl. There was only silence on her sea. That last dose of potion must have sent her deep. But I resolved to try every night, hoping she'd come up enough between doses for me to call her. If nothing else, and in case all else failed, I wanted to say good-bye. I wanted to say I was sorry I hadn't been stronger. I wished, now, that she *had* remained with the Fierae, instead of coming back to me to die.

I didn't fix Tamlyn's wrist. I wondered if Star had noticed I'd healed Lily's. The wedding/coronation would take place the following day, and I hoped against hope that the commotion and confusion would keep Star from brewing another potion. But that night, my hopes were dashed, as Star went over her plans with me. "I will need all my strength, tomorrow, for our very big day," she said. "When the guests have all gone, when husband and wife are king and queen, I'll try the old potion again. If it's lost its potency, I'll find out what I did wrong when I made it and correct all its faults. Then, on the first full day of our reign, I'll brew a new, perfected, more potent batch. My first act as queen will be to dispatch my nemesis once and for all, and banish her from the minds of any who thought to remember her."

It was a warning to me, I knew. Star suspected my tampering, and would find out tomorrow, after the coronation, when she tested her brew. Though she might have still wanted me willingly, I knew she wouldn't hesitate, now, to make me docile, to turn me into her pet. But I would not go as easily as Rosie's girls. I planned to fight. It would be a fight to the death.

When Star finally tired of anticipating the events of the following day, she fell asleep in my arms. With my head touching hers, I called to Pearl, and saw her sleeping face, vague and distant, painted in my mind. "Sleep," I told her. "I'll free you soon, though it may be to a different place than here."

She was fading away when her eyes opened. In a voice I could barely hear, she said, "Yes. Don't hesitate."

Sleep finally stole me from my despair, just before Star woke me. "It is our day!" she said, kissing me. "Rejoice!"

No matter how much I needed to keep up appearances, I could not eat. Nor could I make myself smile. I wanted to take Star by the shoulders and shake her, tell her she was killing Pearl, and herself, and our children. I wanted to tell her that her mind was gone, that she was harming people, that she was drinking these poor girls' blood. I almost did, I almost told her, because it would have saved her and our children, and even Pearl, though she'd never escape the depths of her sea. It would have saved them because Star would have stopped me right then, pacified me and made me her slave. But when my thoughts stopped on that word, everything changed. Star had become a slaver of the vilest sort. Her whip was pleasure, and her shackles, complacency. She was enslaving people without their even knowing it. Her word for it was "efyl."

Star knew something was wrong, but she couldn't read my mind. I'd put a stop to that days ago, but it was harder, now. She could only read thoughts that were mixed with emotion. One can *feel* without emoting, it's an Apprentice discipline called "spoking," but don't ask me why. All I know of a "spoke" is that it's something on a wheel. You figure it out.

Anyway, I'd been spoking for days, and was still able to keep it up, even through my growing despair and anguish. Thirest had taught me well, and I silently thanked him. Finally, as I sat with Star, staring despondently over a table full of breakfast, she said,

"What is it, min lufu? Are you having second thoughts? Are you getting cold feet?" She was smiling. It was some kind of joke, but I didn't understand it.

"My feet are warm," I told her. Then I felt my resolve return. She absolutely *must* trust me. "And my only thoughts are of you."

"I know, min cyning. You're just nervous. It's too much excitement, wedding and crowning all in a day. Let me give you your bath and relax you with my Naiadae."

"No!" I said, too abruptly. Then I calmed and started again. "No. I want no such pleasures until you are in my arms tonight, as my wife and my queen. No love till I sweve you again. No love till then."

Starshine came over and dropped into my lap, put her arms around my neck. "You have always been everything to me, Spaul. Even as a sleepy Charge, I loved you." There was actually a tear in her eye as she spoke, and I believed her. Even through her insanity, the love we'd known came through. And even through that love, I would kill her at my first opportunity.

I bathed myself, sat in that warm embrace and tried to relax, calm my sea, cage my emotion. I would have to get through this day. There was nothing I could do to stop it. I could not act against Star until she tried her potion again. If by some miracle, she couldn't tell it had been neutralized, then I wouldn't be forced to kill. But in my weary heart, I knew that wouldn't happen. She was much too strong, now. She'd know. She'd probably even be able to tell that it was me, who had undone its potency. At the very least, she'd suspect. I'd just have to wait and see, and that meant getting through this day, through this madness, this coronation of insanity.

Star insisted on dressing me. The outfit she wanted me to wear was too bizarre for me to describe. I hardly even noticed as she clad me in it, with its ribbons and ruffles and bows. The shoes bore large, silver buckles, and felt like heavy boxes clumsying my feet. When she was finally satisfied with the clothes, and the way my hair was fixed, she touched me here and there with her fingers wet with perfume. Then she said, "There! You are a king! Look!"

She was pointing to one wall of the room, which suddenly began to shimmer. By some cooperation of Air and Water, the

Naiadae and Zephrae caused the wall to reflect. I looked as ridiculous as I felt and smelled. "It's a wonder," I said to Star, trying to decipher how she'd done that trick.

For some reason, Star wouldn't let me stay while she dressed. "When next you see me, I'll be a bride," she said. "Now go sit in my rocking chair and relax. If you decided to eat, put a towel over you. Rosie will tell you what to do when it's time."

Getting me dressed had taken quite a while, though my woeful state of mind was playing tricks with time, and I hadn't realized. Outside the house were a throng of people, more than I'd ever seen gathered in one place. I'd seen little carnivals here and there in my travels, and this looked like four or five of those combined. People were dressed in outrageous clothes. Tables were laden with food and casks of wine and something these people called beer.

A trellis arch had been built over a raised dais, in front of the house. It was covered with ivy and jasmine. Cut flowers were everywhere, and their scent was on the gentle breeze. For such a large crowd of people, milling about with nothing to do but eat and drink, they seemed subdued, quite calm, and conversation droned at a steady low hum.

I stood at a front window, looking out over this scene for quite a while. How had my life become entangled in such strange events? If only Thirest knew how profoundly true his warnings to me about love had been. I'd allowed myself to love *one* girl, but an entourage of other lovers had come along with her. And, of course, there'd been the Fierae, with their plan to save man from the dying off of the Apprentices. Had their plan been flawed from the start, or had we fugged it up? It would have worked if Pearl hadn't insisted on talking to the Fierae. It might have worked again, if she hadn't come back. Should I try to keep her body alive, save the children? No. "I fear our children would be damaged," she'd told me. I'd allow no one else to be ruined by this failed plan. When I'd done for Star, I'd let them all go. Then I'd find a Charge and join with the Fierae one more time, body and all.

I was going to sit in Star's chair, when Rosie came up to me wearing some kind of shiny, flowing robe that touched the floor. I'd never seen anything like it. "What is that you're wearing?" I asked her.

"Oh!" she said, as if she'd forgotten all about her attire. "I'm the priest."

"I'd heard that world somewhere, but didn't even bother to ask her about it. It didn't matter. It was just one more insanity to crowd the ever-growing list. "It's time," she told me, taking me by the arm and leading me toward the door.

"Where's Star?" I asked.

"We have to go out on that dais, then she'll come. I'll bet you can't wait to see her."

"I wouldn't if I were you," I told her. Then she led me out and all those people applauded. I actually heard several of them say, "It's the king."

It seemed I'd been standing on that dais with Rosie for quite some time when, suddenly, some musicians began to play. I didn't recognize their song, which sounded rather pompous and overdone. Then the door to the house opened, and Rosie's girls came out, dressed in lavender gowns that were quite audacious. They were carrying baskets of flowers, which they tossed on the grass between the stoop and the dais. Then Star appeared at the door.

The dress she wore reminded me of Rufus' party. It was nearly too large to fit through the jams of the door. White as cloud, and sparkling with some sort of Naiadae majick, she looked like a magnificent angel come to take us all out to heaven. Over her head, she wore a netted veil, which paled her brown skin beneath. Tiny white flowers were woven all through her hair.

I expected her to walk down the stairs and onto the flowers the girls had laid, but apparently her desire of spectacle had grown. She no longer cared about hiding her majick. Though no one else could, I saw the two mag lines she was calling between herself and our perch. Slowly, the Zephrae pushed her out onto them, and she floated to me like a fairae princess in a tale told to sleepy children.

Was she beautiful? More so than you can imagine. Did I love her? I did, and it made me want to cry. I wished I could kill her right then, and build a bunker in which to preserve her beauty for a thousand years. I imagined taking new Apprentices there to see her, and telling them, "If you ever see one coming, run!"

Then she was standing next to me. "You're very pretty," I told her, as I'd told Pearl a million years ago in that little room at her father's house.

191

"Gesse," she answered. "And you are a handsome prince."

"Now what?" I asked, as she seemed to be bathing in the splendor of her moment.

"Now Rosie will marry us," she whispered. "She can read, and I've written it all down for her, what she must say."

"I didn't know you can write," I said, clinging to mundane talk to keep from being blown away by this tempest of lunacy.

"I'm not *ignorant*," she giggled, though she seemed a touch miffed. "I know what there is to know."

"Of course you do," I said, as I stood their wanting to release her of all knowledge and majick and breath. It may be the worst thing in World, to long for the demise of what you love most. It's a curse that rises from nightmare and fever and delirium, then hangs in the air like a rotten stench that clings to your skin.

"Dearly beloved!" Rosie sang out, dragging my awareness back to this bizarre scene. "We have come together to witness the marriage of Starshine and Spaul, the future King and Queen of Ginny!"

"Future!" I thought. What a strange word to use for something that would happen the very same day. But it *was* appropriate. The future was crowding me, growing too close, becoming a hallway that leads to a wall. I wanted no part of it, but futures and pasts, it suddenly seemed, were inviolable. Even as your hands devised them, they twisted your fingers to shape themselves in spite of you.

Rosie spoke, but I no longer heard her. I was back at the beach with Pearl, tangled on her blankets in our little nest of sand. I was lost in this reminiscence, and it's a wonder Star didn't see it in my mind. Then I heard Rosie whispering to me, with some kind of urgency, "The *ring*! Give her the ring!"

"What ring?" I asked, wanting to jump in the sea and rinse off the sand.

"It's in your pocket, silly," Star said. I reached into my pants and, sure enough, a ring was there.

It ended with a kiss, which Star took ravenously from my lips. "Forever and ever," she said, "you will be mine. Till world refuses to turn, and the Ball no longer rises."

"That's a very long time, you'll grow tired of me," I told her.

"Oh, no!" I will *not*! My imagination runs infinite, and will keep us amused for a million years!" she sang.

"Now what?" I asked, wanting off of this dais.

"Now we'll have a bit of cake, and drink some wine. Then I must change into my coronation gown, though I love being a bride, and would linger a bit all dressed in white."

"What's your hurry?" I said. "If I understand this correctly, you're only a bride one time, unless I die."

"Oh no! You will not die! I *forbid* it!" she said, and a tear formed in her eye.

"I will live as long as you are alive," I told her, kissing her again, and wiping her tear away.

"I will remain a bride for a while," she told me. "Now come see the wonderful cake I've had made!"

Though the people seemed happy, they also seemed somewhat dull, somewhat sluggish. They congratulated us, and I wondered if they knew what for. Had they ever seen someone marriaged before? I doubted it, but who knew. The Apprentices were dying off, perhaps our influence was already gone. Perhaps people were falling into the wicked ways of the Ancients. But it didn't matter. Soon the Elementals would be blind again, and blow the rest of mankind off the face of World. Then even they would go unaware, and World would cease to be.

Sometime in the afternoon, Star disappeared, and left me alone to be patted on the back, and toasted over and over. I drank too much wine, which was stupid, so I quickly neutraled some of the ethnyl in my blood. This was no time to abandon myself. Tonight Star would drink her potion, and I'd need to be ready for whatever ensued. I'd made it through the wedding, now I must stand and allow myself to be crowned. Great King Spaul, I'd become, ruler of Ginny and all of doomed World! For a moment I wondered what would happen if I allowed Star to live. Would it be better for World and mankind to survive in the grip of her Passions? Pearl hadn't thought so, and neither did I. "All things pass," Thirest once told me, though I'm sure he hadn't anticipated all things passing at once.

When Star reappeared, she floated once more to the dais. The gown she wore now was as ostentatious as her wedding clothes had been, but this one was very blue, almost indigo. Red and white periwinkle flowers adorned her hair, and she wore her emeril on top of her bodice, where it glistened in the afternoon light.

As she floated, she held her arms out to me, and I felt two mag lines rising under my hands. In a moment I was on my way toward her, as the crowd oo-ed and ah-ed. It will all be over soon, I kept thinking. She'll drop crowns on our heads, and these people will go away. I'll be left alone to do murder, so they all might live their lives in blissful ignorance. Just as the Ancients had done, they'll ignore every portent of doom until their tiny lives are stepped on, like invisible gnats underfoot.

Rosie was already on the dais, holding our crowns on a big, red pillow. Star's was gold, studded all over with emerils of many sizes. "You should wear that when you cook," I told her.

"I'll not *cook*," she told me, as if I was being too silly.

The crown she'd had made for me was silver, and covered with gems of every description. "Do you like it?" she asked.

"Best crown I've ever had," I said, and she giggled.

"People of Ginny!" Rosie called out. "Thank providence that you are here to see your queen and king come to their reign! You will be the *first* of their people, always treasured in their thoughts!"

The musicians began to play again, and Rosie took one crown in each hand. Then she placed them upon our heads and cried out, "Queen Starshine! King Spaul! Rejoice!"

Star played with her emeril in her fingers, as the crowd of people yelled, "Long live the Queen and her King! Long may they reign!"

Through the noise of their cheers, I said to Star, "I'd like a piece of that chocolate pie, and some milk. These people should go home, now, and leave us to ourselves, don't you think?"

"Not *yet*," she said to me, smiling. "I must give them the first gift of my reign, which will be a gift to us as well. "My people!" she called, and the crowd went silent. "I give you all a present, now, to ensure our happy future. To my ladies, I give fertile bellies, like dark, rich earth, ready to sow! To my men, I give these ladies' soil, to plow deep, and plant with their seed!"

As she said this, thin clouds gathered, but did not obscure the Ball. Then a fine rain fell, that sparkled in the descended light of day. I watched as the people sighed and moaned, while Starshine's Naiadae played on them. Soon they started pairing off, some heading toward the woods, others beginning to love right where they stood. Before long, there was not a soul standing, all were frantic with love. Even Rosie's girls had been gathered up and taken to mate by some boy or other. Only Rosie was alone, though she, too, seemed under the spell of the rain. "Hmm," Star said, "I should find a girl for Rosie. I can't have *her* pregnant, you know."

When she'd picked out a girl she expected Rosie would like, Star put them together, and said to me, "There, now everyone's happy. Shall we go in the house, min lufu. They'll wander back to the village before long to continue their loving, and we'll have each other to ourselves."

"And all the women will be with child?" I asked, watching this thing take place that she'd called down from the clouds.

"All except Rosie. I need her unencumbered."

I was pretty much out of it by the time we went in the house. I'd witnessed too much, but if nothing else, I'd seen enough to know I'd never allow Star to continue her maniacal reign.

I'd eaten nothing but a forced bite of cake all that day, and was hungry. I went to the kitchen, as Star wandered off to our room. I was pouring milk into a cup, which sat beside a chocolate pie I intended to eat. I wanted to make myself sick with it, as punishment for being hungry after all I'd seen. As I exited the kitchen with milk and my pie, I saw Starshine. She was dressed in that little gown she liked to form out of air, and purred to me, "Cuman ond sweve me, min lufu, tis ure weddung niht. Bring your pie, and I'll feed it to you, and kiss it from your lips."

How she did this next bit of majick, I'll never know, but at that moment my clothes seemed to simply unravel, and fall as a pile of threads to the floor. "Come now," she sang, taking me by the wrist, "and make me your wife for true."

I couldn't. I simply could not. You might think such a spectacle as occurred at our coronation would make one itchy to love, but it had quite the opposite affect on me. Even when Starshine spooned the creamy chocolate into my mouth on her tongue, I remained unmoved. "I'm sorry," I told her. "It was just too much excitement for me today. Come and let me hold you while we sleep."

195

But Starshine was undeterred, and smiling wickedly, putting pie on me and then licking it off. She'd never done anything like that before, and though it surprised me, it also worked, and sparked my arousal. Then she straddled her body over me, and did our loving herself. Apparently, her shyness had finally waned. For a moment, she reminded me of Pearl.

When Star's first love to me was over, she laid herself out in my arms. "See how much I love you, my king? But don't make me do it too often, I'd so rather be beneath your touch."

After a little while of silence, during which I found myself starting to drowse, Starshine said softly into my ear, "My potion, it seems, has weakened by more than half. It's curious how such a strong thing as that could diminish all by itself, corked tightly into a jug. But it doesn't matter. Tomorrow I will concoct another, stronger brew, and I'll drink as much as I dare. It might make me a little drowsy, which would be a wonderful time for you to sweve me, but I think it will also send my nemesis queen very deep. One more time after that, and she'll no longer be a concern. I shall keep the diminished potion for Rosie's new girls. Three or four drops before bed should be just the perfect thing."

"New girls?" I asked.

"Gesse. Those other two have gone listless. Rosie needs stronger help to manage our home."

Star suspected my tampering with the potion, I was sure, though I believed she was uncertain. If she did take enough of the new one she'd brew, to drowse her, that would be my chance. If all worked well, Queen Starshine's reign would come to an end the day after it began.

When Star fell asleep in my arms, I tried to contact Pearl. It would be my last chance to do so. I was hoping the weakened potion, and so many days since Star had last taken any, would allow me to call her. Before long I saw her asleep on her sea, but almost immediately her eyes opened. She saw me and smiled. "Don't grieve," she whispered. "Don't discard your life over me. World needs its apprentice. Live and remember."

"I will," I lied, but tears came into her eyes.

"No," she whispered, as she faded away. "Please live."

196

XIX
Falling Star

I was surprised when Star asked me to help her gather the plants she needed to brew her new potion. "Just find the same things as you did the last time, and I'll gather the rest," she told me. "We will do this together, on our first full day as royals. Our first great deed as queen and king will be to send our only enemy on her way to an inescapable dungeon."

"How will you know when she's gone?" I asked.

"This dose, and one more, will send her too deep to rise, but she'll never truly be gone. I need her on my sea, or I'd become the little nitwit I was before she returned."

"I loved that little nitwit," I told her, feeling suddenly angry with her, as if she'd been the one to destroy that Star I'd loved.

"I know, min lufu," she said, making a pincer with her fingers and grabbing my nose. "I will always be thyn crabba. I am always here for you, any way you'd like, and once I've sent the dark witch deep, nothing can ever take me from you again. So gather my plants, and come back to me soon. I'm anxious to boil my brew."

When Star had everything she needed, we went to the kitchen, where she started a pot full of water boiling. "I'll do this, min lufu, go sit and rock. Rosie will be here soon to cook. They should all have been loved out by morning, but I told Rosie to stay in Ginny till she found us a couple of girls that were to her liking. I was reluctant to let her go off with the crowd, but I wanted us to be truly alone on our wedding night. Are you glad we were?" she asked.

"Of course," I said. "But I want to stay with you while you make your potion. As you've said, it's a thing we both should do."

"Gesse. We should. Crush these morning glory seeds for me and put them into the pot." Then she sing-songed to me, "Don't get any in your mouth. I don't want you seeing things that aren't there. You might imagine a young girl to play with instead of me."

"I'd send her back to the land of hallucinations," I said, "and love you instead."

197

When, finally, that noxious brew was boiled, the whole kitchen stank of it. "Throw open the window," Star said. "Though I don't think these vapors would affect you, it smells as bad as it tastes. Hand me that big jar with the lid, if you please."

Once she'd filled the jar with her potion, Star said to me, "Put this in the cabinet with the jug. Tonight, when it's cool, I'll take it, and then you can love me while I drowse."

I did as she asked, just as Rosie came in the door. She seemed quite lively to me, the way she'd been when she ran the inn. "Let me get to my kitchen," she said, scooting around me. "I'm going to make you a special desert for tonight."

When she entered the kitchen, where Star still stood, she said, "Phew! It smells like a cartload of shite in here!"

"Now Rosie," Star said, "don't be vulgar."

I watched as Rosie cocked her head and stared as Starshine fondled her emeril.

"I'm going for a walk," I said, as that idea seemed to jump into my head.

"Gesse," Star said. "A good idea. I shall have a bath while you're gone. Work up a sweat, and I'll bathe you when you return."

"I didn't know where to go, and really didn't feel like walking after all. Instead, I sat under the lattice arch, on the dais where Star and I'd had crowns place upon our heads. "Tonight," I thought, "once Star's taken the potion, I must find a way to get more of it into her!" That would not be easy, as foul as it tasted and smelled. As I sat there, scheming murder, I watched little clouds roil and fight in the sky. When I listened, I could hear the Lesser Three grumbling sleepily their anger at being compelled. But it was very subdued, and then ceased altogether. Star was powerful indeed, and I wondered what the elements would do when she was no longer there to restrain them.

The rest of that day was strange, considering what I intended to do. I allowed myself to enjoy Star's company, and let myself love her the way I had before she'd changed. Perhaps she could sense that love, because she was happy, and played her crabba game like she used to. "Remember the time you hid from me on the beach?" she asked, and of course, I did.

"That was bad of me," I told her. "Do you remember how sorry I was?"

"Gesse. But you shouldn't have been. Sometimes lessons need to be taught. I never did wander away from you again, did I?"

"No, you didn't. But I still felt awfully bad. I was just beginning to realize how much I loved you."

"I already loved you, had *always*," she said, showing me eyes gone shy. "Now come, let me give you a bath. I will give you your medicine, the way you used to give it to me."

So that day went, as if nothing untoward in our lives was happening. It turned out that Star hadn't bathed after all while I'd been out on the dais, so we climbed in the tub together. Afterward, we walked, and I put little flowers into her hair. We kissed gently under the trees at the edge of our clearing. As we walked back toward the house, Star hummed a tune in her Fierae voice that soothed me as only she could.

Rosie's new girls arrived just before dinner. They reminded me very much of Tamlyn and Lily. Rosie put them to work in the kitchen, as Star and I sat at the table sipping wine. "I'm excited," Star said, smiling widely at me.

"What has you excited?" I asked.

"I *mean*, I'm ex*cited*!" she said, making me understand.

"Well, you'll just have to wait," I told her. "Be patient, my love. Let your passion build, and once you've taken your potion, I'll fondle you unmercifully, and make you beg me to stop."

"You'll hear no such pleas from me," she assured me. "So be ready with many ideas for my lovely torture. I'll be very pliable and willing within the influence of my brew, so please feel free to take advantage of me."

If she only knew, I thought. Then I wondered if she actually did, if she was setting some sort of trap. No, I could see the lust building in her eyes and smile. Tonight, I would love her to death.

After dinner, Rosie set two cups of something chocolate on the table in front of us. "That's called 'mouse,' which is a kind of pudding," she told us. "It's a very old recipe that I learned from my grandmother. Of course, we made it with fruit, not chocolate, back then. If we'd had any chocolate, we certainly wouldn't have eaten it. It would have been like eating gold."

When Rosie went back to her kitchen, I leaned across the table and whispered, "Let's save it, to eat tonight. I'm going to make you very hungry, my love."

"We shall then," she whispered back. "I'll pour wine for these girls, now, and send them all off to bed."

"And we'll be alone," I told her.

"All by ourselves," she smiled. "Go fetch us some perfumed candles from the closet by Rosie's room, while I fix their wine. Try to find ones that smell of jasmine."

"Whatever you like," I said.

I met the girls coming down the hall with their cups of wine. "Good-night, Spaul," Rosie said, to which the girls both giggled. "I mean, your highness," Rosie corrected.

"Good-night, sire," the girls said in unison through their giggles.

When I got back to Star with the candles, she said, "I've had a very big drink of my potion. Take me to bed quick, it makes me tipsy already."

I swept her up into my arms, and said, "We'll take no chances. I'll carry you off to your just desserts."

"Oh yes," she said, "don't forget our chocolate mice."

"I'll come get them later, when you appear in need of something to sustain you."

"*You* sustain me, min cyning."

"Maybe, but I'm preparing to *drain* you now!"

It wasn't so much drowsy, as *dopey* that the potion made Star. Her eyes became glassy and seemed slightly crossed. But she really did become quite submissive, which made her even cuter, and piqued my curiosity as well as my desire.

Our night of love quickly became shenanigans in the bed, and at one point I told her to lie across my lap so that I could spank her. "Have I been bad?" she asked, as she complied with my demand.

"No, I just feel like spanking you," I told her.

"Good. Then I *want* you to," she said.

200

It amazed me that I couldn't bring myself to spank her hard, yet I intended to kill her later. "Harder!" she insisted. "If you don't make me cry, it's no spanking at all!"

Instead, I kissed her bottom, and laid her back down in the bed. Then I fondled her till she begged for my love, which I gave her hard, and for a very long time. When she was sweaty and spent, I told her to lie still while I fed her chocolate mouse to give her strength for our next bout. "I think you *like* me like this, all buzzed and drugged," she said.

"It's your eyes," I told her, "they shine and make me want you. Now rest till I get back."

"Wear your robe," she said, as I was about to leave the room naked. "What if the girls come out and see you?"

"Then they'll have to be spanked," I said, going naked anyway.

"But *I'll* do *that* spanking," she said. "I want you spanking no tushes but mine."

I had to force myself to stop shaking, as I stood at the china closet preparing to construct the instrument of Star's destruction. Kneeling down, I opened the cabinet and retrieved the big jar that sat next to the jug. Then I removed (and ate) several spoonfuls of the chocolate from one of the cups. I'd be lucky to get one good bite of this foul stuff into her before she tasted it, even mixed with the chocolate. I needed it to be strong. When the deadly mouse was ready, I took an empty cup and filled it with the potion, then replaced the jar back into its cabinet. "Don't think," I told myself. "One way or the other, it will all be over in a minute."

When I entered our room, I pretended to be drinking out of the cup full of potion. "Where is *your* mouse?" Star asked me.

"I felt like wine, instead," I told her. "Now give me a kiss, then lie still and let me feed you."

I kissed her hard and had to make myself stop. I did *not* want to do what *had* to be done. "Mmm, you kiss like there's no tomorrow," She said.

"Open!" I told her, scooping a heap of the poison chocolate onto a spoon."

"It's too *much!*" she squealed.

"Open *wider!*" I commanded. "And I want you to swallow *every bit*, all at once! I want you practiced for what *else* I might have in mind."

201

Star opened obediently, and I put the spoon of mouse on the back of her tongue. "Take it! Swallow!" I told her, and she did.

She made a terrible face, and cried, "It's *awful*, what a horrible taste!"

"Here," I said, grabbing the cup full of potion, "drink some wine to wash it down."

Before she knew what was happening, she'd swallowed two big gulps. Then her eyes went wide and she knocked the cup from my hand. "Spaul! What have you *done*?"

"What I had to," I whispered, with tears running down my face. "What I had no choice but to do."

She wanted to run, but I held her. I thought she might scream, but instead, she went limp in my arms. The potion I'd given her, on top of what she'd already taken, was working fast. Faster than I'd expected it to. Before long, her breathing went shallow, and her eyes glazed as she stared up at me. "I'm so sorry," I told her in sobs that I could not control. "I've only ever wanted to protect you. Oh Lords, look what I've done!"

"Don't cry, min lufu," she whispered, her eyes beginning to lose focus. "It's *me*. It's *Starshine*. I've been bad, haven't I, Spaul?"

"No, my love, it was *none* of it your fault. It was dire deeds and schemes of the mighty that stole our tiny lives. You're going to rest now, with Pearl, on her sea. Soon I'll join you both where there is no pain."

"Spaul," she spoke, and I could barely hear her. "I'm scared out here, beon min hus."

"I will always be your house. You will always live in me," I cried, my tears bleeding from my heart to my eyes. "I will always love you, Star. Please, know that I love you."

Then she closed her eyes and I was alone. Suddenly I knew the most dangerous thing about love.

How long I stayed like that, with her in my arms, I don't know. The sobs and gasps that came from me threatened to tear me apart. I had never known such a grief. My love was dead and I had killed her, though her body still breathed in my arms, and her beauty refused to fade. Not only had I killed Star, but Pearl as well. I thought for a moment to stop her breathing and end it now, but I couldn't.

Instead, I crawled into bed, and held her beside me, as the wind outside the house began to moan.

I don't think I slept, but it's hard to tell when you're living a nightmare. I think I spoke, at times, out loud to Star and Pearl. I thought of drinking the potion, and I thought of cutting my throat. But my anguish was a far worse punishment than any I could think to inflict on myself, so I let it have its way, and continued to live.

Night finally fled the torment of that room. The light of day, dimmed by a storm, fell over me and the evidence of my crime. She looked so alive, as if she was merely sleeping, and she was, but she'd never wake. So I lay there and listened to the storm grow louder, as the day wore away, and night, once again, sealed us into its tomb.

I might have just lain there till both of us died of hunger and thirst. I certainly had no will to live beyond what the body of my lovers would endure. But the storm became fierce, and my sea had calmed enough to hear the Elementals screaming. The wanted destruction, *now*, both body and sea, of the one who'd compelled them. "Talk to the Fierae!" I screamed in my mind. "It was *they* who wrought this horror. DAMN YOU ALL!" I howled, and for a moment the wind went calm, and the driving rain ceased. As if I had scared them silent with my curse. As if some great power, insane with grief, had come into their midst.

Slowly, tentatively, the storm came up, but seemed now to be a debate rather than a death sentence. I got up and put on a robe, pulled covers up around my poor, gone love.

No one was in the house when I wandered out of our room. Rosie and her girls must have fled as Star's spells and majick were abruptly cleared from their minds. Though I'm very unclear about what I was thinking then, I remember seeing that other cup of mouse sitting on the table. I may have been thinking to eat it, or perhaps I was going to throw it across the room. But when I got to it, a note was on the table beside it. "I'm going home," it read. "I want my inn back. What did you do to those girls? What did you do to me?"

That was all it said, but those words rang angry in my head. I wondered how many more angry people there were in Ginny, as I fetched two bottles of wine and went back to bed.

"Angry and pregnant," I laughed, as I drank myself stupid. "Here's to Ginny," I said, sloshing wine, "home of the annual bastard's birthday party!"

I'm not sure how many days I passed like that, though it couldn't have been too many. Pearl's body was still alive, and I didn't expect it to live very long. There was no way to make her drink without choking her, and I didn't even try to devise a way. I was waiting for that finality to occur. I wanted that one last grief to punish me further. But she was still alive when the rising storm woke me from wine induced oblivion. Then I could hear what was coming, vaguely sounding in my mind.

As a rule, I cannot read minds, or hear other people's thoughts. Or, who knows, perhaps I simply can't distinguish them from my own. But that many minds, all at once, shouting for my destruction, I couldn't help but hear. The people of Ginny were on their way. When I cleared my sea and concentrated, I could hear it quite well, a chorus of anger and threat. As best I could tell, Star had ceased even paying for all the things she took. And, of course, there was the matter of the orgy she'd made of them. Now that their minds were clear, she'd become a monster, and they were coming with torches and pitchforks and hoes, to take their revenge. They'd be here within the hour. I poured another cup of wine, and took Pearl's body into my arms. "Do your worst," I said to the coming crowd, as I pulled her head onto my shoulder. "You can't kill what's already dead."

I wasn't going to let them in when they got to the house. I was still a very strong Apprentice, and could easily keep them out. But I wouldn't stop their torches from burning down our cottage. It was what they intended to do, I was sure.

It seemed fitting that Pearl and Star and I should be taken together by fire. We were, after all, very much Fierae, though I was the least. Fire would sanitize all sins, consume all guilt, and return all ash to ash. Flame is so pure, it never discriminates. It will take the guilty as well as the innocent. All it asks of breath is combustion. All it wants from flesh is fuel.

Those torches were on their way, they were close. The storm was ratcheting up, as if inspired. As my last act of majick, I sealed the windows and doors against entry, and shooed as much moisture out of the wood of the house as I could. "Burn quickly, burn hot," I said out loud. "Let my love and I vanish without a trace in this pyre."

"It's very romantic for a story, perhaps, but I think I'd prefer to be dead before you consign my body to flame."

I was mad, now, hearing Pearl's voice making jokes. I turned to her to tell her it was almost over, I could hear them in the yard. Then I saw that something had opened her eyes. "You look at me as though you're awake," I said, about to shut them with my fingers.

"It sounds to *me* as if you're drunk," she said, causing me to jump and drop my cup.

"Pearl?" I gasped.

"Yes, my poor, tormented love, it's me. I've been here with you all this time, wanting to comfort you, but I was struggling to rise."

"But I gave Star the potion. *Lots* of it! How can this be? It was *very* strong, I helped her make it! I was sure I had killed you both!" Then I broke down and cried, as she took me into her arms.

"She *switched* them, Spaul," Pearl said into my ear. "She put the new potion into the jug, and the weak one into the jar. She wasn't sure if it was you who'd weakened it the first time. She wanted to see if you'd try again, but she didn't want her new batch spoiled. I'm actually surprised that what you gave her was enough to send her to my sea, as your majick was still at work, weakening it day by day. It almost seemed as if, at some point, she stopped fighting and came to me willingly. She's resting now, you killed no one, Spaul. I'm sorry it took me so long to rise and tell you. Actually, I wouldn't have made it if Star had opposed me, but she actually *helped*. She sent me to you, to save you, and to save our children. Our daughter will be very much like her. More of her will show in that child than I."

As she spoke, the relief that coursed through me was like rain on a parched desert. I wanted to laugh, to scream, but all I could do was continue to cry. Emotionally, I was an invalid, now. I don't think I could have majicked a spark to light a candle. I tried to kiss Pearl, but her mouth was so dry our lips stuck together. "Give me some of that wine," she said. "The last liquid to pass these lips was that foul tasting potion. I wish we had time to eat, but they're setting fire to the house right now," she said, drinking wine like it was water.

"I take it you don't want to stay for our funeral," I said.

"Not while my eyes are open," she answered. "Now let's put some clothes on and get out of here. You did a gollam good job of drying out this house."

205

"I had a good teacher," I told her.

"I had *two*," she said. "One was a Fierae elemental, the other an Apprentice, who came one day and lured me from my Papa's farm."

"He must have been a real charmer," I said.

"Oh, he was! Now I'm pregnant with twins, and am being chased from my house by a mob!"

"I'm sure he meant well," I told her. "How are we getting out of here?"

"Straight up, my love. I'm afraid this is seeming all too familiar."

"Fierae live to love," I told her, "but I think a good fire amuses them, too." Then I noticed the smoke coming under the door.

"I'm not amused," she said, seeing it, too.

Pearl was concentrating, eyes closed, when the Zephrae finally started buzzing around us. I was wondering why she was having trouble, if struggling to rise had weakened her, when she said, "They're very angry, but I think I've convinced them. Here we go!"

The roof directly above us suddenly blew out. The force of it sucked the bedroom door in, followed by a gout of flame. "Let's go!" I yelled.

"I'm trying!" she assured me. Then, slowly, we rose.

Though the storm didn't touch us in our cocoon, it immediately grew as we floated out into it. I could see the people of Ginny scattering in its increasing wrath. The hole in the roof made a chimney of the cottage, and it exploded into an inferno that seemed to be reaching for us. "Higher!" I said.

"I *know*, higher!" Pearl yelled. "I'm trying!"

Though it took a good while to get there, we were finally very far up. Still, it seemed we couldn't get above the storm, which was a furious tempest all around us. "What now?" I asked

"We're going to have to get out of here. They're seriously thinking about dropping us. The Fierae are trying to calm the Lesser Three, but Star had them righteously angry! Elementals aren't overly concerned with right and wrong, but compulsion the pretty much see as *evil*. Star compelled them to compel other beings. Even the Fierae can't seem to assuage their anger. It's very nearly a civil war out here."

206

Suddenly, I felt a lurch in my stomach. "They're going to drop us!" I yelled.

"I'm calling up lines!" Pearl hollered back. "We'll have to go north, the storm is building from the south."

"Will you be able to get them to stop us?"

"We'll have to go very far, to where the Elementals aren't so mad!"

"Not good for the hands," I told her.

"Look down there," she said, pointing toward the conflagration of flames that was so far beneath us. "If they drop us now, you'll get some use out of your pyre!"

"Yowza! Let's go!"

Pearl had just gotten mag lines under us, when the Zephrae let go. "Did you do that?" I asked her as we grabbed the lines.

"No! They dropped us!"

As we fell on the lines, I was sure the storm was going to blow us off, but it didn't. I could see the lines stretching down into the distance, and it seemed like a very long way to go. I was wondering what life would be like without hands, when a cloud beside us began to glow. Three tendrils of lectricals reached from that light, and wrapped our hands in cold fire. "It's Blitz!" Pearl yelled. "He's charging our hands!"

"Will that work?" I asked her.

"I don't know, it's not something he taught me. But the Fierae don't do anything for no reason. It'll do *something*, I'm sure."

"Can you shield us and make us go faster?" I asked.

"Not yet. We're still in the war zone."

"We seem to be going so slow," I told her.

"It's the storm. They're fighting our escape, but don't worry, I'm fighting back, and so is Blitz. I'm reaching out, even now, to Zephrae who are unconflicted by this fight. I think I'll have a wind shield up before long."

Shortly after she'd said that, the scream of our passage through Air ceased, as she formed a shield. The sky began to clear, showing us stars. "I can't see the ground," I told Pearl.

"Me either, but it shouldn't be long, now. There's no telling how fast we're going."

"It's coming!" I shouted.

"Oh shite!" Pearl answered.

The Zephrae wind she called to stop us hit me in the face like something solid. I was seeing stars that weren't in the sky. Then we were rolling, tumbling over the ground, until we hit something that was, unfortunately, made of stone. I was conscious, but bruised and bleeding. I helped Pearl up, and took her in my arms. "I think we're alive," I told her. "And look! My hands aren't so much as marked!"

"What did we hit?" she asked me, rubbing herself here and there.

"Well I'll be gollammed!" I said, looking down and across the Ninety-five. "It's Mason Dicksin's line! I finally made it!"

XX
Grandpappy

Pearl and I, propped up against Mason Dicksin's wall, watched the storm rage far to the south. "The Fierae will calm them, eventually." Pearl told me. "The memory of the Lesser Three is as short as the Fierae's is long. But I'm afraid the village of Ginny is getting a storm *they* won't soon forget."

"Not to mention a boon of babies nine months from now."

"Speaking of which, I think we need to have a little talk, Papa Spaul," she said, kissing my lips.

"Do you think we could save that for morning. I'm a little tired right now."

"Too tired to love me?" she asked.

"No, for *that* I'm too sore. Besides, wouldn't Star join and make you both Drea?" I said. "That's just what we need, her coming up and wanting to get into that war back there in Ginny."

"That's just what Drea would want to do, I think," Pearl told me. "Maybe we should let her. I believe she could whip that entire contingent of the Lesser Three."

"Don't even *joke*! I said.

"I'm sorry," she lamented. Then she smiled, and told me, "Star won't join with us anymore, Spaul."

"Really? How do you know?"

"I don't, but I think you should ask her about it. She's very sleepy, but I'm sure your call will rouse her enough to speak."

I didn't answer Pearl, nor did I hesitate. When my sea calmed enough, I called from it. "Star?"

"Gesse, min lufu," her voice came, barely awake.

"Are you alright?"

"Ic drem of thyn hus o'er me."

"I love you," I said.

"Gesse. Ond lufu Pearl, nu. I will stay on her sea and feel the ripples of you. Look for me in thyn daughter, Spaul. I go to her, and will rise no more. Gode niht, min swete, swete, lufu."

Pearl and I fell asleep against the wall old Mason Dicksin had built. Though no love occurred, we held one another tightly, even in our sleep. When day dawned, the storm to the south was gone. I stood and pulled Pearl to her feet. "How do you feel?" I asked her.

"A little sore. How about you?"

"A *lot* sore. But look," I said, pointing north. "Somewhere just beyond this wall lay the great rubble piles of the Ancients! And maybe there are more Apprentices up there! And *snow!*"

"If you go there, I can't go with you, Spaul," Pearl said. "In one respect, Starshine was right. I'm pregnant with twins. I need a place to be, and a place to care for our babies, at least until they can walk and talk. I'm going home to Papa's farm. I'm going to make him a Grandpappy. These children, especially our daughter, are going to need a *lot* of love. She'll be *very* powerful, Spaul. I must teach her to love, most of all, but also many other things."

"Have you thought of her name?" I asked, though I had one in mind.

"I think I already know what you'll call her, so I claim the right to name our son."

"Any ideas?" I asked.

"No, but it won't be Spaul. I won't make him live up to the name of a hero father."

"Hero?"

"Oh, yes. You are definately my hero," she smiled.

"Because I rescued you twice?"

"If I'm not mistaken, both times you 'rescued' me you had already given me up for gone."

"Fate is cruel," I told her, "and must be *tricked*. It's called reverse psychology."

"I'm sure," she cooed. "But you are my hero because you loved. Because you always tried to do what was right as the light of your love showed it to you. Will you come with me now, my hero, and live for some years at my Papa's farm?"

"I don't know," I said, looking north. "I really wanted to see those rubble piles." But I smiled, and so did Pearl, as Zephres whirred around us and faced us south, so high, high up in that clear blue sky.

"Wait!" I shouted, just as Pearl was calling up lines. "Put us back down!"

"What *is* it?" she cried, bringing us quickly down to earth.

When she did, I ran and grabbed a stone off Mason Dicksin's wall. "I promised this to Smith," I said, running back to her.

"If you scare me like that again, you'll get spanked!" she scolded.

I laughed, and wondered if she'd really spank me hard.

Epilogue

On that morning after Pearl and Spaul first loved, high over the beach in Two Carolines, Fargus Macreedy pulled his boat into the sea. With a long board of driftwood, he paddled it toward the storm. As he approached the syphus, he opened his pouch, and pulled out another little bottle made of glass. Then he shook it, and touched it to a line of force, which pulsed momentarily into the east. A tiny, dark face formed in the bottle, wearing a pointed hat with an eye in a triangle painted on. "Fargus," the image spoke.

"Aye, 'tis me. Ay may have found what we need, something more precious then what I came to find. Ye must follow me here, and seek a brown beauty named Pearl. She travels with an Apprentice called Spaul. I believe she'll survive a fusion with a Fierae Charge. She could be the mother of a whole new race of Apprentices."

"Is she marked?" the image asked.

"Aye, she smashed the other bottle. But you'll nay be able to call her till you're close. Last I knew, they were traveling north from here."

"Can you return, or will you await us?"

"Neither. I'm done for, now. A syphus will take me soon. I can nay live with this betrayal of one who saved me and is so pure. But I know it must be done. I am a Mason, always. Save our World, but be as kind as ye can to Pearl. She's a treasure, indeed!"

Then Fargus opened the bottle he held, and cast it into the sea. "Come take me, now!" he called to the storm. "Come end me wretched life!"

Author's Note

I don't speak Old English very well, and sometimes even Starshine's goes a little pidgin on her (though I'm sure they'd have understood her in jolly old Old). My intention in using the language was only to pilfer its beauty, and use it for my own selfish purposes. I admit to abusing it mercilessly, and wrenching the syntax to suit my ear. I've also changed spellings to make words read the way I wanted them to. I freely acknowledge my crimes, and ask, as Starshine might, "Forgiefan me?"

Out Now:
Women Writing the Weird
Edited by Deb Hoag

WEIRD
1.   Eldritch: suggesting the operation of supernatural influences; "an eldritch screech"; "the three weird sisters"; "stumps . . . had uncanny shapes as of monstrous creatures" —John Galsworthy; "an unearthly light"; "he could hear the unearthly scream of some curlew piercing the din" —Henry Kingsley
2.   Wyrd: fate personified; any one of the three Weird Sisters
3.   Strikingly odd or unusual; "some trick of the moonlight; some weird effect of shadow" —Bram Stoker

WEIRD FICTION
1.   Stories that delight, surprise, that hang about the dusky edges of 'mainstream' fiction with characters, settings, plots that abandon the normal and mundane and explore new ideas, themes and ways of being. —Deb Hoag

RRP: £14.99 ($28.95).

featuring
Nancy A. Collins, Eugie Foster, Janice Lee, Rachel Kendall, Candy Caradoc, Mysty Unger, Roberta Lawson, Sara Genge, Gina Ranalli, Deb Hoag, C. M. Vernon, Aliette de Bodard, Caroline M. Yoachim, Flavia Testa, Aimee C. Amodio, Ann Hagman Cardinal, Rachel Turner, Wendy Jane Muzlanova, Katie Coyle, Helen Burke, Janis Butler Holm, J.S. Breukelaar, Carol Novack, Tantra Bensko, Nancy DiMauro, and Moira McPartlin.

Out Now:
Bite Me, Robot Boy
Edited by Adam Lowe

Bite Me, Robot Boy is a seminal new anthology of poetry and fiction that showcases what Dog Horn Publishing does best: writing that takes risks, crosses boundaries and challenges expectations. From Oz Hardwick's hard-hitting experimental poetry, to Robert Lamb's colourful pulpy science fiction, this is an anthology of incandescent writing from some of the world's best emerging talent.

Featuring
S.R. Dantzler, Oz Hardwick, Maximilian T. Hawker, Emma Hopkins, A.J. Kirby, Stephanie Elizabeth Knipe, Robert Lamb, Poppy Farr, Wendy Jane Muzlanova, Cris O'Connor, Mark Wagstaff, Fiona Ritchie Walker and KC Wilder.

Out Now:
Cabala
Edited by Adam Lowe

From gothic fairytale to humorous pop-culture satire, five of the North's top writers showcase the diversity of British talent that exists outside the country's capital and put their strange, funny, mythical landscapes firmly on the literary map.

Over the course of ten weeks, Adam Lowe worked with five budding writers as part of the Dog Horn Masterclass series. This anthology collects together the best work produced both as a result of the masterclasses and beyond.

Featuring
Jodie Daber, Richard Evans, Jacqueline Houghton, Rachel Kendall and A.J. Kirby

Out Now:
Nitrospective
Andrew Hook

Japanese school children grow giant frogs, a superhero grapples with her secret identity, onions foretell global disasters and an undercover agent is ambivalent as to which side he works for and why. Relationships form and crumble with the slightest of nudges. World catastrophe is imminent; alien invasion blase. These twenty slipstream stories from acclaimed author Andrew Hook examine identity and our fragile existence, skid skewed realities and scratch the surface of our world, revealing another—not altogether dissimilar—layer beneath.

Nitrospective is Andrew Hook's fourth collection of short fiction.

RRP: £12.99 ($22.95).

Acclaim for the Author

"Andrew Hook is a wonderfully original writer" —Graham Joyce

"His stories range from the darkly apocalyptic to the hopefully visionary, some brilliant and none less than satisfactory"
—*The Harrow*

"Refreshingly original, uncompromisingly provocative, and daringly intelligent" —*The Future Fire*

ND - #0486 - 270225 - C0 - 229/152/18 - PB - 9781907133381 - Matt Lamination